PRAISE FOR SHERIDON SMYTHE!

HOT NUMBER

"A fast-moving story with loads of sexual pressure and plenty of hot scenes."

—*Romantic Times*

"An engaging romance. . . . Vivid characterization and heated and entertaining dialogue move the story forward at a rapid pace."

—*Romance Reviews Today*

THOSE BABY BLUES

"A compelling, sexy romp that leaves you smiling!"

—Christine Feehan, *New York Times* bestselling author

"The interaction between the characters is first rate and highly entertaining . . . a fast, fun and tender story sure to touch the reader's heart."

—*Romance Reviews Today*

"Sheridon Smythe has created a warm and touching tale of love that just keeps expanding."

—*Romantic Times*

A PERFECT FIT

"Lots of good chuckles and a modern relationship that goes from zero to racing speed in seconds flat."

—*Romantic Times*

"Brooke and Alex's sexy interactions will keep you reading."

—*All About Romance*

MR. HYDE'S ASSETS

"A warmhearted and charming tale of secrets, lies and true love."

—*Romantic Times*

A WHOLE LOT OF MAN

With every step, she grew more nervous. "He's just a man," she muttered beneath her breath. "Probably drop-dead gorgeous, but just a mortal man who gets paid for sex. Nothing more, nothing less."

Lydia stopped dead in her tracks as the butler and her hired escort came into view. Her jaw dropped. She felt her eyes stretching wide, then wider still.

He was standing with his feet braced apart and his hands on his lean hips. His posture drew Lydia's attention to his incredibly tight-looking butt. She'd never told anyone, but she'd always had a thing for tight butts.

His chest was completely bare, and *lord* what a chest. Bronzed, rippling with muscles, gleaming beneath the overhead chandelier as if he'd rubbed himself with oil. . . . As shameless as his species was, he probably had, she mused.

"Dear God."

He swung around at her muttered words, his firm, sensual mouth curving in a smile that knocked the air from her lungs as if someone had punched her in the stomach. The moisture in her mouth dried up as he strode toward her . . . wearing a wicked, downright naughty smile. Was that smile a requirement? she wondered.

"You must be Ms. Carmichael." He stuck out his hand, his smile widening. "I'm Luke."

Other *Love Spell* books by Sheridon Smythe:

HOT NUMBER
HEAT WAVE (anthology)
THOSE BABY BLUES
A PERFECT FIT
MR. HYDE'S ASSETS

MR. COMPLETE

SHERIDON SMYTHE

LOVE SPELL NEW YORK CITY

LOVE SPELL®

April 2004

Published by

Dorchester Publishing Co., Inc.
200 Madison Avenue
New York, NY 10016

ISBN 0-505-52556-9

Printed in the United States of America.

Visit us on the web at www.dorchesterpub.com.

MR. COMPLETE

This dedication goes to my niece, Melissa Parker. You'll always be Sweet Pea to me, although you're a gorgeous, grown woman now, with a sparkling personality and a very definite mind of your own. I treasure the special closeness we share, and pray each night that God will bless you with everything you desire in life (well, within reason!).

All my love,
Aunt Sherrie

Chapter One

The man's muscles bulged as he flexed his arms. His thighs looked hard and powerful, his buttocks firm, and his chest broad and well-muscled. His eyes were a stunning baby blue, his hair and lashes the blackest black, and his jaw a square show of strength and latent sexuality with a heart-stopping hint of five-o'clock shadow.

But there were definitely a few extra inches around the man's waist, giving him those dreaded love handles.

Slowly circling the nearly naked man, Luke Reynolds took his time assessing his employee. He detested this part of his job, but it was necessary. He knew better than most that when a woman paid a man for his services, she expected to get her money's worth.

Just to be fair, Luke turned and bellowed for his secretary.

Mrs. Scuttle poked her tiny head out of his office, her thick glasses magnifying her eyes two-fold. She was seventy-eight, widowed and childless, and had been working in a soup kitchen when Luke placed the ad for a secretary more than five years ago.

"Do you have to scream, Luke? I'm not deaf, you know."

Luke suppressed a smile. "Sorry."

"Huh?" Perversely, Mrs. Scuttle cupped her hand to her ear and snapped, "Speak up, will you? Land sakes, Luke! I'm seventy-eight years old! I don't hear like I used to."

Managing a straight face, Luke waved her over. He indicated Ivan, who was standing in his boxers giving *him* the evil eye. Like the rest of his employees, Ivan knew that Mrs. Scuttle's word was law. "Take a look at Ivan, if you don't mind. Tell me what you see."

Mrs. Scuttle shuffled up to Ivan, standing nose to chest, with a scant inch or two between them. She looked him up and down, then slowly shuffled around him, her nursing-style shoes hardly leaving the carpet. Her head bobbed on her scrawny, wrinkled neck.

Luke suspected that if she touched Ivan, she'd give him a nasty shock.

"Hmm. I see," she mumbled as she moved. "Oh, dear. Yes, I see what you mean, Luke. Poor Ivan's turning to fat." She clucked her tongue and shuffled in the direction of the door. "Ladies won't like it.

They won't like it one bit. I'm going to lunch, Luke. I'll be back in an hour or two—if you're lucky."

The moment the door slammed behind her, Luke turned back to Ivan. He stared at him silently, his brow arched in question.

"Come on, Luke!" Ivan cried as if Mrs. Scuttle had just given him a death sentence. "It's just a few measly pounds! I told you, Diane's eating everything in sight. She's buying potato chips, candy bars, and every flavor of ice cream known to man. When the baby's born, things will get back to normal, I promise." He paused, then added almost desperately, "The very same thing happened when she was pregnant with Joey. Don't you remember?"

Luke sighed and folded his arms. He couldn't afford to be soft, not in this business. For his sake and for the sake of Ivan's tips. "I'm not going to fire you, Ivan, so calm down. You've worked for me how many years?"

"Three. Three years of good service," Ivan emphasized. He tried to suck his gut in and failed. Nervous sweat popped out on his brow.

"And in those three years, you've been happy with the extra money you make working for me?"

"Yes, sir. *Very* happy. In another year or two, Diane and I will have a down payment for a house."

"So you agree, then," Luke said softly.

Ivan looked puzzled. "You lost me."

"You agree that this job is important to you."

"Well, yeah. I told you that already."

"Then you'll understand when I tell you that you have to come in three times a week for the next month and work out in the gym."

"Aw, Luke! If I'm not home to help with Joey—"

"Bring your son with you. I'll keep an eye on him myself while you work on getting rid of those love handles." Luke ignored Ivan's groan as he hurried in the direction of his office to catch the ringing phone.

His mind had already turned to other pressing problems by the time he snatched up the phone. "Mr. Complete Escort Services. L. J. Reynolds speaking."

"Mr. Reynolds. Detective Parker."

Luke stiffened. His earlier warmth vanished. "How can I help you, Mr. Parker?" Chances were slim to none, Luke knew, that Parker needed an escort.

"*Detective* Parker," the man corrected. "There's been another complaint filed against your company."

Two complaints in two months, Luke thought with a savage, inward snarl. After five years of building a sterling reputation with absolutely no complaints.

Striving for a casualness he didn't feel, Luke asked, "And what is the nature of this complaint?"

"Same as the last one. You're aware that one of your employees—" Papers rustled before he continued. "A Mr. Anthony Cuff, engaged in sexual relations with one of your clients?"

Rubbing the bridge of his nose, Luke said coolly, "Yes, I'm aware. Are *you* aware that Mr. Cuff was immediately terminated?"

"Lucky you," Parker said with a sneer in his voice.

"This is your last warning, Reynolds. All I need is a solid piece of evidence and you're going down, understand?"

Luke clenched his jaw so hard he thought he heard something pop. Would he ever get used to the prejudices some people harbored about the nature of his business? "I understand perfectly. It won't happen again."

It shouldn't have happened in the first place, he thought to himself as he hung up the phone. The fact that it had happened twice in a short period of time aroused Luke's suspicions again. Was he being set up? Could his competition feel that threatened?

He suspected that his competition, At Your Service, headed by his embittered foster brother, Rhew Burgess, had planted a couple of bad seeds in his flawless garden, hoping to put him out of business.

He had nearly succeeded.

Time to reinforce the Golden Rule, he decided, reaching for the phone. Mr. Complete couldn't afford another mistake.

Thirty minutes later, three of Luke's five employees had agreed to meet him at Danny's Bar and Grill on Sixty-seventh Street.

The remaining two were scheduled to work and would have to be reinforced another time.

"Mr. Complete Escort Services!" Lydia Carmichael's lip curled in an uncharacteristic snarl of contempt. She flipped the business card onto the table. "Even the *name* is suggestive! Why doesn't this L. J. Reynolds person just put up a sign that reads SEX FOR HIRE?"

Sitting across from her in a booth near the window of Danny's Bar and Grill, her best friend and co-worker, Casey Winters, regarded her with worried eyes. Lydia knew she was obsessing, but she couldn't help herself. Aunt Tempera had been wronged, and she had to do *something* to avenge the sweet, generous woman who had raised her.

She watched as Casey drummed her fingers on the tabletop. Together, they ran a successful spa that catered to the working middle-class people of Atlanta. The idea of making previously out-of-reach luxuries available—and affordable—had been a hit from the start.

There was even a rumor floating around that *Style* magazine was considering doing a feature story about the startling success of their small business.

It was exhausting work for embarrassingly little pay, but the rewards were well worth the effort.

"I take it your aunt still hasn't left her room?" Casey asked. She popped a stuffed mushroom into her mouth, rolling her eyes. "Mmm. God, these things are great! What do they put in them, I wonder?"

Lydia didn't know and didn't care. Morosely, she picked at the shrimp salad she'd ordered. Like her poor aunt, she didn't have much of an appetite these days. "No, she hasn't. It's been two weeks. I'm really getting worried about her, Case."

"I don't blame you. Tempera always had such energy and drive. Just look at what she's accomplished in her charity work. Because of her, a lot of homeless people now have housing and jobs."

"Yes, she's wonderful," Lydia agreed wholeheartedly. "Which is why I feel I should *do* something constructive, avenge her in some way."

Casey laughed. "God, Lydia! You sound like a Viking or something with that avenge stuff." She pushed her plate aside and leaned closer. "Look, you did all that you could. You filed a complaint with the police, the Better Business Bureau, and *Consumer's* magazine."

"Not that it did any good," Lydia grumbled. "According to Detective Parker, my complaint wasn't the first. To think there might be someone else like Aunt Tempera, pining away in her room because of some miserable, conniving gigolo who had nothing more on his mind than to take her for all he could before he dumped her." Lydia gathered steam, an image of Aunt Tempera's embarrassed, yet sorrowful expression still vivid in her mind. "The saddest part of all is I think Aunt Tempera really loved this fiend."

"There you go with that Viking talk again. And is it just my imagination, or do I detect a gleam in your eye? You've got something up your sleeve, don't you?" Casey sat back and folded her arms, as if preparing herself for a juicy bit of gossip.

Lydia shrugged, but the look she shot Casey was anything but casual. "I was thinking about what Detective Parker said to me. If I can get evidence that proves Mr. Complete is nothing more than a cover-up for a male prostitution ring, then he'll close them down."

Casey's eyes narrowed. "What kind of evidence? And how would you get it?" When Lydia continued to gaze steadily at her, Casey's jaw dropped. She sucked in a sharp gasp of disbelief. "You—you aren't serious? Lydia! You *can't* be serious! If you're thinking what I think you're thinking, it could be dangerous, not to mention immoral—"

"I don't think there's anything immoral about ridding the world of something as potentially devastating as this—this sickening, parasitic, conniving, cruel—"

"I get the picture, and I agree. But, Lydia, do you really mean to have *sex* with one of those gorgeous, hunky, mouth-watering . . . parasites?"

Although her face felt hot just thinking about it, Lydia nodded. "If it means closing them down, then yes, that's exactly what I intend to do." Her mouth firmed with resolution. "Sometimes a girl has to make sacrifices to protect those she loves."

"Sacrifices?" Casey laughed and shook her head. "You have to admit, Lydia, that Tony was a *babe*. They don't call the service Mr. Complete for nothing, so be careful you don't fall into your own trap."

It was Lydia's turn to laugh, but the sound was more bittersweet than humorous. "Not a chance of *that* happening. Remember, I'm next to impossible to arouse."

"So your ex-boyfriend says." Casey grimaced, but had the good sense to lower her voice. "Just because you've never experienced the Big One with a man doesn't mean that you can't. With the right one—"

"Don't, Case. I'm not ready to go there again."

"But it's been a year—"

"Not long enough, in my opinion." Lydia shook her head to emphasize her statement. "Besides, Aunt Tempera has a calendar full of engagements, and she's asked me to fill in for her, which leaves me little time to worry about dating."

"Oh my God!" Casey squealed, making Lydia wince as several customers at a distant table turned around to look. "You're going to need an escort, am I right?"

Lydia smiled tightly, feeling her face flush again. "Right. I'm going to need an escort." She scooped up the business card again along with her credit card and stuffed it into her purse, exasperated and puzzled by the envious gleam in Casey's eyes. "Casey, are you and Brett having problems?"

Casey's expression fell as if someone had wiped a hand down her face. She suddenly smiled brightly, falsely. "Having problems? Me and Brett? Why, no, I don't think so." She shrugged, her gaze dropping to the half-eaten mushroom on her plate. She picked up her fork and gave it a vicious stab. "Just because he fell asleep while we were making love last night doesn't mean we're having problems, does it?"

"Oh, Casey, I'm sorry!" Lydia grabbed her hand and gave it a sympathetic squeeze. "Brett's been working a lot of hours, hasn't he? I'm sure he couldn't help himself."

With a sigh, Casey said, "I'm sure you're right. But

we've only been married six months. . . ." She let out a frustrated growl. "And here I was so determined not to add to your problems."

"We're best friends. We're supposed to tell each other our problems." Lydia glanced at her watch. "Hey, what do you say we check on Aunt Tempera, then have a girl-to-girl chat in the kitchen over a dish of ice cream?"

"Got anything chocolate?"

Lydia laughed as she signed the credit slip the waitress had brought them earlier, then slid from the booth. "What a silly question! I'm a woman, aren't I?"

"I'm a woman, aren't I?"

Sitting in the booth directly behind Lydia and Casey, Luke might have opined that Lydia wasn't a woman, but a menace.

Then she walked by him, and his mind emptied of all thought, save one. Or two. Make that three.

Beautiful.

Graceful.

Sexy.

She was tall and lithe, yet all luscious curves and tempting softness. The dark blue conservative dress she wore reached mid-calf, but the stretchy material fit her like a second skin, outlining one of the finest bottoms he'd ever seen.

Luke's mouth went dry. Belatedly, he realized he'd been holding it open. Gaping, in fact. Possibly even drooling. He snapped it shut and pulled his gaze from the woman now disappearing through the door.

Due to his proximity, he'd heard every word the two women had exchanged. At first he hadn't been paying much attention.

Then the woman called Lydia—the Everyman's Dream—had mentioned his escort service by name. After that he had shamelessly eavesdropped.

Good thing, too, considering the plot she'd been hatching with her friend to bring down his business. Luke stared thoughtfully at the empty doorway. Not that he blamed her, if her aunt was truly in the shape she indicated. Damn Anthony Cuff for smearing Mr. Complete's pristine reputation!

Well, almost pristine, anyway.

The first smear had happened a month ago when another new employee broke the Golden Rule. Graham Prescott had claimed the client got him drunk, then seduced him, but when Luke questioned his client, she had reluctantly admitted *Graham* had seduced *her*. Luke wasn't a fool, and he could tell the woman had considered lying for Graham, had already half fallen for the jerk.

Fiend, Lydia had said. How quaint, Luke thought, glancing at his watch. He had fifteen minutes left to think about Lydia, and just how he was going to handle the situation.

His first thought was to confront her with his knowledge of her plot the moment she called. Damage prevention, Mrs. Scuttle would say in her dry, raspy voice.

His second thought was to assign the very happily married Ivan to her, and watch her frustration grow. Then there was Collin, who'd been married to his childhood sweetheart for fifteen years and whom Luke was reasonably certain couldn't be tempted by any other woman.

Even one as tempting as Lydia.

Luke smiled wolfishly, thinking Lydia would get exactly what she deserved if he gave her the blond Adonis, Greg, instead. Greg was about as foolproof as he could get, considering he was one hundred percent gay.

Or . . . he could give Lydia what she needed. What, in fact, she deserved for her naughty intentions.

He could give her himself, and make her rue the day she ever thought to sabotage Luke Reynolds's business. Luke warmed quickly to this challenge. His life had been so full of business and more business that he literally couldn't remember the last time he'd had some fun.

The fact that he knew Lydia's most intimate secrets helped fuel his anticipation. Fire flashed deep and low in his belly as he thought about being the first for Lydia as she experienced the Big One. Wasn't that every man's dream? To be the first?

But no, that couldn't happen. He of all people had to abide by the Golden Rule. He had to be a perfect example for his employees.

Luke smiled as he slipped into the booth the two women had vacated and read the name on the credit slip she'd signed. He'd just thought of at least one way to get around the Golden Rule. If he never accepted a penny of her money, if he immediately shredded her checks, she would never be able to prove anything, and he wouldn't be breaking the Golden Rule.

Because she wouldn't be a client.

But he would let her *think* she was a client. A smart woman like Lydia would know that she couldn't pay in cash, not if she wanted proof of the exchange.

By the time Luke was finished with Miss Lydia Carmichael, she would realize that his business was on the up and up, and harmed no one. Did, in fact, help hundreds of women needing a last-minute escort to some function or other.

Sometimes they just needed a friend or someone to hold their hand. Sometimes they needed the confidence a handsome man could give them.

Maybe, after a few dates, he would tell her about the time Collin had surprised a burglar at the home of a client. Collin had knocked the burglar senseless while his client called the police.

What might have happened if Collin hadn't been with her? Granted, the woman might have clobbered the intruder herself, but the fact that Collin was active in the army reserve had honed his instincts, making him a force to be reckoned with.

Then there was the time that Greg had helped his client make her wandering husband so jealous, he'd dumped his mistress and given up his adulterous ways. To this day Greg was treated like family by the client, who was now expecting her first child after ten years of marriage.

They planned to name the child after Greg.

There were more stories Luke could share, heart-warming, enlightening stories that would surely melt Lydia's misguided heart in regard to the escort business.

He lifted the credit card receipt and glanced at the business card she'd left for the waitress. *Lydia's Affordable Spa, owned and operated by Lydia Carmichael and Casey Winters.*

For the first time in a long, long time, Luke felt a stirring of anticipation.

Chapter Two

The next day, when Lydia called to acquire his services, Luke barely had the breath to answer the phone. He couldn't imagine how Ivan had gained an ounce of extra flesh while running after Joey.

Joey was now busily chasing his panicked goldfish with his dirty little hands. Dirty, because he'd just upended Mrs. Scuttle's pride and joy, a vibrantly green peace lily. Dirt also covered the plush jade carpet Mrs. Scuttle had so proudly selected. It matched his eyes, she'd declared.

His eyes were hazel, not green, but he hadn't had the heart to correct her.

Luke blew out a sigh, keeping one eye on the murky water in the aquarium that three-year-old Joey was stirring. He was breathless as he answered the phone. "Mr. Complete Escort Services, Lu—" He clamped his mouth shut in the nick of time, remembering that he was waiting for a very important call from someone who didn't need to know his real name. Panting, he said instead, "Luis speaking. How may I help you?"

"I'd like an escort," a sultry, sexy voice responded.

It was she, Lydia. The walking, talking wet dream. He swallowed hard, focusing his full attention on the caller. The hell with his fish. He could always buy more. "Yes, I believe I can help you." Luke deliberately deepened his voice, trying to mask it. "What are your requirements?"

When she didn't immediately answer, Luke smiled. No doubt her dirty little mind was dreaming up all sorts of implications.

"Um, I've got a charity function to attend—"

"Ah, you'll be wanting Luke, then." When Luke remembered the dozens of charity functions he'd attended with his foster mother, he was able to add honestly, if a little devilishly, "He's very talented with his hands."

He was certain he heard her squeak.

"Excuse me?"

"His hands." Luke bit back a grin. "Isn't there a lot of handshaking at those events?"

When she let out an adorably relieved sigh, Luke let his grin widen.

"Oh." Her breathless little laugh made his groin tighten. "Yes, there is. I thought you—never mind. Luke will do nicely. I need him for tomorrow night, around seven. Is that enough notice?"

"Yes. Tuxedo be okay?"

"Ye—yes."

"Anything else?" He ceased to hear her breathing, which made the sound of splashing water dreadfully clear.

"What—what do you mean?"

God, he couldn't wait to turn those tiny, hesitant sighs into full, throaty moans of pleasure. And he would, or he wasn't an orphan. "I didn't get your name," he said, though he knew it from her business card, of course.

"Oh. It's Lydia Carmichael."

"And the address?" Luke scrambled for a pen, only to find the pen-holder completely empty.

He'd forgotten that Joey had dumped it into the wastebasket moments before the plant had caught his interest.

Luke bent over the trash can, knocking his elbow against the corner of the desk. He stifled a moan. "Wait just a moment. Okay, I'm ready."

He looked up just in time to see Joey triumphantly lift a flopping goldfish from the murky water.

He gasped, dropping the phone as he decided he couldn't leave the goldfish to such a cruel fate. Mrs. Scuttle talked to the damned fish as if they were the children she'd never had.

Come to think of it, she'd done the same thing to the poor plant, which had already begun to wilt.

Reaching Joey, he rescued the fish, lifted the toddler to the floor, and kicked aside the chair that the enterprising little tyke had pulled to the tank. Were *all* three-year-olds this bright? he wondered, staring down at the black-haired, blue-eyed miniature of Ivan with a mixture of exasperation, yearning, and outright terror.

When he picked up the phone again, Lydia was saying, "Did you get that?"

Breathless again, Luke answered. "No, I'm sorry. Could you repeat that?" He was scribbling the address when Joey fell headfirst into the trash can. "Oh, God," he said, just before he slammed down the phone.

Lydia stared distastefully at the buzzing phone, goose bumps popping up along her arms. The way the man had been panting, the way he'd gasped, his unorthodox hangup—it could only mean one thing.

He'd obviously been engaged in—in *sex* even while he talked to her! It was not only disgusting, but rude! She had a good mind to call back and demand to speak to his superior and file a complaint.

But she didn't because she was deathly afraid his boss would laugh in her face!

She took a deep breath, determined to maintain her cool. So what if the man had been having sex? It wasn't any concern of hers, was it? She should be thrilled because she was *counting* on her escort possessing the morals of a tomcat.

She wasn't at all certain of her own ability to seduce a man. Oh, she'd been told by many that she was attractive. A few had even gone so far as to say they thought her beautiful.

But when it came to playing a seductress, Lydia knew she was out of her league. She didn't have the moves or the experience. In fact, she lacked the drive as well.

So she would have to fake it—it wasn't as if she hadn't done *that* before. Yet she couldn't forget that she would be pitting her lack of knowledge against a professional in the art of sex.

Lydia sat abruptly in the chair in front of her cluttered desk, suddenly overwhelmed with misgivings. What had she been thinking when she hatched this plot? That *she* could pull it off, convince a man she was everything she wasn't? She couldn't recall a single time when she had deliberately set out to seduce a man. She had always dreaded the natural advance to intimacy, fearing she would disappoint not only her partner but herself.

And she had. Over and over again. Okay, so she'd only slept with three different men, but for her it felt like a dozen failures.

Casey was constantly trying to analyze the reasons Lydia failed to get aroused. She'd once hinted that maybe it had something to do with Lydia's parents' desertion. At the time, Lydia had scoffed at her friend.

But later . . . she'd taken the possibility out and examined it. Could this be the reason she didn't experience passion like other women? Could she have closed herself off emotionally because of her parents?

Lydia didn't think so, simply because she felt other emotions just fine. Take her aunt, for instance. She felt not only fury that Anthony had so callously dumped her beloved aunt, but a strong need for vengeance.

Not *revenge*, but vengeance. Lydia felt there was a vast difference. Revenge often involved hurting, and that wasn't what she intended.

Vengeance, on the other hand, implied noble intentions. She intended to make the world a better place by shutting down Mr. Complete, thus ending its employees' harmful, cruel actions toward innocent, gullible women like Aunt Tempera.

When the door to the office opened, Lydia gave a guilty start. She relaxed when she saw that it was only Casey. She put a hand to her pounding heart, laughing. "Oh, it's you."

Casey lifted a questioning brow. "And you were expecting . . . ?"

Lydia shook her head. "Nobody. I mean, I was just thinking about—"

"Later," Casey interrupted. "We've got a situation on our hands out here, and I need you."

"A situation?" Lydia frowned, getting to her feet. "What kind of situation? A dissatisfied customer?"

Rolling her eyes, Casey dropped her voice to a whisper. "No. At least, not yet. There's a gorgeous blond giant out here stirring up the customers. He wants to know if we can do an emergency waxing of his, um, legs and chest."

It wasn't the first time a male customer had used their spa services, but it was certainly the first time one had caused a *stirring* of this magnitude. "Well? What's the problem?" Lydia asked.

"The problem," Casey said, "is that he's making the ladies swoon. Mrs. Solton had to be revived with a bottle of developing solution Mrs. Jamerson happened to have in her shopping bag. She's decided to go platinum."

Lydia was lost. "I still don't know why you need me, Casey. He's just a man. We do have male clients occasionally."

But Casey was shaking her head before Lydia had finished. "No, Lydia, he's not *just* a man. He's from Mr. Complete. The escort service? Calls himself Greg." She smiled as Lydia gaped at her. "Yeah, thought that might catch your interest. By the way, did you get in touch with them?"

"Yes." Her voice was a mere whisper, so she tried again. "Yes, I did. Just—just now, in fact." Which meant there was no way they could have sent someone over that fast, even if they'd gotten confused about the date and time. Besides, she had given the gasping, moaning, breathless man on the phone her home address, not her work address.

And then the rest of Casey's announcement sank in. "Did you say he wanted his *legs* waxed?" When Casey nodded, Lydia put a hand to her forehead. She felt flushed, and wondered if she was coming down with something.

"Not only that, but his magnificent chest, as well."

"Mag—magnificent?" Had Casey actually said magnificent?

"Yes."

Lydia didn't really want to know, but she couldn't resist asking anyway. "How do you know his chest is magnificent?"

"Because he took off his shirt. That's when Mrs. Walters screamed. I'm surprised you didn't hear her. Then he dropped his pants—"

"Whoa!" Lydia's face got hotter. She was definitely coming down with something. "He did *what?*"

"He dropped his pants," Casey repeated. "We can't wax his legs with his pants on, Lydia. That's when Mrs. Solten fainted. I don't blame her. You should see the size of his—"

"Wait!" Lydia shouted. "Don't tell me. I don't want to know."

Casey chuckled. "I was about to say—"

"No!"

"—you should see the size of his—"

"Stop!"

"Tattoo. He's got a tattoo of a shark across his butt. When he walks, it makes the shark undulate. Looks neat as hell."

Lydia let out a breath she didn't realize she'd been holding, bracing her hands on her desk to support her wobbly knees. "Take him into the torture room. I'll be there in a moment."

"You're going to do it?"

Her friend sounded so disappointed, Lydia felt avenged for the way Casey had teased her. "It will be *my* pleasure," she said.

And meant it.

Chapter Three

Luke was trying to decide what type of luxury car he would rent for his date with Lydia when Greg burst into his office. Luke's eyes widened at the sight of his employee.

Greg's two-hundred-twenty-pound, six-foot-five-inch frame visibly trembled. His dark blue eyes held the look of a wild, frantic animal running from a hunter.

"Luke, you can't do this!" Greg blurted, sounding agonized. "You can't go near that—that—"

"Calm down, Greg." Luke spoke in a soothing tone, indicating the sofa against the south wall. "Have a seat and tell me all about it. It can't have been that bad."

"Yes, it was!" Greg ignored the sofa and began to pace, casting nervous glances at the closed door as if he expected an axe murderer—or Lydia Carmichael—

to come bursting in. His fists were clenched. "I did what you asked. I went to check out this spa place, pretending to be a client." He stopped suddenly and jerked up his shirt, exposing his red, blotchy chest—his hairless chest.

Luke bit down hard on his tongue to keep from grinning. Soberly, he said, "I take it you had your chest waxed?"

Greg nodded vigorously, his face contorting in remembered pain. "And my legs. You said to make sure I didn't arouse suspicion."

"You didn't have to go to that extreme, Greg." But it hadn't been a bad idea, Luke mused to himself. He didn't think Lydia would suspect anyone who would actually go through that kind of hell just to snoop.

"I didn't know it would feel like they were skinning me alive!" Greg's blue eyes gleamed with unshed tears. His full bottom lip actually trembled, reminding Luke of Joey's expression when he'd rescued him from the trash can. "I can't *believe* women actually go through this voluntarily! And that woman—*that woman* is some kind of monster! She was smiling while she ripped off my skin!" Greg shuddered. "And I think she actually laughed when I screamed!"

A chuckle slipped through Luke's lips. Greg glared, and he sobered fast.

"I'm warning you, boss. Stay away from her! She's wicked. She'll eat you alive."

If he could be so lucky, Luke thought. His pulse picked up speed. "Find out anything interesting?"

The question seemed to calm Greg somewhat. He gingerly rubbed his burning chest and flopped onto the sofa. "I can't remember much beyond the pain," he whispered dramatically. "I remember a woman fainting when I dropped my pants—"

Another chuckle slipped out. Luke tried to look innocent when Greg shot him a suspicious glance. He cleared his throat. "Must have been the shark. The first sighting can be a bit of a shock."

Greg nodded. "Except for this Lydia person. She didn't seem shocked at all. Just . . ." Greg frowned as if searching for the right word to express what he wanted to say. "She just seemed *contemptuous*. And mean. As if she had a grudge against *me!*" He sounded wounded, as if he couldn't imagine anyone not liking him. "I mean, I'm used to women being disappointed when they find out I'm gay, but this woman didn't know that I was gay."

Luke figured she might have had a pretty good idea, considering Greg had asked for a chest and leg waxing, but he kept his silence. Instead, he said, "I explained to you what was going on. It's nothing personal—she's upset because of what Anthony did to her aunt."

"Well, I still think you should change your mind about this plan of yours." Greg shot from the couch and approached Luke's desk, his expression earnestly concerned for his boss. "She's a devil, Luke. A devil with long legs and buns that would make a straight man weep."

"So you noticed," Luke said dryly.

"Of course I noticed! I'm gay, not dead."

"Well, don't worry. I can take care of myself." Luke felt very confident about that. He'd handled difficult women all his life; he could handle Lydia Carmichael.

In fact, he looked forward to it.

"You look ravishing," Tempera Foster said as Lydia reluctantly emerged from the huge walk-in closet. "Turn around."

As she obeyed, Lydia tugged self-consciously at the plunging neckline of the black sequined evening gown she was borrowing from Tempera. In her opinion, it revealed too much of "God's blessing," as her aunt was fond of calling her more-than-ample breasts.

"Stop yanking at it," Tempera ordered. "Be proud you fill out the bustline the way you do. Lot's of women aren't so fortunate."

Lydia didn't consider herself fortunate. So far her big chest had been more of a hindrance than an asset. Men tended to become fixated. She'd trade her big boobs for a smaller nose in a heartbeat. She swept her hand over her chest. "I feel overexposed, Aunt Tempera. Maybe I should change."

"Don't you dare!" As if Tempera realized she'd sounded too sharp, she changed her tone. "Don't hide your light under a bushel, darling."

It was on the tip of Lydia's tongue to remind her aunt that *she* wasn't the one hiding, but she resolutely swallowed the words.

Tempera, dressed in a frilly, seventies-style peignoir

in a feminine shade of pearl pink, glided across the room to inspect Lydia at close range. She frowned thoughtfully as she looked her over. Finally, she nodded. "If this date of yours doesn't ask you out again, I'll be surprised. Who did you say he was again?"

With skill and effort, Lydia managed to shrug. "Oh, just someone I met at work."

Her aunt's finely plucked brows rose. "He came into your spa?"

"Um, yes. He's a salesman." Lydia hated lying to her sweet aunt, but she couldn't tell her the truth—that she had hired an escort from Mr. Complete. She didn't want to resurrect bad memories, and she didn't want Tempera asking questions.

"Oh? What was he selling?"

Lydia met her aunt's sharp gaze evenly. "Cold wax. He was selling a new brand that's supposed to help numb the area so it doesn't hurt so much." If only it were true, Lydia thought, maybe she wouldn't still hear the blond giant's screams echoing in her ears. It was obvious the poor man hadn't had a clue what was in store when he'd asked for a chest and leg wax.

And she was absolutely certain he wouldn't be back.

"Well, I would go down with you and meet him, but I'm not feeling very well." Tempera's voice trembled slightly, and her beautiful hazel eyes brimmed with tears. She turned away, but not before Lydia saw them.

Feeling her own eyes grow moist, Lydia put a supportive hand across her aunt's shoulders and led her to the bed. The sorrow Tempera obviously felt was almost tangible. "You'll feel like your old self before you know it," Lydia encouraged softly. "You're the bravest, strongest woman I know." It was the truth, which made it all the more alarming that a mere man could bring her aunt to the brink of collapse. Lydia had never been in love, and if this was any indication of what it was like, she never wanted to be.

Tempera wiped her eyes and drew a deep breath. The smile she flashed at Lydia was both brave and gut-wrenching. "I really thought he loved me," she whispered. "I feel like such an old fool."

"You're not a fool, and you're certainly not old. Forty-five isn't old." Lydia stopped short of clenching her hands. She hated seeing her aunt this way, and it made her more determined than ever to close the escort service responsible.

Suddenly, Tempera swung around and grabbed Lydia's hands. Her expression was earnest as she said, "Don't let what happened to me color your outlook on men, Lydia. Promise me."

"I—"

"I know that your parents are partially to blame for your mistrust in the human race, and I don't want to add to that mistrust."

"Well, I—"

"Because love really is a beautiful thing, Lydia. What your uncle and I had was a wonderful example."

Lydia's throat closed at the mention of Uncle Theo. Big-hearted and jolly, he'd died with a smile on his face. The cancer had take his life, but his optimism had been untouchable and eternal. He had made Lydia and Tempera promise they would not think of him with sadness, but with joy. Only joy. Lydia tried hard to honor that promise. Sometimes it was almost impossible.

"Promise me, Lydia."

"I promise." Lydia managed a smile. She glanced at her watch, suppressing a relieved sigh. It was nearly time for her "date." Anything had to be better than continuing to lie to the woman who had been a mother and a friend to her. "I should get going."

As if on cue, the doorbell rang.

Tempera stopped Lydia with a hand on her arm. "Let Sweeney get it, darling. You don't want to appear too eager."

This time Lydia's smile felt a little on the sick side. The truth was, she *did* want to appear eager. Eager and available. The sooner she got him into bed, the sooner she could wash her hands of him. She kissed her aunt on the cheek and made her way downstairs.

With every step, she grew more nervous. "He's just a man," she muttered beneath her breath. "Probably drop-dead gorgeous, but just a mortal man who gets paid for sex. Nothing more, nothing less."

Voices reached her as she rounded a doorway into the foyer. She immediately recognized the butler's voice, but she couldn't make out the words. He was obviously talking to her escort. . . .

Lydia stopped dead in her tracks as the butler and

her hired escort came into view. Her jaw dropped. She felt her eyes stretching wide, then wider still.

He was standing with his feet braced apart and his hands on his lean hips. His posture drew Lydia's attention to his incredibly tight-looking butt. She'd never told anyone, but she'd always had a thing for tight butts.

His chest was completely bare, and *Lord* what a chest. Now she knew what Casey meant by magnificent. Bronzed, rippling with muscles, gleaming beneath the chandelier as if he'd rubbed himself with oil . . . As shameless as his species was, he probably had, she mused.

"Dear God."

He swung around at her muttered words, his firm, sensual mouth curving in a smile that knocked the air from her lungs. His eyes were a beautiful hazel, outlined by thick dark lashes.

The moisture in her mouth dried up as he strode toward her, wearing a wicked, downright naughty smile. Was that smile a job requirement? she wondered.

"You must be Ms. Carmichael." He stuck out his hand, his smile widening, revealing—not surprisingly to Lydia—dazzlingly white teeth. "I'm Luke."

Lydia swallowed hard, feeling dazed and curiously off balance as she allowed him to take her hand. "Luke . . . ?"

"Just Luke." He gave an embarrassed shrug. "Boss prefers it that way . . . for security purposes."

The man was embarrassed about an understandable security precaution, but not embarrassed about standing in her foyer half naked? Lydia shook her dazed head. She swallowed again. "What happened to your shirt?"

He looked surprised, as if he'd forgotten. "Oh, that. Just a little spill on the way over. Sweeney said he had something that would get the spot out."

Thank God it wasn't his pants! Irrationally irritated by his blatant tactics, Lydia turned away from him momentarily and checked her watch. "We're going to be late."

That confident, naughty smile never faltered, giving Lydia the impression this man rarely failed in his quest to knock a woman off her feet. Well, she might be affected by his fantastic physique, but her feet were firmly planted on the marble floor. She planned to keep them there.

"Sweeney promised that it wouldn't take long. While we're waiting, maybe I could help you with your dress."

Lydia gave a start, her hand automatically flying up to cover the generous expanse of cleavage left bare by the dress. "My—my dress?"

Luke inclined his head. "You forgot the top hook." Before she could respond, he gently turned her around again and fastened the hook, his fingers brushing the sensitive skin on the back of her neck.

When he'd finished, his big hands settled lightly onto her shoulders. Lydia felt a peculiar shudder ripple over her body. She tried to shrug his hands away, but he held fast.

His breath was warm against her ear as he said in a low, sexy voice, "You look great, by the way."

What was wrong with her? She was acting like a star-struck teenager at a rock concert! *Remember Anthony. Think about Tempera upstairs in her room . . . grieving over an unrequited love.*

Remembering did the trick. Lydia moved forward and away from his hands. She turned, forcing herself to smile at her clueless victim. "Thank you." Deliberately, she let her gaze roam over his bare chest, then down along his muscled thighs, superbly outlined by his tight black pants. "You don't look too shabby yourself."

He chuckled, the husky sound skittering over her nerve endings in a way that made Lydia suck in a sharp breath. She could no longer deny her reaction. Dismay filled her. She'd finally met a man who could stir her libido, and he was a conceited, drop-dead gorgeous gigolo! Just her fat luck . . . but it might, however, make her quest a tad bit easier to accomplish. At least she wouldn't have to fake an attraction. It would be difficult enough to hide her self-disgust!

To her relief and yes, reluctant disappointment, Sweeney returned with Luke's shirt and jacket. The middle-aged butler helped him don the shirt, then held out the jacket. "I brushed your jacket down as well, sir."

"Thank you," Luke said, flashing him a winning smile.

Lydia blinked as a pleased Sweeney palmed a folded bill that Luke offered. If the butler knew exactly who and what Luke was, she doubted he'd be so congenial, considering Sweeney's devotion to her aunt. Smothering an exasperated sigh, she said, "We should get going. I'm the hostess, so I shouldn't be late."

Luke took her arm and walked her to the door. "I hope the limo is appropriate."

"It's fine." Lydia kept her eyes forward, hoping he didn't feel her quivering. She'd forgotten to tell the man on the phone that she would provide her own limo—courtesy of Aunt Tempera, of course. "In the future, we'll use my aunt's limo."

"Okay. That'll save you a hundred bucks." Like a perfect gentleman, he opened the front door and stood aside.

So Luke didn't know about her aunt and his co-worker Anthony, Lydia mused as she stepped outside. Otherwise he'd know that money was no object for Tempera. She hoped he remained ignorant. The last thing she needed was for L. J. Reynolds to become suspicious and start asking questions.

"Money's not a problem." Lydia's Uncle Theo had not only been a successful businessman, but a keen investor as well. Tempera had more money than she could possibly spend in her lifetime. Lydia, on the other hand, was lucky to own a Volvo on her meager salary. Not that she complained—and not that Tempera didn't *try* to help her financially. From the moment she'd turned eighteen, Lydia had been determined to make her own way. Her one concession was living in the mansion with her aunt, and she chose that path because she liked living with Tempera.

"Must be nice," Lydia heard Luke murmur as he followed her to the limo parked in the circular drive. The limo driver stood waiting to help her inside.

Lydia deliberately allowed the scandalously high slit in her gown to part as she slid onto the cool leather seat, revealing her silk-covered thigh. She darted a quick glance at him, but was disappointed to find that his attention was on the driver instead. Her self-esteem slipped a notch. What if he wasn't interested in her? What if she couldn't tease an indecent proposal out of him?

The limo moved forward and Luke leaned back with a sigh, his strong, tanned hands dangling between his knees. Lydia kept her hands folded primly on her lap, trying to control her erratic breathing.

"So," Luke said, looking at her with a mysterious half smile on his lips. "Why would a young, beautiful woman like yourself hire an escort?"

Lydia opened her mouth, not with the intent to speak, but from shock at his outrageously personal question. He reached out and closed it with one finger, his gaze dropping to her mouth and his finger lingering far too long for comfort. Her lips began to tingle, and Lydia found herself resisting the alarming urge to suck his finger into her mouth.

"And don't tell me you can't get a date," he continued huskily, leaning closer, his gaze still riveted on her mouth.

Not her breasts—the customary area of choice for most of the men she'd dated—but her mouth, Lydia thought dazedly. Her body went weak with relief when he finally removed his finger and sat back against the seat again. But he wasn't finished shocking her. Not by far.

"Because if you do, I'm afraid I'll have to call you a liar."

Chapter Four

"Well?" Luke drummed his fingers on his thigh.

Lydia stared at those tanned fingers as if she couldn't believe what she was seeing. She definitely couldn't believe what she was hearing! She licked her lips, considering her options. Her first instinct was to sharply remind him that her business was none of *his* business, that he was a hired date.

Her second thought vetoed the first. She was supposed to get him to proposition her, not alienate him.

With that objective firmly in mind, she tossed her head in what she hoped was a coy way. "I'm flattered, but the truth is . . . the truth is I can't seem to find a man with all the right qualifications." She looked him over slowly, letting him know that she liked what she saw. "When a friend of mine recommended Mr. Complete, I decided to give it a whirl. I, um, was intrigued by the company name and wondered if it lived up to its claim."

"And?" he asked softly.

"So far, I'm impressed." Lydia hoped it was dim enough in the limo to hide her uncontrollable blush. She felt ridiculous, really, coming on to a complete stranger. Especially a cocky stranger who didn't appear to have a bashful bone in his body.

"Well, let's hope I don't disappoint you."

Lydia couldn't imagine a man like Luke disappointing any woman in a physical way, and that startling thought intrigued her more than she was ready to admit. It also bothered her in light of the fact that she had yet to find out if there was any substance beneath his surface charm and breath-taking physique.

"Tell me . . . Lydia. What is it about me that's impressed you so far?"

"Fishing for compliments?"

"In my line of work, a guy can't be too confident," he drawled with a wolfish grin. "And I'm always looking to improve myself."

A disturbing image of rippling muscles and a fine, washboard stomach came to mind. Then there was his tight butt. She swallowed hard. "I've only known you for a few moments. Ask me again at the end of the evening."

His brow rose, but he let her comment slide. "All right, then. I'll do that." The limo hit the freeway just as the sun sank below the horizon. "Tell me about yourself, Lydia. I find it helps to know something about the client before we appear in public together. It makes us seem more natural as a couple."

"You take your job seriously," Lydia murmured, just managing to keep the distaste from her tone. She hoped. "What can I say? I own a successful spa, I'm single, and I have an independent streak that not everyone appreciates."

"You're referring to men."

"Yes, I'm talking about men. Aside from my stubborn independent streak, there's my money." The lie came surprisingly easily. But then, her subterfuge was for a good cause. "Men find the fact that I'm independently wealthy intimidating, too."

Luke laughed. "The dumb ones, perhaps. I can't imagine an intelligent man disliking a woman because she has money."

Lydia frowned. "Strangely enough, it's the intelligent, successful ones who seem to have the most trouble." She was basing her facts on Tempera's experiences, not her own, but that didn't make the facts any less true.

"You don't say."

He sounded so surprised, she found herself smiling. "You're a man; you can't be all that surprised."

He shrugged. "Speaking for myself, I'd have to disagree. I like money just fine, and I'm not particular about who pays the bill."

Neither was Anthony, Lydia thought bitterly. "You sound ambitious."

"Anything wrong with that?"

She eyed the defensive angle of his chin with mild surprise. So her hired date had feelings—along with a charming dimple in the middle of his chin. "Not a thing. I take it you make good money at this job?"

"Enough."

His brief answer sparked the reckless question, "Do you lie to people about what you do for a living?"

He leveled his powerful gaze her way. "Never. Do you?"

Lydia blinked. "Why should I?"

"Why should *I?*" He was smiling, but his eyes had narrowed slightly. "Maybe you shouldn't presume to know something you couldn't possibly know."

She inwardly winced. *Touché.* "Maybe I shouldn't. I apologize." Changing the subject, she asked, "Don't you want to know what type of function we'll be attending?"

Luke pulled his sleeves over his wrists and checked his jacket for lint. "I already know." His eyes gleamed with wicked amusement. "Despite what you think you know, our jobs involve more than looking good in a tuxedo. I did my research, so you don't have to worry that I'll embarrass you at an inopportune moment."

She decided she wouldn't give him the satisfaction of showing her surprise at this revelation. "I wasn't worried. I did my research as well, so I know your company has a pristine reputation. Otherwise I would have chosen At Your Service." If she thought mentioning Mr. Complete's competition would get to him, she was mistaken.

He laughed.

"Ouch. The lady has claws. I have to admit I find that a turn on."

Lydia gasped before she could catch herself. Her face flamed. "Do you talk dirty to all your clients?"

"No," Luke drawled. "Not all of them. Just the ones that bring out the bad in me."

Luke was having the time of his life.

Meeting Lydia Carmichael face to face had turned out to be quite an eye-opener. He stole a covert glance at her magnificent breasts, which, at the moment, were rising and falling rapidly above the low neckline of her form-fitting evening gown. The creamy mounds begged to be kissed and fondled. . . .

He shifted uncomfortably in the seat, sternly reminding himself that his pants were revealingly tight, and Lydia, though unaware that he was the owner of Mr. Complete, was nobody's fool. If she had the slightest inkling of who he was, the game would be over and the opportunity to change Lydia Carmichael's mind about Mr. Complete would be lost.

And yes, his fun would be over.

Was it so wrong to want to get close to this goddess of a woman? To rise to the challenge of making her moan his name? Luke was a man, after all, and Lydia was an interesting woman. He was also sympathetic to her quest, even if he didn't agree with her reasons. Because of that snake Anthony Cuff, she believed his company to be something it wasn't, a den of iniquity, as he could easily imagine the surprisingly old-fashioned Ms. Carmichael saying.

He had to set the record straight eventually, if only for his own peace of mind. He *could* come clean with her now, of course. The thought had crossed his mind, but the end result wouldn't be as satisfying. No, first he wanted to teach Lydia a lesson. When he finished with her, maybe next time she wouldn't be so quick to judge others by the actions of one rotten snake of a guy.

"How long have you worked for Mr. Reynolds?" Lydia asked, scattering his thoughts to the four winds.

Luke looked at her, deciding her eyes were definitely her best feature. They were dark brown, so dark it was hard to see where her pupils ended and her irises began. Mascara darkened her lashes, but Luke doubted she really needed the artifice. Her hair, which he remembered from the bar as flowing slightly past her shoulders, was a rich dark brown, almost matching the color of her eyes. Tonight, she wore it piled high and held with a clip in one of those artless fashions that Luke decided he liked. The result left her long, graceful neck on display.

Her skin was fair, almost alabaster. Luke was more accustomed to skin browned by tanning beds or bronzed with sunless creams, as a majority of the wealthy seemed to favor. He didn't think Lydia spent much time in tanning beds, or worrying about how pale she might look.

He liked her natural tone. It suited her.

As his gaze drifted to her eyes again, he found one dark brow arched in question. And a faint blush staining her cheeks.

"Change your mind about the way I look?" she challenged.

It was the blush that gave her away. Luke plucked her hand from her lap and brought her fingers to his lips. He kissed each fingertip, watching her from the corner of his eye. He was pleased to notice an increase in her breathing rate. "You are exquisite, but you already know that, right?"

Her blush deepened. She turned her face to the window, revealing a haughty profile that reminded Luke of a regal queen. Her nose was a bit long, but Luke decided that suited her as well. Everything about Lydia Carmichael suited him.

With the exception of her mistaken notion that Mr. Complete needed to be shut down.

He turned her palm up and kissed the very center. She jerked. "Have I embarrassed you again?"

She shot him a sharp glance and pulled her hand out of his grasp. "You never embarrassed me in the first place. But you might like to know before we arrive that I don't care for public displays."

Luke chuckled, refusing to take her pompous tone seriously. Which was the real Lydia? Time would tell. "Thanks for the warning," he said. "By the way, do you want to agree on a signal?"

"Beg your pardon?"

"A signal, when you need rescuing from some boring billionaire who can't stop talking about his bunions or something."

Her lips twitched. "Those billionaires are the reason we're going to this function. Their money helps provide food and clothing for the homeless, and helps fund Hope House."

"Hope House?"

She nodded. "An old plantation house my aunt founded. It provides temporary shelter to homeless women and children. Aunt Tempera's lobbying for more funding to supply computer and secretarial training for the women. We have volunteers who then help the women find jobs."

"We?" Luke's heart thudded as she brought her hand up to tug at the plunging neckline of her dress. It was an absent-minded gesture, giving Luke the feeling that she wasn't at all comfortable with the exposure.

"I'm a volunteer," she said, almost reluctantly, as if she feared he'd think she was bragging. "You'd be surprised how many homeless people are wandering the streets of Atlanta."

Luke wasn't surprised. He didn't keep his head in the sand, but she'd find that out eventually. "You asked me how long I've worked for the company."

"Yes."

"Since the beginning." He didn't miss the way her lip curled slightly at the corners. She quickly coughed and covered her mouth. Luke sighed inwardly. He hated to think this stunning creature was so narrow-minded, but so far he had no proof that she was otherwise.

She fidgeted on the seat, placing her hands in her lap again as if she couldn't figure out what to do with them. Luke could have made a few suggestions, but he didn't want to shock her too badly.

"You must like working for Mr. Reynolds," she ventured.

"The job has its . . . perks," Luke drawled, hiding a smile when her eyes widened. Was she that bad an actress? Or was it just because he knew what she was plotting? Luke supposed he'd never know the answer to that question, but it did bear remembering that Lydia Carmichael was determined to destroy him. It was just a fluke—or destiny—that he'd been sitting in Danny's precisely at the moment she'd revealed her intentions.

"What . . . what kind of perks?"

Her eyes were like magnets; he couldn't seem to pull away. He shrugged. "Oh, you know. Dates with beautiful women . . . exotic food . . . good liquor . . . big tips . . . *perks.*" Yep, Luke thought, watching her tongue dart out to moisten her lips, he'd definitely caught her interest.

"Aren't there risks involved in your line of work?" she asked—too casually. "I mean, do you ever find yourself getting involved with your clients?"

"Occasionally." He waited a heartbeat before he added wickedly, "But everything has its price, doesn't it?" Her chest swelled as she took a deep breath. Luke held his, wondering if she had the courage to ask what she so obviously wanted to know.

Would she?

And what would he say this early in the game? If he told her, the night might have an unforgettable ending—for both of them.

But that was the problem; Luke didn't want an ending, not yet. Lydia not only intrigued him, she made him feel alive. He found that he wanted to know every inch of her luscious body, from head to toe, and he didn't think he could accomplish that in one night. Besides, his main objective wasn't revenge or satisfying his lust, but to give her time to realize she was wrong about Mr. Complete.

Wasn't it?

"Do *you* have a price, Luke?"

Oh, God.

Never in a million daydreams since hatching her plot to bring the escort business down had Lydia thought she would be asking *the* question after only an hour in her escort's company. She'd assumed there would be several dates, giving them time to get to know one another.

But then, she hadn't dreamed her escort would be so bold so quickly, or that she'd be courageous enough to respond just as quickly.

Was she ready? Could she go through with it? Her aunt's tearful confession came back to her. *"I feel like such a fool . . . an old fool."*

Yes, she had to do it. For Aunt Tempera and any number of gullible women out there who might fall prey to these parasitic animals.

"Everyone has something they want," Luke said finally, and evasively.

Instead of disappointment, Lydia felt a surge of relief. She needed more time, and it seemed she would get it.

She jumped as Luke reached out and brushed his fingers against her shoulder. Her startled gaze flew to his face.

He was smiling that devilish smile she was beginning to recognize.

"You had some . . . lint on your dress," he explained softly. "Tell me, Lydia. What is it that *you* want?"

Lydia didn't realize she was holding her breath until her chest began to ache. Oh, he was good, she mused, letting her breath out slowly. He was *very* good.

But then, Anthony had been good as well. He had wined and dined Tempera, romanced and seduced her, convinced her that the ten-year age difference didn't matter. Then he had left her heart bruised and bleeding, and her self-esteem shattered.

Left her feeling like an old fool . . .

Lydia clenched her teeth. She turned her face to the window, away from Luke's self-assured, cocky smile, and thought about his question. What did she want? She wanted to *feel* something.

She wanted *passion* in her life.

But not with someone like Luke, dammit! An attraction to Luke would be paramount to her sleeping with the enemy. She needed to despise him. To think of him with contempt. He was a leech who made his living by taking advantage of lonely, wealthy women.

Abruptly, she turned back to him. "Does your boss approve of your techniques with the clients?"

His brow rose. "Techniques? I thought I was making conversation. Getting to know you."

Her tiny smile called him a liar. "If that's your intention, shouldn't we start with the basics?"

His teeth gleamed. "We don't have that much time. We're almost there. If I know a few personal things about you, people will automatically assume we're a couple."

"Why do we have to be a couple? Why can't you just be a friend or a cousin?"

This time he laughed outright. "Lydia, *you* may be determined to ignore the spark between us, but other people will notice. Still want to be cousins?"

She felt the heat creep into her face and knew that she was blushing. Still, she had to deny his claim. "Spark? There is no spark, Luke. We've only just met."

His lids dropped as he let his gaze roam slowly and thoroughly over her until she shivered. "See what I mean? Attraction has nothing to do with time. It can happen in an instant, as it did with us tonight."

Fortunately, the limo came to a stop outside the hotel where the fund-raiser was being held. Lydia didn't wait for the driver to open her door. She launched herself out of the limo, her heart thundering and her mind rebelling at the idea of Luke being right.

He was beside her in an instant, looking breathtakingly handsome in his tuxedo. Holding out his arm, he waited for her to take it. They started walking toward the entrance.

"Do you prefer boxers or briefs?"

Lydia stumbled, grabbing Luke's arm with both hands to steady herself. Was there anything the man wouldn't say? And why was she complaining? He was making her job easier, wasn't he? It was just that she hadn't expected it to be this easy. Luke must have graduated at the top of his gigolo class, she mused.

"Boxers," she said, hoping her embarrassment didn't show. "Silk, preferably." Ten more steps to the door; then they would be surrounded by dozens of people, people who would serve as a buffer so that she could catch her breath and think about what she was going to do. She had started the ball rolling, but it was rolling too fast.

And unfortunately, they not only had three more steps to go, they had the rest of the night as well.

Just before they reached the doorman, Luke held her back and bent close to her ear. "This is your lucky night," he whispered wickedly. "I just happen to be wearing black silk boxers."

Chapter Five

Lydia made a beeline for the ladies' room.

Luckily, it was empty.

She sank onto a bench and eyed the chic chrome-and-gold line of basins with longing. Her face burned, and she wanted more than anything to splash it with cold water, but such a luxury was out of the question; she would ruin her makeup.

Black silk boxers.

Oh, Lord. She fanned herself with her hand. When that didn't work, she tried fanning herself with her little black purse.

It was no use. She couldn't get the image out of her mind.

Luke in black silk boxers.

Bare-chested, his bronzed skin gleaming with a light sheen . . .

Would she find a tattoo of a predator on his incredibly tight-looking butt? His co-worker, Greg, had caused her patrons to swoon. What would Luke do to Lydia that Greg had failed to do? Or rather, what *more* could he do? He already had her hiding in the bathroom, hyperventilating and fantasizing about what she would find beneath his black silk boxers.

"You're crazy," she muttered, grabbing a tissue and dabbing carefully at the sweat beading her upper lip. "He's not really wearing black silk boxers. I mean, what would be the odds? He's taunting you, seducing you. It's his game, and he's probably played it a hundred times."

Just as Anthony had with Aunt Tempera.

"Well, he can play games with *me* anytime," an amused, envious voice drawled from the bathroom doorway.

Lydia muffled a startled screech, her hand flying to her heart as she swung around on the bench. She recognized the woman from the society pages of the newspaper, and she knew from Aunt Tempera that the socialite was married to the building magnate Don Catalina. Aunt Tempera had gone over the guest list with Lydia, feeding her necessary information and sharing personal tidbits about those she knew. Lydia knew Tempera was counting on the Catalinas to donate an impressive amount of money tonight for Hope House.

And Fran Catalina had just overheard Lydia mumbling about her escort's black silk underwear.

She forgot about her makeup and buried her flaming face in her hands.

"I'll pay you a hundred dollars to find me a pair of black silk boxers."

At Luke's bizarre and desperate-sounding proposition, the bellboy's eyes darted here and there, as if he were mapping his escape from this obvious madman. He stammered, inching along the hallway wall toward the elevator. "I—I'm not that kind of guy, s-sir!"

Luke's mind was blank for a moment. When the boy's meaning sank in, he slapped his forehead and gave a resounding imitation of Ricky Ricardo, "Ai-yai-yai! No, no, I'm not a—I'm not suggesting—oh, hell!" He looked left and right, ascertaining they were still relatively alone in the hallway leading to the kitchen. "It's like this: My girlfriend has this fantasy about me in black silk boxers, and I would like to get lucky tonight, only I'm not wearing any underwear at all, you see?"

The nervous boy's gaze darted to Luke's crotch, then quickly back up again, his eyes bigger than ever. He clearly wasn't convinced that Luke wasn't some wacko. "Man, I—I can't help you."

Swallowing an exasperated sigh, Luke pulled out his wallet. He withdrew two one-hundred dollar bills and held them out. "I swear I'm not trying to proposition you, kid." He jerked his head toward the reception room. "I'm with that party in there, and I just need a pair of black silk boxers. Doesn't this hotel have a boutique?"

The bellboy licked his lips, but he'd stopped inching along the wall, which Luke took as a good sign. "Um, yeah, they got one, but I—"

"Three hundred," Luke said grimly, adding a third bill and silently hoping he wouldn't need cash before he got to an ATM.

"You—you swear the other guys didn't put you up to this?" He was eyeing the folded bills Luke held out with a mixture of greed and fear. "Because if they did, I'll go to the manager this time."

"I swear."

"And—and you're not some creep—"

"Take the damn money!" Luke growled, out of patience. Lydia would be back from the powder room and wondering where her escort had gone off to. "When you get them, put the package behind the waste can in the men's room."

"O-okay." But the boy just stared at the money as if afraid to take it.

Luke grabbed his hand and shoved the money into his fist. "Thanks. Now, get going, will you?" He didn't have to ask the boy twice; he was off like a cannon, darting an apprehensive glance over his shoulder at Luke before disappearing into the kitchen.

Replacing his empty wallet, Luke went to find his stunning, vengeful date. There was always a chance he'd run into someone who recognized him, but he knew the odds were low since he was originally from

West Virginia. Luke had spent most of the past five years in Atlanta training his men and running his business from his office, which left little time for socializing. The arrangement suited him fine. He'd gotten enough of the wealthy party scene when he'd lived with his foster parents in West Virginia.

He wasn't surprised to find the few early birds who had arrived were gathered at the bar. Atlanta's social peacocks, he mused rather cynically, all decked out in their finest feathers.

Lydia, on the other hand, was nowhere to be seen. Luke's immediate reaction was concern. Had he moved too fast? Upset her? Frightened her? He gave his head a wry shake, amused with himself that he'd be so concerned about a woman who was trying to ruin him.

But the situation wasn't all Lydia's fault, and Luke was man enough to admit that. He preferred to think of her as misguided, rather than vicious.

Knowing didn't stop him from wanting to see just how far she'd go, and knowing wouldn't stop him from enjoying every moment of it.

Luke knew exactly when Lydia walked into the room. All three men at the bar stopped talking. One nudged the other, and the other nudged the man beside him. They all turned to stare. Luke didn't blame them, for she was obviously a cut above the other women in the room. Oh, Luke knew from the background check he'd done on her that she wasn't from money, and he didn't think she had any to brag about—although she wanted him to *think* she did, for obvious reasons—but Lydia was proof that money didn't necessarily equal class.

She was classy, all right. Classy, curvy, and definitely rattled, if her fast breathing and wide eyes were any hint. But she didn't look frightened, much to Luke's relief.

Just rattled. His lips curved with pleasure. Rattled was good. Very good. Luke straightened his bow tie and went to do the job he'd been hired for. Later, he planned to cash in on a few of those "perks" he'd hinted about to Lydia.

Life was good.

Life was great.

And with any luck, it would just keep gettin' better.

"It was gruesome, but I insisted on watching in the mirror above me. The surgeon cut my toe open and took a grinder and ground the bone. I could see it, but I couldn't feel a thing."

Lydia smiled, nodded, and tried to look suitably horrified as Liam Westmoreland, a shrewd businessman who owned a chain of automotive part stores, explained in gory detail, from beginning to end, his terrifying toe operation.

It hadn't taken her long after emerging from the restroom to start questioning why she'd agreed to fill in for her aunt. Now, three head-bobbing hours later, she understood completely why she preferred the hands-on work of helping with the homeless.

Aunt Tempera, however, was excellent at charming the wealthy and sucking up. If only she'd get over her melancholy and get back with the program. Damn Mr. Complete and his army of heart-breaking gigolos, anyway!

"Hey, gorgeous."

Speaking of the devil . . . Perversely, Lydia had never been so happy to see a familiar face. Next time—if there was a next time—she'd take him up on that silly offer of a signal. In fact, she'd insist on Luke sticking by her side, instead of running off to the men's restroom every ten minutes. What was he doing in there? Admiring himself in the mirror? Checking to see if he had a muscle out of place? Shining his teeth?

Oiling his chest?

Or maybe he was checking his sexy black silk boxers for wrinkles.

The moment Mr. Westmoreland paused for breath, Lydia pointed to Luke's drink and asked sweetly, "Having a problem holding your liquor?"

Luke grinned to show he'd caught her meaning. "Miss me?"

Aware that Mr. Westmoreland was watching them with an indulgent smile, she said, "Of course."

The millionaire of car parts cleared his throat. "I can't believe Tempera didn't mention you finally had a new man in your life, Lydia. She told me she was afraid you were taking this little hobby of yours far too seriously."

Lydia's smile froze in place. She knew Aunt Tempera had said no such thing. Politely—because he was an old friend of Uncle Theo's and he had just handed her a check with six digits—she said, "I love my work."

Mr. Westmoreland chuckled as if she'd said something funny. "You own a spa, isn't that right?"

"That's right." Lydia struggled with her temper, remembering another reason she wasn't comfortable mingling with the rich. They had a knack for being patronizing and not even realizing it.

"I should get Leanne to give you a try." He lowered his voice to a stage whisper. "Maybe one of your mud packers could succeed where others have failed."

"I'm one of those mud packers, Mr. Westmoreland, and I don't think your wife would like my spa."

"Oh? Why is that?"

"We serve lemonade instead of champagne, raw veggies instead of caviar, and for the kids, we—"

"You let children into your spa?" Mr. Westmoreland sounded downright horrified.

Beside her, Luke smothered a chuckle. The sound of it made Lydia feel strangely comforted. *Luke* was picking up on her sarcasm, even if Mr. Westmoreland seemed imperious. "On Saturdays, we provide a daycare area for the kids, yes."

"I can't imagine that being cost-effective."

Lydia tried not to sound smug as she said, "It is when your clients volunteer to watch the kids. It's amazing what women will do for a free massage." This time Luke didn't bother smothering a chuckle. "But there's another reason why I don't think your wife would like my spa."

"What's that?"

"I don't charge enough."

For a moment, Mr. Westmoreland looked blank. Then her joke sank in. He threw back his gray head and laughed heartily. Lydia and Luke joined him, and the tension inside Lydia started to fade away.

Then Luke slipped his arm around her waist and blew her comfortable feeling all to hell. Almost immediately, her breathing changed. She felt her breasts tighten, and she shot him a disgruntled look that made him smile knowingly.

The man undoubtably knew the extent of his power over women. No wonder he was conceited!

"Excuse us," he said with a pleasant smile at Mr. Westmoreland. "I think someone's trying to get our attention."

The moment they were out of earshot, Lydia muttered ungraciously, "Thanks. You can remove your arm now."

Luke leaned close, his voice disturbingly low and husky. "Is that an order? Because if it isn't, I'd like to keep it there. It feels good."

Lydia would be lying if she disagreed, and she suspected Luke would know it. She bit her lip and kept quiet as they approached another group of potential donators. Aunt Tempera would be pleased, she thought, when she saw the number of donations she'd gathered tonight.

Her heart quaked when her gaze collided with Fran Catalina's. Fran wore a tiny, amused smile as she looked from Lydia to Luke. Lydia noticed she spent a lot more time looking at Luke, her bold, exploratory gaze hinting that Fran Catalina wasn't a stranger to infidelity. She squashed an irrational surge of jealousy.

"Introduce this gorgeous hunk, Lydia," Fran demanded, her hungry eyes still fastened on Luke.

"This is Luke." Lydia prayed that Fran wouldn't mention the bathroom encounter. All she needed was for Luke to have proof of his effect on her! "Luke, this is Fran Catalina, Leanne Westmoreland, and Dana Creed."

Luke effortlessly captivated the women with his wicked smile and honeyed words. "Having so many beautiful women in one room could make a man's head spin," he said, lingering over each bejeweled, manicured hand.

That's it, Lydia thought, watching him with something akin to awe. *He's a mastermind at making women—any woman—feel as if she's the only one in the room.* Where had he learned these talents?

Dana Creed was the last to fall. She fairly simpered as Luke placed a chaste kiss on the back of her hand. "Tell us your secret, Luke. How do you keep yourself in such . . . excellent shape?"

She sounded breathless; Lydia knew exactly how she felt. There was something about Luke's personality that seemed to suck all the air from the room.

"If I told you," Luke drawled teasingly, "then it

wouldn't be a secret. Now, if you beautiful ladies will excuse me?"

A bathroom break again? Lydia frowned at his retreating back, momentarily forgetting that she was now the center of attention.

"Earth to Lydia!"

Fran's openly amused voice cut into Lydia's thoughts. She gave a guilty start and turned back to the group of women.

All three were staring after Luke.

Lydia cleared her throat. They all began talking at once.

"Where did you find *him?*"

"Does he have a brother?"

"Two brothers?"

"I wonder who tailors his suits?"

How should she answer? She knew nothing about Luke, other than the fact that he cost more money by the hour than she probably made all day.

"Come on, Lydia," Leanne cajoled. "We're not trying to steal your man. It's obvious that he's madly in love with you."

Ha! Lydia fought back a smile over that very mistaken observation. She was saved from having to answer as a man wearing a hotel uniform touched her shoulder.

"Excuse me. Are you Lydia Carmichael?"

"Yes, I am."

"Could you come with me, please?"

He sounded so serious that Lydia's heart gave a

frightened leap. Had something happened to Aunt Tempera? "W-what's this about?"

The hotel employee hesitated, glancing pointedly at the listening women. "I really can't say just now, Ms. Carmichael. Will you come with me?"

Seriously concerned now, Lydia followed him from the banquet hall. What could be wrong? And why couldn't he tell her?

Chapter Six

When Luke was a teen, he'd shattered his elbow playing basketball.

It had hurt like hell.

When he was twenty, he'd dislocated his shoulder during a crazy trip down white-water rapids. Having a bunch of amateur, half-drunken colleagues popping it back into place had been sheer hell.

But this . . . this was the worst pain Luke had ever experienced.

He held very still in the bathroom stall, his hands gripping the top of the stall for balance, sweat pouring from his face. The slightest movement was agony. The simple act of breathing was excruciating.

In a hasty attempt to undress and slip on the three-hundred-dollar black silk boxers the hotel boy had finally delivered, Luke had caught the tender skin covering his unmentionables in the track of his zipper.

Absolute, sheer hell.

That's what he got for not wearing underwear, Mrs. Scuttle would say in her tart, I'm-old-so-I-can-say-anything voice.

Well, Luke could reassure his sage secretary that he was now a believer.

If he ever got out of this mess without losing his manhood . . . literally.

His eyes flew open as he heard the faint squeak of the men's restroom door. He swiftly closed them again, his embarrassment at an all-time high. God, what he wouldn't give if he could start the night over. He'd start by not lying to Lydia about wearing black silk boxers! Again he heard Mrs. Scuttle's righteous voice telling him that he'd gotten exactly what he deserved for lying in the first place.

For once, he agreed with the cranky old woman.

"Luke? It's Lydia."

Her voice was hesitant, concerned. Not amused, thank God, because Luke found nothing remotely funny about his situation. He let out a very slow, careful breath.

"Which stall is he in?"

"The third one, ma'am. Should I call 911?"

Luke hissed out, "No!" Their silence informed him that he'd been heard. "Lydia, come to the door." He heard her approach the stall door. When she stopped, he carefully wiped sweat from his eyes, trying to decide how to instruct her.

"Luke, we really should call the paramedics," she said. "I know it's embarrassing, but—"

"No." Luke closed his eyes, enduring the wave of pain that washed over him. Once again he was reminded that talking hurt.

"Well, what do you suggest we do?" Lydia sounded both baffled and sympathetic. "You must be in pain."

"That's an understatement," he gasped. "Hold on a moment." Very slowly, with his teeth clamped together hard, he pushed the notorious silk boxers into the pocket of his tuxedo.

Then he grabbed the top of the stall again and rode the waves of pain. Excruciating. Hellish. It made him physically sick.

His voice came out in a pained whisper this time. "I want . . . you . . . to try to . . . help me get . . . it unstuck." He held his breath. Sweat trickled down his cheek. She was silent for a long, painful moment, scaring the daylights out of him.

"Luke, I—I can't. Please let me call the paramedics. I'm sure they'll know what to do."

And have everyone in the hotel—including the crowd of wealthy people in the banquet hall—know what was going on? Luke thought not. Despite what Lydia believed about him, he did have his pride.

He took a deep, slow breath and said one word: "Please."

A moment ticked by. The stall door began to inch inward, as if she were a virginal, brave heroine creeping around an old castle in a gothic romance. From the corner of his eye, Luke watched it open until her face appeared.

Her gaze flew downward, then swiftly up to his sweat-drenched face. She turned red, then white. Her eyes widened in horror. "Oh, my God," she whispered. "Luke, that's gotta hurt."

With clenched teeth, he said, "Take my word for it. It does."

She pushed the door inward until it bumped gently against the wall. She kept her gaze trained on his face. "What do you want me to do?"

It was a damn good question, Luke mused, nearly biting his tongue in two at the thought of anyone touching him. Even Lydia. "I don't know," he confessed. "Have . . . any . . . suggestions?"

Her gaze darted downward. This time it stayed, as if she were fascinated. Any other time, Luke might have rejoiced.

Not now. Not this time.

"Well, I guess it has to come out the same way it got in there, right?"

Luke gave a small, jerky nod of agreement. He didn't like her solution, but he had to admit it was probably the only one that made any sense. Short of taking a blow torch and melting the metal zipper, there was no other way.

Lydia went to her knees before him, her gaze glued to his crotch. She tentatively reached out as if to touch him.

"Don't," Luke ground out as a new horror rose to

join the first. He slammed his eyes closed to shut out the erotic sight of Lydia kneeling before him, her hand inches from his crotch. *God in Heaven*, he prayed, teeth clenched, *please have mercy!*

He was getting an erection!

"I think . . ." Lydia shook her head, as if she couldn't believe what she was about to say. "I think maybe it will help."

Luke didn't have to ask her to define "it." He knew, and he wished that he didn't, because thinking about it only made things worse.

And more painful.

She touched him, her tentative fingers following the growing outline against the material.

He sucked in a sharp breath as he continued to swell. It was obvious to Luke that Lydia was no stranger to arousing a man, but there was something oddly innocent about her actions. As if she truly didn't know her own power.

He continued to grit his teeth, forcing himself to look down. Looking down gave him an enticing view of Lydia's well-endowed cleavage, as if he needed anything more arousing than her soft, hesitant fingers stroking him!

He was swelling . . . and yes, he conceded, swallowing a groan, the swelling was stretching the skin, pulling it away from the tracks of the zipper. It hurt like hell, but there was a small measure of relief, too.

Without warning, Lydia grabbed the zipper tab and

yanked it downward, releasing him entirely from its steely clutches.

"Ahhhh!" Luke fell to his knees, grabbing her shoulders for support. He buried his face against her neck, breathing hard. His erection still throbbed, but it was such a drastic difference from the previous pain that he barely noticed it. "Why didn't you warn me?" he asked, inhaling the delicious scent of her perfume on a ragged breath. Now that his crisis was over, he realized that she was breathing hard as well.

"Because it would have hurt worse," she explained breathlessly. "Ever notice that the dentist doesn't warn you before he sinks that needle into your gums?"

With his face still buried against the spicy, wonderful silkiness of her neck, Luke shook his head.

"Well, that's why. If he told you ahead of time, you would anticipate a pain that you might not have otherwise felt."

"Makes sense. Thank you from the bottom of my heart." His voice was thick with sincerity. "And my future children thank you, too."

He felt her laugh, and it was all he could do not to groan and lower his face to that delectable valley between her breasts. She had just saved his life; he couldn't start pawing her in a men's room stall, even if that were his style, which it wasn't.

She brought her hands to his face, framing it as she tugged his head up and back. Her expression was solemn, but her face was flushed as she said, "Are you . . . bleeding? Should we go to the emergency room to make sure there's no permanent damage?"

Luke wanted to kiss her. He stared at her full, painted lips with a longing that jolted him. Dragging his gaze back to her intense, expressive eyes, he said, "I don't think that's necessary, but I'll check—"

She scrambled to her feet, nearly knocking him backward. "I'll—I'll just wait outside for you."

He smothered a chuckle as she flew out of the stall. Moments ago she had been stroking him intimately; now she was fleeing as if her life were in danger.

Lydia Carmichael, Luke decided, was full of surprises. His gaze fell on the small purse she'd left behind in her haste. Perfect, he thought. Just perfect.

He reached into his pocket and pulled out the now infamous black silk boxers.

The limo pulled away in a crunch of gravel that sounded loud in the still night air. Lydia used her key to let herself in, hoping that Aunt Tempera had given up on her. She wanted desperately to be alone so that she could spend a few hours going over all the reasons she shouldn't—couldn't—be attracted to Luke.

"How did it go?"

She jumped, her startled gaze searching the shadowy foyer for Tempera. At least she was out of her room, Lydia thought, taking this as a good sign. She closed and locked the door. "I could use a cup of your homemade cocoa."

"You've got it. It's the least I can do considering the sacrifices you're making for me and Hope House."

Her aunt had no idea, Lydia thought, blushing despite herself. "I don't mind, Aunt Tempera. You should know that by now."

The flourescent lights in the kitchen shone brightly on Aunt Tempera's pale, sad face, reminding Lydia—and she did need reminding—that her beloved aunt was suffering.

Because of a man like Luke.

"Do I have to wait for the cocoa before you spill the beans, or will you put me out of my misery now?" Tempera asked as she retrieved the milk, powdered cocoa, and sugar. She brought out a small saucepan from under a counter and began adding ingredients.

Lydia slid onto a stool at the breakfast bar and placed her purse on the counter. She kicked off her heels and sighed. "I think it went very well. Nearly everyone on the list showed up, and even a few whom I didn't recognize."

"Word of mouth," Tempera explained. "Tax cuts and all that. Most people would rather give money away than pay it to the government." She stirred the ingredients, checking the flame beneath the pan. "How did your date go?"

"Um, fine. It went fine." Lydia prayed her aunt wouldn't turn around until she got her color under control. Damn her silly tendency to blush! To distract herself, she opened her purse and reached inside for the bundle of checks.

Her fingers encountered something soft and silky. She let out a squeak, jerking her hand from the bag.

Checks went skittering across the breakfast bar, along with a pair of black . . . silk . . . boxers.

She watched, paralyzed with horror, as the silk boxers slipped off the end of the bar and floated to the floor. They landed directly behind Tempera's pink fuzzy house shoes.

Tempera turned at the sound of her squeak. "What is it? Is it a mouse? I'll call the exterminator. . . ."

Lydia nearly fell off the stool in her haste to reach the damning boxers before Tempera looked down.

She didn't make it. Just as her fingers touched the silk, Tempera glanced down.

"My, my, my." She *tsk*ed *tsk*ed, laughing as she pulled the boxers from Lydia's fragile grasp. "You're holding out on me, darling." She held the boxers up by one finger and wiggled them, grinning at a red-faced Lydia. "Come, come. Spill it. My niece gets laid for the first time in a year and I don't get to hear about it?"

Lydia prayed for an earthquake—monsoon—*anything.*

No force of nature came to her rescue.

"Lydia?"

"Um, I didn't exactly get laid, Aunt Tempera."

"Exactly?" Tempera shook the cocoa-coated spoon at her. "So what *did* happen? Something must have, or you wouldn't have ended up with these." She tossed the boxers onto the breakfast bar and went back to the business of stirring the simmering cocoa. When she spoke again, it was in a more subdued tone. "Tony wore boxers. Not always silk, but I thought he looked sexy in any kind." She paused. Her voice wobbled with abject misery as she added, "Especially none at all."

Her dejected sigh went through Lydia like a hot knife through butter. She snatched the silk boxers up and threw them into the trash, dusting her hands with satisfaction. With her back to Lydia, Tempera missed her symbolic gesture.

"Did I ever tell you that Tony had a daughter?"

"Um, no, I don't think you did." Lydia decided it would be best to let Tempera talk about Creepo Anthony, even if she had to bite her tongue until it hurt.

"She's twelve. Lives with his ex in San Antonio, Texas." Tempera turned off the flame and divided the cocoa into two big mugs. She carried them to the breakfast bar.

Beneath the lights, Lydia saw that her aunt's eyes were shimmering with unshed tears. She took one of the steaming cups from Tempera and patted the bar stool beside herself.

Tempera slid onto it. She sighed and stared into her cup. "You know, I never thought I'd fall in love again after Theo."

Her sad smile broke Lydia's heart.

"He was one of a kind, wasn't he?"

"Yes, he was," Lydia agreed quietly.

"Tony said he wanted me to meet his daughter," Tempera whispered. A lone tear trickled down her cheek. "Her name is Autumn. Isn't that a pretty name?"

Lydia nodded and took a sip of her cocoa. Listening to her aunt kept her mind off *him*. Which was a good thing. A very good thing.

Tempera propped her chin in her hand. Tears rolled slowly down her face. "He told me he loved me over and over again. He told me that he'd never felt that way about a woman, not even his ex-wife. We made so many plans. He wanted to take me to Bridgetown in Barbados to meet his best friend."

Yeah, on *your* money, Lydia thought, scowling.

"You know, Lydia, I believed him. I think I *still* believe him. Something happened. Something scared him off."

Lydia covered her aunt's hand and gave it a squeeze. "Maybe he just got cold feet." *Or maybe he just got enough of your money.* She couldn't speak her mind because she felt instinctively that Tempera needed to come to this conclusion on her own. Lydia suspected she wouldn't get over Tony until that happened.

"Are you going to see him again?" Tempera asked abruptly.

Hot cocoa sloshed onto Lydia's hand. She sucked in a sharp breath and raced to the sink to run cold water over her red skin. With her back to Tempera, she was able to say evenly, "I don't think so. We don't really have much in common."

"How can you tell from just one date?"

A question Lydia couldn't answer, not without revealing more to Tempera than she wanted her to know. She opted for being as honest as she could.

"He's too full of himself for my taste." Although she had seen a more humble side of him tonight. Her fingers began to tingle. She jerked them out of the water and hastily dried them on a towel.

The entire happening seemed like a dream. Had she really gotten on her knees and stroked Luke in the men's room until he swelled to an impressive length?

"Lydia . . . you're drooling, darling."

Lydia gave her chin a self-conscious swipe, mortified to discover her aunt hadn't been just teasing. She *had* been drooling!

That settled it then, she decided firmly. In the morning she would call Mr. Complete and ask for a different escort. Luke was too—too *assuming*, and he left her too unsettled. She wanted to be the one in command. She wanted to call the shots . . . set the pace.

With Luke, the pace so far had been fast and furious, leaving her thoughts muddled and her resolve shaky. Although the idea of enjoying sex—for a change—appealed to her, enjoying it with the enemy smacked of disloyalty.

And Luke *was* the enemy.

Chapter Seven

Luke was in the office by eight-thirty. By nine o'clock, he had the brand new caller I.D. hooked to the phone and Mrs. Scuttle's tea brewing on the hot plate.

He put a napkin on her desk and set a warm cheese Danish on top of it. He prepared her tea in her favorite cup, added two teaspoons of sugar and a dollop of real cream, then set it alongside the freshly baked Danish. By the time she arrived at nine-fifteen, Luke was ready.

Mrs. Scuttle took one look at the Danish and called him on it. "What's going on, Luke Reynolds?" She shuffled up to him and stared long and hard into his flushed face. "You're up to something—any fool can see that—but what? What are you up to?" When he remained silent, she looked carefully around the office.

Her owl-eyed gaze landed on the new caller I.D.

"What's that?" she barked, shuffling over to take a closer look. She poked at it as if she expected it to wiggle. "Haven't I told you I don't like a bunch of gadgets cluttering the office?"

Wisely, Luke kept his mouth shut and let her wind down. He feared little, but Mrs. Scuttle was an exception.

"Cheese Danish. My favorite, although it gives me gas." Finally, she turned back to him. Her owlish eyes were narrowed to slits now, reminding Luke of a cat he'd once had. "Is my paycheck going to bounce? Is that it, boy?"

She'd called him boy. That was not good. He cleared his throat and tried to look casual. "Um, no. Your check's not going to bounce." The woman had a mind like a steel trap, he mused. When she first had come to work for him five years ago, he'd miscalculated his checkbook and had inadvertently bounced her first paycheck.

She had never let him forget it, and Luke doubted she ever would.

"You closing the business?"

"Nope."

Mrs. Scuttle propped her hands on her hips. "You firing me?"

"No, of course not."

"Because if you are, I want you to know that I understand. I'm an old, useless woman and I know you keep me on out of pity."

"Nonsense."

"So you're not firing me? Because if you are, I was going to remind you that my grandmother practiced voodoo, and she taught me everything she knew."

"I'm not firing you."

"Did you break my typewriter? Because if you did, I'm still not going to use one of those stupid computers."

"No, I didn't break your typewriter."

"Hmm." She stared at him a moment longer, then shuffled back to her desk. She picked up the rich Danish and threw it at him.

Luke easily ducked before the pastry reached him. It bounced off the wall behind him and fell harmlessly to the floor. He bit his tongue to keep from telling her that he'd gone five blocks out of his way to get her that Danish.

"That might not have bothered you," Mrs. Scuttle bawled out, "But this hot tea will."

The moment she reached for it, Luke found his courage and blurted out, "I need you to lie for me."

"*What?*" his secretary bellowed. "You want me to *lie* for you?"

She said it as if Luke had asked her to dance naked on her desk—in front of a dozen of her church buddies.

He crossed his arms over his chest, prepared to leap out of her way if she got feisty with the tea. "It's important," he said, disgusted by the pleading note in his voice. Only his secretary could bring him to his knees.

Well, her and a flesh-eating zipper.

"What could be so important you'd coerce your poor old widowed secretary into lying?"

Luke winced at her deliberate choice of words, but stuck to his guns. "The welfare and reputation of this company."

"Ha!" Mrs. Scuttle blinked her owl eyes at him. "You in trouble with the law?"

He hesitated, trying to decide just how truthfully he could answer that question. Technically, he wasn't. But on the other hand . . . he *could* be, if Mrs. Scuttle didn't cooperate with him and Lydia managed to get to one of his men.

One night spent in her company and he was even afraid to assign Greg to her.

"Well?" Mrs. Scuttle prompted in an irritated voice. "This office doesn't run itself, you know. Are you in hot water?"

"Um, sort of. I'm expecting a woman by the name of Lydia Carmichael to call and request an escort. I need you to tell her that I'm the only one available."

There was shocked silence for a long, tense moment.

Mrs. Scuttle blinked about fifty times before she ventured, "A woman, huh? She a new client?"

"No. I want no record of her calling and no file made on her. Just tell her that I'm the only one without prior assignments, and don't mention my last name or the fact that I'm the boss."

"You gonna tell me why you're asking me to lie? Because you know I hate to lie, Luke."

Luke softened, sensing victory. "I know, Mrs. Scuttle, I know. But I wouldn't ask you if it wasn't very important." He hesitated. "She's the niece of one of our former clients, Tempera Foster."

"Ah. She's out for a little revenge, is she?" Mrs. Scuttle had been present at the emergency meeting Luke had called after the Anthony incident, and she obviously hadn't forgotten.

"She prefers to call it vengeance," Luke said dryly. "Thanks to Anthony Cuff, she's convinced we're all scheming heart-breakers." He avoided using the nastier term of "gigolo" in deference to his secretary's delicate nature.

"Thinks you're running a brothel, huh?" Mrs. Scuttle said without a hint of a blush. She nodded. "I guess if I were in her place, I might want restitution, too." She shuffled around and sat down at her desk. Taking a sip of her tea, she looked at him over the rim of her cup. "You planning on setting her straight?" When Luke didn't immediately answer, she picked up a stapler and aimed it at his head.

"Eventually," Luke told her hastily.

"Eventually?" She slammed the stapler down. "Are you up to no good, Luke? Because if you are, I want no part of it."

Luke ran a hand through his hair and took a seat as far from his secretary as he could get. "I like her," he said bluntly. "And I plan on telling her the truth after she gets to know me. I don't think she'd believe me if I told her now."

"You planning on sleeping with her?"

"That's none of your business." He knew his face had turned red, but he'd been caught off guard by her blunt question.

"What about the Golden Rule? You can't expect everyone else to abide by it if you're going to go around breaking it left and right."

"She's not a client."

Mrs. Scuttle took a sip of her tea. The cup rattled ominously in the saucer as she set it back down. "So if she calls here wanting to hire an escort, I'm to give her you—for free? Is that the plan?"

"Yes." Luke realized he was clenching his jaw and forced himself to relax. He not only held the utmost respect for Mrs. Scuttle, but she was the closest thing he'd ever had to a mother. "She's planning on sabotaging my business by sleeping with one of my escorts. I can't take the chance that she might succeed."

His secretary cackled. "Sounds like my kinda woman!"

Lydia was his kinda woman, too, but Luke wasn't about to let his secretary in on that bit of juicy news.

"Well." She drummed her gnarled fingers on top of her desk. "I guess I could do it . . . if it will help save the company and finally get you a good woman."

Oh, hell. Luke started to argue with her, but the phone interrupted his protest.

He froze.

Mrs. Scuttle cackled again as she reached for the

phone. "Mr. Complete Escort Services. This is Madeline speaking."

She winked at Luke. He forced himself to relax and listen.

"Yes, Ms. Carmichael. I understand, Ms. Carmichael." She paused, her head tilted and a grin on her face that made Luke uneasy. "Any particular reason you don't want Luke again? Because if he's done something wrong, I'm certain Mr. Reynolds will take care of it."

Luke pinched the bridge of his nose. Everything has a price, as he was certain he was about to find out.

"You say he was an excellent escort? Then what's the problem?" She nodded. "Ah, a personality clash. He too chatty for you, is he? I have that problem around the office sometimes. I'm trying to work and he just keeps on talking. But what really boils me is that touchy-feely problem he has. You didn't have that problem with him? Lucky you. No, age doesn't matter to him. I think he needs to have his testosterone level checked. I'll mention that to the boss."

Grabbing a pad and pen, Luke scribbled furiously on it, asking Mrs. Scuttle to please shut up.

She winked at him again and shoved the pad back at him. "Yes, I know all about that sexual harassment crap, but I don't care. When you get to be my age, you're not choosy about how you get your kicks. Did I shock you? Sorry, honey. I forget myself sometimes. Working around all these horny men—"

"*Mrs. Scuttle,*" Luke hissed, louder than he intended.

"Yeah, I guess we should get down to business. Wouldn't want that boss of mine to fire me for goofing around."

She cackled, and Luke would have given his eyeteeth to know what Lydia had said in response to that.

"Well, honey, I'm afraid you're going to have to put up with Luke if you need an escort. He's the only one available." Her voice dropped to a confidential whisper.

The sound of it made Luke break out in a cold sweat.

"You know . . . with that nonstop chatter and that touchy-feely thing he's got going on, he doesn't get as many assignments as the other guys do. I feel kinda sorry for him."

By the time she hung up the phone, Luke was close to tears. He glared at his smug-looking secretary. "You were having fun," he said, stating the obvious.

Mrs. Scuttle shrugged her bony shoulders. "I figured if I was going to tell a lie, I might as well tell a whopper and help you out."

Luke shook his head. "Now she thinks I'm an oversexed pervert. How is that going to help me?"

"If you don't know the answer to that one," Mrs. Scuttle said dryly, "then I'd say you definitely need to get out more." She glanced up as the door behind Luke opened and one of his employees came in.

"Jet!" Mrs. Scuttle cooed, making Jet instantly wary and Luke suspicious.

Jet, whose full name was Jerome Elliot Thomas, had

been with Luke for three years. His golden, honey-toned skin and flashing black eyes earned him good tips and girlfriends galore. But Jet resented being called a player; he claimed he was looking for Ms. Right.

"Mornin'," Jet said, keeping a cautious eye on Mrs. Scuttle as he poured himself a cup of coffee.

It didn't take long for Luke to figure out that something more than the usual fear factor was present in the room. He folded his arms and glared sternly at his secretary, who blinked her owlish eyes innocently back at him. "What's going on?" Luke demanded. "I feel like I missed something."

"You didn't miss a thing," Mrs. Scuttle said—too innocently. She hooked a finger in the handle of her tea cup and shot a warning look at Jet.

Luke caught it. "Jet?" He cocked a brow and waited. It was obvious Jet was bursting to tell someone. It was also obvious that he was afraid of Mrs. Scuttle.

Finally, Jet turned to face the room with his coffee. As he lifted his cup to his mouth, the cuff of his shirt sleeve dropped away from his wrist.

Luke straightened in his chair. "Is that a bite mark on your wrist?"

Jet hesitated. He glanced accusingly at Mrs. Scuttle, then down at the floor.

And said nothing.

"Is someone going to tell me what happened? Or am I supposed to guess . . . ?" After another moment of stubborn silence, Luke heaved an exasperated sigh and rubbed his jaw. "Okay, I'll take a wild shot. You tried to steal Mrs. Scuttle's granola bar and she bit you."

Mrs. Scuttle took offense. "I'm not stingy with my food, you numbskull."

But she didn't say that she didn't bite. Luke pounced on the oversight. "But you did bite Jet. Am I right?" Lucky for him that Mrs. Scuttle hated to lie.

She wasn't, however, above using technical evasion tactics. "I didn't break the skin, so I don't see what the fuss is about."

Luke's brows rose in disbelief. "You admit that you bit one of my employees, and you don't see what the fuss is about?" He shook his head over the bizarreness of the conversation. Maybe he *should* consider hiring a new secretary—one with a little less bite and a lot more bark. Never again, he mourned, could he joke about his secretary's bark being worse than her bite.

Hell. He rubbed his eyes to make absolutely certain he wasn't having a nightmare. Then he said, "I want to hear the whole story, and I'm not picky about who tells it." It wasn't often that he used his authority with his employees to get what he wanted, but this was an exception.

Jet responded to that authority, his respect for Luke overriding his fear of Mrs. Scuttle. "She . . . she was sitting straight up in her chair and she had her eyes closed. I couldn't wake her up, and I thought—" his honey-toned skin turned a shade darker "—I thought she wasn't breathing, so I put my hand on her chest to see if she had a heartbeat."

"I take it you found one," Luke concluded dryly. "Is that when she bit you?" When Jet nodded, Luke sighed and looked at his secretary. He was relieved to catch a flicker of shame in her magnified eyes. "Mrs. Scuttle, why did you bite Jet?"

She clamped a hand to her bosom. "I thought some scumbag had walked in from the street and was trying to have his way with me. I didn't know it was Jet until I'd already bitten him." Her eyes watered. She blinked and sniffed. "Can't blame an old widowed woman for being cautious, can you?"

Inwardly, Luke softened. Outwardly, he maintained a stern expression. "Did you tell Jet you were sorry?" he asked gently.

She made a show of blowing her nose with a hanky covered in big pink roses before she answered. "I guess maybe I forgot. He gave me some scare, I'll tell you that." When Luke stared pointedly at her, she added reluctantly, "I'm sorry, Jet, for biting you. But next time I suggest you try a little harder to wake me before you decide I've kicked the bucket. I was just having a little afternoon nap. When you get to be my age, you'll be doing the same."

Jet gave an embarrassed shrug at her backhanded apology. "I didn't mean to scare you, Mrs. Scuttle."

Luke clapped his hands together, eager to get this ridiculous conversation over and done. "Okay, that's settled. Jet, try to keep that . . . mark covered. We're standing on shaky ground as it is. The last thing we need is for a client to see it and draw her own nasty little conclusions." A client like Lydia, Luke thought. "Jet, how did your assignment go with our V.I.P. client?"

"She's jumpy, but I managed to make her laugh a time or two. I can't blame her for being paranoid, though, after that last attack."

"What happened?" Luke asked. Cameron Rose, a rock singer on the rise to stardom, had formerly used At Your Service when she needed an escort. Luke was pleased and flattered that she'd turned to him.

Jet poured himself another cup of coffee, finally relaxing in Mrs. Scuttle's presence. "Her stalker shot an arrow over the ten-foot wall surrounding her property, with a love note attached. The arrow landed three feet from where she was lying beside the pool."

Luke winced, immediately concerned for Jet's safety. "Maybe this job's too dangerous."

"She's paying double, Luke, and she knows I used to work for Congressman Baily. She feels safe."

"But didn't you say you got out of the bodyguard business because of the risks?"

"Yeah, but this is different." Jet's dreamy smile alarmed Luke. "Besides, she's a hell of a woman and a great singer. She's really fun to be with."

"Don't let all that glitter go to your head," Luke warned. "Detective Parker is just looking for a reason to close us down."

"So is that Carmichael woman," Mrs. Scuttle added sagely.

Jet blinked in confusion. "What Carmichael woman? What's she talking about?"

"Oops."

Luke suspected his secretary wasn't at all sorry she'd slipped up, but he swallowed a sigh and said, "I held a meeting, but you were working. I'll bring you up to date at lunch." He hadn't gone into detail with the others—except Greg, for obvious reasons—on the slight chance that his foster brother had managed to bribe one of his employees into helping him with his nasty little sabotage, and Luke didn't plan to go into detail with Jet, either.

He hated to think any of his loyal employees could be bribed, but when he'd told Lydia everything had its price, he'd really meant *everyone.*

And unbeknownst to Lydia, Luke's price had nothing to do with money, and everything to do with a whole lot of lovin'.

Chapter Eight

"What time is this function you have to go to?" Casey asked, grabbing a bottle of spring water out of the compact fridge in the office they shared. She uncapped it and drank half before lowering the bottle.

Lydia tapped her personal appointment book with her pen. "Eight. It's some kind of presentation. Aunt Tempera said there would be plenty of money floating around for me to gather. All I have to do is mention her name and Hope House in the same sentence."

"Wow. That must be a heady feeling to know you have the power to help a lot of unfortunate people."

"Aunt Tempera doesn't think of it that way. She donates the interest from her savings account every year and still frets that she hasn't done enough."

"As if buying a plantation house and doing a zillion dollars' worth of renovations isn't enough." Casey propped her butt on the edge of the desk and sighed. "I can't believe we've been so busy." She took a sip of her water and grinned at Lydia. "You know why, don't you?"

Lydia groaned and arched her stiff back. "Because we work like dogs and we're so damned cheap?"

"Not just that, but because word's gotten out about that hunk Greg dropping his drawers. Half the women who came in today were hoping they'd get lucky. If we stay this busy, we'll have to hire a couple more people or work even longer hours ourselves."

"Count me out, at least until Aunt Tempera gets back into action."

Casey sobered. "How's she doing, anyway?"

"I don't know." Lydia wiped a hand over her brow, pushing a lock of hair away from her eyes. "She just can't seem to get motivated. I wish she'd see a doctor."

"You mean a shrink."

"I'd settle for anyone with a degree right now, if they could help Tempera get over Tony."

"Bastard."

"Rat."

"Creep."

"Scumbag."

"Gigolo."

Lydia had to laugh. "Okay, you win. You're better at name-calling than I am. Suffice it to say he's all of the above."

"That's what *I'm* saying," Casey muttered. She hopped down from the desk and pitched her empty water bottle in the trash can. "Guess I'd better get back to work. Thank God tomorrow's *my* day to play boss. I think I've got mud in my eye and wax in my ears, not to mention seaweed in my hair."

When she'd gone, Lydia opened her personal day planner and stared at the red ink she'd used to mark each function she had to attend for Tempera the following week.

Three. Three more times she'd have to be close to Luke just in the following week, unless she wanted to get him into trouble by filing a complaint. What could she say? That he was too sexy? Too appealing? That he had trouble zipping his own pants?

Her face heated as she pictured him in that stall, climbing out of his pants so that he could take off his boxers and prove to her that he hadn't been lying.

She could think of another way he could have proved it, but that was dangerous thinking. Finding that intimate garment in her purse had been dangerous and shocking enough.

How could she face him again after that . . . that embarrassing episode in the stall? And how could she *not* face him, knowing he was the perfect gigolo for the plan she had in mind?

She had to keep her personal feelings out of it. She was doing this for Tempera, and if it was turning out to be more complicated than she'd first anticipated, then so be it. But from now on, *she* was going to set the pace. When she decided the moment was right, she would sleep with him and have the evidence she needed.

In the meantime, she just had to be good. Behave. Resist. Remind herself that she wasn't in the vengeance business for her own pleasure.

The door burst open again. Lydia looked up to find Casey hidden behind a gigantic flower arrangement. "Where did those come from?"

Casey set the arrangement carefully on a small table and plucked the card from the basket. She handed it to Lydia. "See for yourself, and hurry so I can get back to work. I left a very slippery Mrs. Dalton on the massage table to sign for this."

Curious, Lydia opened the small, oil-stained card and withdrew the note. "It says, 'Thanks for coming to my rescue. Looking forward to Thursday evening.' " Lydia felt her face flush. "It's from Luke."

"The escort?"

Lydia nodded.

"What did he mean by coming to his rescue?"

She'd been afraid Casey would ask that question. Instead of confiding in her best friend, she had tried to put the incident from her mind.

So far she hadn't succeeded, and now she not only had to think about it, she had to talk about it. "Um, he had a little trouble with his zipper."

Casey's eyes widened. "Are you saying that you and he—that you had *sex* with this guy and you didn't tell me?"

"No!" Lydia fanned her hot face. "Why does everyone assume that?"

"Everyone?"

"Aunt Tempera said the same thing. Well, something like it, when she saw the black silk boxer shorts—"

"Whoa, Nelly!" Casey dragged a chair over to the desk and sat down. "I don't care how busy we are, I'm not leaving this room until you tell all."

"Casey, I don't want to—"

"If you spill it now—and don't leave out any details—I'll forgive you for waiting two whole days to tell me."

As quickly as she could, Lydia told Casey about her date with Luke. Only it really wasn't a date. Just because it had *felt* like a date, didn't make it a date.

She had paid the man for his time, for Heaven's sake.

She finished by telling Casey about the black silk boxers in her purse. Casey clamped a hand over her mouth to stifle her laughter. Lydia's lips twitched, but she sternly chided them into order. "How can you laugh? The man was in pain!"

"And you care?" Casey challenged. "I thought you hated him and everything he stands for."

Lydia hesitated a second too long. "Of course I dislike the man. He's a gigolo."

"What if he isn't like the others? Would you like him then?"

"Why are you asking me this?" Lydia felt confused

by Casey's badgering questions. "You forget, Detective Parker said Anthony wasn't the first employee working for Mr. Complete to sleep with a client. I'd say that's pretty good evidence that they all make their living that way."

Casey shrugged. "Well, all I'm saying is that I'd hate to be in your high heels. This one sounds pretty irresistible."

Lydia had the perfect comeback, something that would promptly end this ridiculous conversation. "Yeah. Apparently Anthony was, too."

Lydia watched for Luke's arrival from the window. Aunt Tempera's driver Roger had brought the limo around and was waiting in the driveway. She had left her aunt upstairs going through her photo album. Lydia grimaced. The album contained pictures of Tony. Pictures of Tony with Tempera; pictures of Tony with Uncle Theo's Jaguar, which Tempera had given to him a week before he left town; and more pictures of them together at Savannah Beach: Tony standing in the waves with a laughing Tempera on his shoulders; Tony with Tempera, sitting on a blanket, feeding Tempera grapes and staring into her eyes as if he adored her.

Aunt Tempera appeared to be getting worse instead of better. What was Lydia to do? She had to do something!

Maybe *she* should see a psychiatrist and get some

advice. She'd made no headway in getting her aunt to go.

Parting the curtain, Lydia looked out the window again. A set of headlights turned into the driveway. Almost immediately, her heart began to hammer and her mouth went dry.

The vehicle pulled up behind the waiting limo; it was a huge black SUV that must have cost someone a small fortune. Lydia's lips twisted. Had a woman bought it for him? Was this one of the perks Luke had bragged about? Did it still count as prostitution if he accepted gifts instead of money? She made a mental note to ask Detective Parker.

"Oh. I thought you'd gone already."

Lydia jumped at the sound of Tempera's voice. She whirled around, her heart in her throat as the doorbell sounded. Luke! Luke was at the door and her aunt was poised on the bottom of the stairs. She couldn't let them meet!

Snatching up her purse, Lydia rushed to the door, flinging a smile over her shoulder. "Just leaving! See you later, Aunt Tempera."

"Wait."

Lydia froze, swallowing a groan. She heard Sweeney's precise footsteps approaching. If she hadn't been so preoccupied thinking about Luke, she could have beaten him to the door.

"I'd like to meet your date, Lydia." There was a smile in Aunt Tempera's voice as she added, "I promise not to mention the black silk boxers."

"Um—" Lydia tried to think of a logical excuse. The best she could come up with was, "We're running a bit late, Aunt Tempera. Maybe next—"

"Ah, there's Sweeney. Sweeney, get the door so I can meet the mystery man Lydia doesn't want me to see."

Sweeney reached Lydia and moved around her to open the door.

Lydia's heart stopped. Her apprehensive gaze clashed with Luke's. His smile faded as he stepped into the foyer. He was dressed in a charcoal-gray suit that outlined the width of his broad shoulders.

As if he needed it.

"Am I late?" He checked his watch, then glanced at her again with eyebrows raised. "You did tell the secretary eight o'clock?"

She should have warned him. She should have told him that she didn't want Tempera to know she'd hired an escort.

"Lydia?" Tempera prompted in a slightly strained voice. "Aren't you going to introduce us?"

She knows, Lydia thought, trying not to panic. *He's too perfect to be an ordinary date. Like a Ken doll.* Lydia stifled the urge to laugh hysterically at her silly simile.

Slowly, with dread swamping her, she turned to face Aunt Tempera. She opened her mouth to lie through her teeth to the woman she loved most in the world. What was one more lie? And wasn't it a good lie, since she was doing it for Tempera?

But she didn't have to lie, not this time.

Luke stepped forward before she could say a word. An engaging grin spread across his face as he strode to meet Tempera at the bottom of the stairs. He lifted her hand and brought it to his mouth. "You must be the aunt Lydia's always talking about. I'm Luke Smith."

Smith? Lydia's mouth fell open in shock. She quickly closed it as Tempera looked at her.

"You didn't tell me what an absolute gentleman he was," she chided Lydia. "And how handsome. No wonder you were drooling."

"Aunt Tempera!"

Luke's eyes brimmed with laughter. Lydia wanted to sink through the floor.

"And she didn't tell me how beautiful you were." Luke dropped her hand and winked at Lydia. "Maybe she was afraid of the competition."

Lydia unlocked her jaws before her luck ran out. "We should be going, Luke. I have to stop at Hope House on the way and drop off a check for the housekeeper." To her relief, he joined her at the door, taking her elbow. "Good night, Aunt Tempera. Don't wait up."

"Bye, darling. Have a good time."

When the door closed behind them, Lydia sagged against Luke. "How did you know?" she asked as she climbed into the limo.

He got in and closed the door before answering. "The horrified look on your face tipped me off," he said dryly. "Don't worry, we're used to it."

"And it doesn't bother you?" For some reason Lydia couldn't fathom, it bothered her.

Luke shrugged. "Women just feel more comfortable with people not knowing they've hired an escort. I understand perfectly."

"You do?"

He glanced at her and smiled. "Yes, I do. I think it has to do with that whole wallflower complex. Do we really have to stop at Hope House?"

"Yes." She was relieved that she didn't have to lie. "I really do have to give the housekeeper a check."

"That reminds me." Luke fumbled in his suit coat pocket and withdrew a check. He handed it to Lydia. "I told my boss about Hope House. He wanted to make a donation."

Lydia stared at the check with a revulsion she wasn't completely successful in hiding. How could she take a check from a man she was trying to destroy? She couldn't. She just couldn't. How to decline tactfully and without arousing Luke's suspicions?

"Something wrong?" Luke's voice was silky smooth. "You do take individual donations?"

He knew that she did. He'd watched her do it. She cleared her throat, reaching to take the check. She'd take it and tear it to shreds later, she thought. With glee. Maybe she'd even stomp on the shreds and let off some steam.

Then she glanced at it.

And choked.

Luke slapped her on the back until she recovered.

"I would hope," he drawled, "that your shock is a good sign."

The check was for ten thousand dollars. Yes, she'd seen bigger checks—much bigger—but she hadn't expected such a generous check from someone like L. J. Reynolds. She glanced at the check again.

It was made out to Tempera Foster.

"Something wrong?" Luke repeated, staring at her quizzically. "You look as if you bit into a lemon or something."

Lydia didn't doubt him for one moment. She searched his face for some sign that he was mocking her. "Did—did your boss tell you about my aunt?" she asked, the intensity of her gaze making her eyes burn.

"Just that she was an amazing, generous woman who did wonders in the community."

He sounded totally innocent. Generous, indeed, Lydia thought bitterly. No doubt L. J. Reynolds thought Tempera the most gullible of fools when it came to generosity.

"Why do I get the feeling I'm missing something here?"

She shook her head. If Luke didn't know about Anthony and Tempera, she wasn't going to enlighten him. No doubt L. J. Reynolds was ashamed of himself and guilt had prompted the generous donation.

As if ten thousand dollars could make up for all the pain and suffering his company had caused Tempera.

Not even close.

But she couldn't in good conscience tear up the

check. It belonged to Hope House, and would go a long way toward helping the homeless.

Trying not to gag, she put the check in her purse, making a mental note to deposit it to the Hope fund herself so that Tempera wouldn't see it.

"Lydia?" Luke prompted softly.

Lydia snapped her purse closed and set it on the seat. She didn't want to hold it any longer than necessary. "It's nothing," she said with a shake of her head. "I was just thinking about something unpleasant." Which wasn't a lie.

"Maybe I can take your mind off it," Luke said in a low voice. He picked up her hand, bringing it to his lips. He feathered a kiss over her sensitive skin, making her shiver.

She wanted to snatch her hand back, but sternly reminded herself that this was exactly what she'd been hoping for. Trying to ignore her thumping heart, Lydia stared out the window as the limo approached the plantation.

"Tell me more about Hope House," Luke said, settling her hand on his thigh and covering it with his own.

When she tried to tug it free, he applied just enough pressure to prevent the motion without an obvious struggle. She let it rest, feeling his muscles flex beneath her palm. The man was made of steel, she thought. Was he that hard all over? If her plan worked, she would find out soon enough.

The provocative thought made her belly flutter with

shameful anticipation. She hastily focused on his question. "It's not the original plantation house. During the Civil War, the owner burned it to the ground to keep the Yankees from using it as a military post. He was luckier than most because he'd invested in several factories in the North, so he was able to rebuild after the war."

"He used the same blueprints?"

"Yes. Right down to the cypress lumber he had imported from Louisiana for the first house."

"No wonder it's in such good shape," Luke murmured, gazing past her to look out the window at the huge plantation home. "Cypress is almost indestructible." He pointed to several large shipping crates backlit by the security lights. "What are those?"

Lydia followed his gaze. "Playground equipment. One of our former residents hit it big with a company he went to work for and he talked his firm into donating the equipment."

"There's a success story."

She sighed. "Yes, it is. Now if we can just find some volunteers to put it together . . ."

Suddenly, a piercing scream rent the air. The limo came to an abrupt halt, throwing Lydia forward and sending her heart into her throat. "Roger? Please tell me we didn't just hit someone!"

The limo driver sounded shaken as he said, "No, ma'am. I think a kid just fell from one of those crates."

"Dear God," Lydia said, reaching for her door latch.

Chapter Nine

Luke reached the little boy first. Roger had left the headlights on, so Luke could see how white and pinched the little guy's face was as he lay sprawled on his back, trying to catch his breath.

He was definitely in pain.

"What happened?" Lydia demanded.

When Luke glanced at her, he saw that she'd taken off her high-heeled shoes and held them in her hand. She was directing her question to a solemn group of boys standing a few yards away.

"Jeremy? Colte?"

A black-haired boy of seven or eight with huge brown eyes reluctantly answered Lydia's sharp question. "We dared him to jump."

"*You* did!" the other cried, his voice hitching as he fought tears. "I told him not to!"

"Colte, where's your mom?" Lydia asked, gingerly approaching the boy on the ground. She knelt, seemingly oblivious to the destructive combination of wet grass and sheer hose.

"She got a job today, working at a coffee shop," the younger one said with obvious pride.

Leaning over the boy, Lydia reached out and smoothed the hair from his forehead. She spoke softly. "Are you in pain, Bart?"

Bart gulped and nodded, then moaned.

Luke gently explored his shoulder. "I think he dislocated his collarbone," he said. "We'll have to get him to the emergency room." He looked over his shoulder and spotted Roger hovering in front of the limo. "Roger? Can you get the door?"

"He gets to ride in a limo?" Jeremy asked with awe. "That ain't fair!"

A horrible image came to Luke's mind; he could easily imagine Jeremy and Colte leaping from the crate in the hopes of getting to ride in the limo.

He hadn't forgotten what it was like to be a boy, especially a boy enthralled by the finer things in life.

"Is it okay if they come with us?" he asked Lydia.

Lydia nodded. Luke could tell by the look they shared that she'd been thinking the same thing.

She spoke to the oldest boy, Jeremy. "Go tell Ms. Ruth what happened and where we're going, and hurry back."

Very, very gently, Luke gathered Bart in his arms and took him to the limo. He laid him carefully on the seat, breaking into a cold sweat when the boy cried out in pain. "You sit with him," he instructed Lydia, who obeyed without question.

He saw that she had grass stains on her knees and a big hole in her stocking; she didn't seem to care or notice. Gently, she lifted Bart's head and settled it on her lap. She began to talk softly to him, soothing him with her voice, stroking his forehead.

"Don't worry, Bart. Everything will be just fine."

Watching her with Bart put a lump in Luke's throat. He wanted her more than ever. Wanted to haul her into his arms and kiss her like there was no tomorrow. Wanted to tell her how much he admired her loyalty, her spirit, and her loving nature.

Wanted to make love to her over and over again, and watch the sunrise, holding her in his arms.

Then Luke had a terrible thought, one that made his blood run cold. What if he never convinced Lydia that he was anything other than what she believed him to be?

"I want my mom," Bart whimpered. Tears trickled down his dusty face.

"Ms. Ruth will let her know what happened. She'll probably meet us at the hospital, okay?" When she glanced at Luke, she must have read the question in his eyes. "Ms. Ruth is sort of like the babysitter, housemother, and housekeeper rolled into one. She's a wonderful volunteer."

"Should they have been outside at this hour?" Luke asked, trying his best not to sound critical.

Lydia smiled faintly. "My guess is they sneaked out when she wasn't looking. Am I right, Bart?"

Bart gave his head a tiny nod.

"Colte and Bart are brothers. Jeremy is a cousin who lives with them. A few months ago, his parents died in a fire that razed their apartment building to the ground, leaving a lot of families homeless, including Bart's."

"My cat got burned up," Bart whispered sadly. "So did Jeremy's. He cries himself to sleep at night."

The odd lump returned. Luke tried to swallow it. He suspected Jeremy cried for more than his cat, poor guy. "I lost my dog when I was about your age," Luke said, feeling compelled to share with the boy. He'd lost more than his dog that day, too, but he didn't want to burden Bart with the awful details.

Bart's pain-filled eyes brightened a bit. "How?"

"It was a car accident. It was dark, and a garbage truck didn't see our parked car. Our dog was sleeping in the back window."

"Why was he in the car?"

"Because . . . that's where I was." Luke shifted and looked out the window, regretting his impulsiveness. He hadn't figured on the boy asking questions, and Lydia was staring a hole through him already. And there wasn't just sympathy in that look; there was understanding.

"We lived in our car once," Bart said, startling Luke with his perception. Luke hadn't actually said they'd been living in their car at the time, but Bart had figured it out on his own. "Until we came to Hope House. It was fun, but kinda crowded."

Luke was saved from responding as Jeremy and Colte came running up to the limo, followed by a visibly shaken woman he assumed was Ms. Ruth. He opened the door to let the boys in, pointing to his own seat opposite Lydia and Bart. The boys had that wet puppy smell to them, and their eyes glittered with excitement.

"We'll call you as soon as we know something," Lydia told Ms. Ruth. "Call his mother and tell her to meet us at the hospital."

The limo moved forward, pinning the boys to the back of the seat and causing Lydia to brace herself and Bart to keep from pitching forward. Bart cried out, and Luke felt his pain as if it were his own. He muttered a nasty curse beneath his breath and growled at Roger through the open partition. "Take it easy, will you? The kid's in pain!"

"Sorry, sir." Roger sounded rattled, which explained his reckless driving.

Luke clenched his jaw and tried to look anywhere but at Bart's pained little face and Lydia's silent, questioning one.

Me and my big mouth, he thought.

Lydia felt a reluctant admiration for Luke as he carried Bart inside and barreled right past the security guard. She followed with the goggle-eyed boys.

Luke walked up to the receptionist with his burden.

"Point me to a room. I think his collarbone is dislocated, so I don't want to move him twice."

The receptionist, a young girl with blond hair and dark roots, blinked at him as if blinded by a bright light.

Despite the somber situation, Lydia felt her lips twitch; she knew exactly how the girl felt.

"You—you haven't signed him in," the receptionist stammered. "He has to wait his—"

"Never mind," Luke growled. "I'll find an empty room."

"Wait! You can't go back there!"

"The hell I can't."

Her alarmed shout alerted the security guard. He came trotting up, but Luke had already disappeared through the door leading into the emergency treatment area. Lydia hesitated to follow him with Jeremy and Colte.

"Take a seat in the waiting room, and don't move a muscle," she instructed. They obeyed without question, and only when she was reasonably convinced they'd stay did she go after the security guard.

Luke wasn't hard to locate; she just followed the sound of raised voices. He was arguing with the security guard and the e.r. nurse in one of the partitioned rooms.

"He's in pain! You can't move him again," Luke was saying.

The security guard sounded like a man trying to calm a loose cannon. "I understand what you're going through, mister. If it were my son I'd feel the same way, but we have rules in this hospital—"

"You're not moving him." This time Luke didn't raise his voice. He was stating a hard fact. "So stop wasting everyone's time and get a doctor in here."

The e.r. nurse and the guard exchanged a resigned look. "It's okay, Bill, I'll handle it from here," the nurse said. She pasted a bright smile on her face and moved to stand beside Bart. "What happened?" she asked.

"He jumped from—"

The nurse cut Lydia off. "I'm sorry. I have to hear it from him."

Bart looked at Lydia, then Luke. They both nodded. "I jumped off a big box," he said. "Jeremy dared me."

"Who's Jeremy?"

"My cousin. He's older than me."

"Can you tell me where it hurts?"

Bart tried to move his left arm. He gasped and cried out. "There! It hurts right there!"

Luke started to bolt forward, but Lydia grabbed his arm to hold him back. "Wait," she whispered urgently.

"Okay, okay." The nurse spoke in a soothing voice that immediately calmed Bart. She took Lydia and Luke aside and said softly, "You'll have to wait in the waiting room when the doctor gets here. There's no way to do this painlessly."

"Can't you give him a shot or something?" Luke demanded.

Beneath her fingers, his arm was rock-hard. Lydia wondered if he realized he sounded exactly like a hysterical father—and he hardly knew Bart. In fact, she was almost certain the nurse thought she and Luke were Bart's parents. Was he putting on a show for her benefit?

The moment the thought entered her mind, Lydia felt ashamed. Just because Luke was a gigolo didn't mean he couldn't possess the capacity to care. "Come on," she said, tugging on his arm. "Let's go check on the boys. Bart's in good hands."

He allowed her to lead him away, but Lydia noticed he did it reluctantly, as if he couldn't bear to let Bart out of his sight. *He'd make a good father.* The realization came to her unbidden and unwanted.

Lydia ruthlessly pushed the thought from her mind. She couldn't let her emotions get in the way of doing what she knew she had to do. There was usually a thread of good in the worst of villains.

Luke was no exception.

It was after midnight before they were able to leave Hope House. Bart was resting in the room he shared with his mother, brother, and Jeremy. His mother had arrived at the hospital moments before the doctor popped Bart's shoulder into place.

Lydia didn't think she'd ever forget Luke's agonized expression when he heard Bart scream. In fact, she was fairly positive he had come close to fainting.

Now, as they pulled away from the plantation

house, she studied Luke's handsome face in the dim interior of the limo. Reluctantly, she admitted that she was curious about him. She wanted to know why a man like Luke, a man who exploited his looks and charm, would care so much about a homeless boy.

"You've got questions," Luke stated softly, startling Lydia. "Your eyes are full of them."

He looked at her, and she saw his lips twitch in the beginnings of a wicked smile.

"Do you mind?"

"Do *you?*" he countered swiftly. "And are you sure you want to know? Because sharing brings a certain intimacy to any relationship, don't you think?"

The soft, seductive sound of his voice enveloped Lydia like a warm, satin cover. She shivered, hoping he'd missed her betraying reaction in the dim light. Did she want to take that chance? Wouldn't it be easier to sleep with Luke if she *didn't* know him?

Maybe easier for her conscience, but not easier for her admittedly old-fashioned ideas about sex. The thought of sleeping with someone she didn't know made her feel sick inside.

She took a deep breath. "We shared a crisis together. I think it's only normal that we feel . . . closer."

"Okay. I'll buy that. What do you want to know?"

"Well, for starters, do you have family?" She held her breath, half expecting him to balk at her question.

His lips twisted in a cynical smile. "Leave it to a woman to go straight for the throat."

Lydia flushed. "I'm sorry. If it's too painful for you, you don't—"

"It was a long time ago," he said. "And no, I don't have any family. Along with my dog, my parents were also killed in that car accident. The only reason I'm alive is because I was asleep in the backseat, surrounded by blankets and pillows and every stitch of clothing we owned. We were living in our car at the time."

"Oh God, Luke. I'm so sorry." Lydia's throat burned with tears of sympathy. "That must have been awful for you. How . . . how old were you?"

"I was eight. My mother hemorrhaged to death in the emergency room. One minute she was talking to me, telling me everything was going to be all right, and the next minute there was blood dripping from her left eye. Then she just . . . died." He stared out the window. His features were rigid, unsmiling. "I was lucky enough to be placed with wealthy foster parents who spoiled me rotten."

He'd said he was lucky, but Lydia didn't think he meant it. She suspected his foster parents had denied him what he needed most: love.

"Your turn." He turned abruptly to look at her. "Do you have family other than your aunt?"

Lydia shook her head. "No. My aunt and uncle raised me. My parents left me with them when I was five."

"Where are they now?"

"Dead," Lydia said flatly. "They ran a salvage operation, cruising the seas for sunken ships and looking for mythical treasures. Their boat got caught in a hurricane. They were never found." She let out a bitter laugh. "I guess someday they'll become someone else's salvage. Ironic, isn't it?"

"You're still angry with them."

"No, not really. Tempera and Uncle Theo were very good to me. I know I was better off with them. I guess maybe my parents knew it, too."

"So we have something in common; we're both orphans."

"Yeah." She hated that he was right, but loyalty compelled her to add, "Although my aunt and uncle never made me feel like an orphan."

"You're lucky to have them."

Another clue that he didn't know about Tempera and his ex-coworker, Lydia mused. "My uncle died when I was sixteen, so it's just me and my aunt now."

The limo came to a smooth halt in front of the darkened three-story mansion. Lydia made a mental note to thank Roger properly tomorrow for his help in getting Bart to the hospital. Maybe she'd give him a gift certificate for a full-body massage.

Roger opened the car door and helped her out. Luke surprised her by following her to the front door. She fumbled with her key, extremely conscious of Luke standing next to her. Finally, she got the door open.

She turned to Luke, feeling flustered and warm and confused. "Thanks so much for all your help tonight," she said. "I'll make sure you get a bonus."

"I don't need a bonus. In fact, I'm going to ask Mr. Reynolds to waive tonight's fee."

Surprised, Lydia stared at him in open-mouthed shock. "That's not necessary. In fact, I insist that you get paid."

Luke chuckled, reaching out to tilt her chin. "In that case, I want to be absolutely certain I've earned that bonus."

Before Lydia could question his meaning, Luke kissed her, his warm, firm mouth exciting and full of wicked promise as it moved over hers. His tongue swept over her lips, demanding entrance.

With a tiny moan Lydia couldn't suppress, she melted against him and opened her mouth. His hot tongue darted inside.

She shuddered and clutched his shoulders, lost in a fog of desire and anticipation. Luke was a great kisser. A marvelous kisser, and Lydia suspected he would rock her world if she gave him the chance.

When, not *if*, she reminded herself. The reminder shot her blood pressure up another ten notches.

As if he could read her naughty thoughts, Luke pressed her against the wall beside the door and let her know the shocking truth; he was hard and throbbing. Lydia was astonished to find herself growing damp between her legs, as if he'd touched her with those warm, talented fingers.

What would happen when he did touch her? Would she go up in flames, like so many of her friends claimed? Lydia spread her feet apart so that she cradled his hard length. So that his erection pressed against the very part of her that throbbed and burned.

He moved slowly, languidly, against her, as if he knew exactly what he was doing to her. Lydia gasped and clutched his shoulders as his tongue darted in and out of her mouth in an erotic rhythm she wanted to copy with her hips. She whimpered, shamelessly dropping her hands to clutch his hard butt cheeks.

She pulled him hard against her, wanting more, not caring if her aunt slept upstairs, or if Roger could see them from his apartment over the garage. It was dark, and she was on the verge of . . . on the verge of . . .

Luke broke the kiss, resting his lips on her jaw. "Goodnight, Lydia," he whispered huskily.

It took a full moment for his words to sink in. Heat rushed up her neck and into her face. She dropped her hands from his butt cheeks as if they'd turned into twin burners. Her voice sounded strangled as she choked out, "Um, goodnight."

She couldn't get in the door fast enough.

Chapter Ten

He'd nearly blown it with Lydia.

Luke grabbed a crowbar and pried the lid from one of the crates, popping the nails into the air. They landed harmlessly on the grass. Mindful of bare little feet, he picked them up and shoved them into his pocket, pausing to wipe his face with the T-shirt he'd tied around his waist. It was only nine o'clock in the morning and the Georgia sun was already scorching his back.

He looked at the other guys busy opening crates, heard their laughter, and felt their enthusiasm. Collin, his bare chest gleaming with perspiration, strode over to Luke.

"Found the instructions, Luke." He handed over a thick book, grinning at Luke's dismayed expression.

Luke opened the book, tried and failed to focus on

the tiny print, and pitched it aside. "We don't need instructions, do we?"

Collin laughed and clapped him on the back. "Nah. But I expect we could use some strapping young boys to help." He jerked his head at the group of boys watching them, squinting in the bright glare of the sun.

Bart was among them, looking pale but hopeful with his arm in a sling. Luke smiled and waved them over. "Bart, we could sure use something cold to drink. Think you could manage that?" Bart nodded happily and shot off like a rocket toward the house. Luke studied the rest of the boys—six in all—including Jeremy and Colte. The oldest appeared to be in his early teens and was nearly as tall as Tyler, who at five-eleven was the shortest of Luke's men. "The rest of you boys pair off and help the others. We want this equipment up and ready before the sun goes down."

"Yes, sir!" The oldest gave him a dignified, if clumsy salute; the rest whooped for joy.

Retrieving the crowbar, Luke went back to attacking the crate. Collin hung around, dodging the nails that rained down around them.

"Something bothering you, Luke?"

"No." Luke grabbed the stubborn crate top with both hands. The cords in his neck stood out as he pushed upward. Rusty nails squeaked in protest, then finally surrendered. To his relief, Collin gave up and went back to work on his own crate.

Collin was astute, because something was definitely

bothering Luke. After nearly exploding during that sizzling encounter with Lydia, he'd tried a cold shower the moment he got home.

Afterward, he'd still been able to hang a towel on his erection.

An early morning workout—after a restless night—hadn't worked, either. Now he was hard at it, hoping the hot sun and work would take his mind off Lydia's erotic whimpers and butt-clutching hands.

Unless he was mistaken, she had been close to experiencing the Big One right there in the doorway.

And *that* was his problem. He couldn't get the image out of his mind. Couldn't erase the memory of her hot little mouth sucking on his tongue, couldn't forget how she'd opened those long, gorgeous legs of hers so that she cradled his erection like a glove.

"Think about something else," he muttered, dragging a heavy cluster of steel bars from the crate. "Think about how you spilled your guts about your pathetic childhood. Think about that; then think about how little she'll care when it comes time to stick it to you."

"They say," Ivan said from behind him, "that only crazy people talk to themselves."

Luke shot him a glowering look over his shoulder. "I'll agree to that. What's up?"

"Just thought I'd let you know that we have an audience."

"What?" Luke frowned at Ivan, then followed his amused gaze to the plantation house. He shaded his eyes. On the long, elegant porch stood a group of women, perhaps a dozen or more. "And your point is . . . ?"

"Just thought I'd let you know."

The moment the words left Ivan's mouth, Bart appeared in the doorway. He was carefully balancing a tray filled with glasses. The women leaped at him, fighting over who would carry the tray. Finally, a tall blonde held the tray triumphantly over her head. Luke was amazed that none of the glasses appeared to be damaged.

Bart's chagrined expression made Luke and Ivan chuckle. "Looks like we're about to have company," Luke said. "Tell the men to be on their best behavior—and to tone down the charm."

"Will do, boss."

"And don't call me that. Remember, I'm just plain ole Luke today." He looked around at the five men who had volunteered to help assemble the playground equipment. There was Greg, Collin, Ivan, Tyler, and Jet. Collin, Ivan, and Tyler were married, but that didn't lessen their talent for making a woman feel confident, beautiful, and unique.

Luke knew because he'd trained them. It was their job and they did it well. Pride swelled Luke's chest. Yes, dammit, he was proud of each of them, as proud as any football coach of his team. His men did their jobs with style and sensitivity.

And by God, he wasn't going to let a skunk like Rhew Burgess sully Mr. Complete's reputation and cause his men to lose their jobs, and he wasn't going to let a misguided woman like Lydia bring them down, either. He knew Ivan and his wife were very close to having that down payment for their first house, and that Collin and his wife were planning a second honeymoon in Hawaii.

Jet had just bought a Jaguar, and Tyler, who was an out-of-work actor with three kids, was still out of work.

They all had something to lose if Rhew or Lydia succeeded with their plans.

Heaven forbid the two should ever meet!

"Ms. Ruth called," Casey informed Lydia shortly before closing time. "She wants to know if we can do a house call at the plantation, something about a few emergency manicures."

Lydia's brows rose as she made certain all the lids were tightly closed on the gallon jars of seaweed, Dead Sea mud, sea salt, and hot wax. Because of the spa's low prices, they couldn't afford to be anything but frugal. "Must have been a lucky day for more than one job hunter today." She glanced at the clock, then back to Casey. "I don't have anything planned tonight. Do you?"

Casey shook her head, a shadow flickering in her eyes. "No. Brett's working late . . . as usual. Oh, and Ms. Ruth asked if we had anything to treat a sunburn."

"Shall we go together, then? I'm eager to see how Bart's doing."

"Sure. I'll get the aloe gel for the sunburn."

"I'll get our manicure case."

They gathered the necessary items, turned out the lights, and met at the door. Lydia had an envelope clutched in one hand and the manicure case in the other. "I thought we'd pass out a few gift certificates while we're there. Some of these women will never see the inside of a spa otherwise."

"I know. Good thinking. My car or yours?"

Lydia muttered a curse. "I knew I was forgetting something this morning. I forgot to get gas, so I guess we'll take your car. Afterward you can drop me off and I'll have Roger bring me to work in the morning."

The Georgia sun was setting as they drove out to the plantation house located about ten miles from the heart of Atlanta. When Casey sighed for the third time in as many minutes, Lydia took the hint, "I take it things are not getting better between you and Brett?"

Casey grimaced as she navigated around some construction work on the exit ramp. "I guess maybe my idea of a good marriage isn't the same as Brett's."

"What do you mean?"

"I mean that Brett seems to think it's perfectly natural to make love once a month after just six months of marriage."

"You lived together for two years before you got married," Lydia reminded her. "Did a piece of paper make that much difference?"

"Yes, it did." Casey shot her a bewildered glance. "I've heard men say their sex lives changed drastically after marriage, but I've never heard another woman complain."

"Have you thought about seeing a marriage counselor?"

"When I mentioned it, Brett went through the roof. He claimed I was overreacting and reminded me that I knew he was going to be working impossible hours until they made him a partner." She sniffed, sounding miserable. "I think he's having an affair."

"What? That's ridiculous! Why in the world would he marry you if he wanted to sleep around?"

"Believe me, I've asked myself that same question, Lydia. The answer I keep coming up with is that *I* was the one who suggested we get married. Maybe he wasn't ready."

"Marriage is a big step, and Brett's an intelligent man. I doubt he'd do something that serious without thinking it through."

Casey was silent for a moment. Then she said, "Maybe you're right. I hope you are." She peered through the windshield, frowning. "Hey, you didn't tell me that you finally found some volunteers to put together the playground equipment!"

"That's because I didn't. . . ." Lydia gawked at the shiny new equipment. Children squealed and played, chasing each other from one activity to another. There were two heavy-duty swing sets, monkey bars, slides, a merry-go-round, and teeter-totters.

Shiny and new and put together.

Lydia resisted the urge to rub her eyes. Last night

Bart had jumped from a sealed crate containing a daunting array of poles, bolts, and screws. Now the crates were nowhere in sight. It would have taken more than a few men to do that much work in so little time.

Who? Had Tempera come back to the land of the living long enough to rustle up some volunteers? It would be great news, of course, but somehow Lydia doubted it. Just this morning she'd left her aunt moping around in her bedroom. It was clear from the dark shadows beneath her eyes that she'd had another sleepless night.

Casey stopped her car in front of the plantation house and cut the engine. She stared through the windshield as the motor ticked while it cooled.

Her miserable expression made Lydia want to shake Brett until his teeth rattled. Didn't he see how insecure Casey was? Didn't he realize she needed to be needed? To know that he loved her, and only her?

Men.

Lydia stifled a sigh and got out of the car, grabbing the manicure case and the gift certificates. She hoped she'd brought enough. "You coming?" she asked Casey, wishing she knew how to cheer up her friend.

"Of course I'm coming," Casey muttered. "And I may just stay here all night and see if Brett even notices I'm missing."

As they climbed the steps and approached the front door, Lydia heard the sounds of shouting and laughter coming from inside. She frowned. Normally, the people staying at Hope House moved about in a cloud of depression.

Laughter? Shouting? What was going on?

She and Casey exchanged curious looks before Lydia opened the door and went inside. The noise was coming from the dining hall where three simple meals were served each day. There was always a volunteer around to plan and supervise the meals, but everyone staying at Hope House pitched in with the cooking, serving, and cleaning.

Lydia supervised when she could; Casey often helped on weekend nights while Brett worked until the wee hours of the morning for the firm. She told Lydia it was the only thing that kept her from going insane.

"It sounds like a party," Lydia said, moving down the hall in the direction of the noise. Maybe someone's birthday, she thought.

She stopped dead in the doorway. Casey ran into her, bumping her on into the big dining room. Lydia blinked, then blinked again. She heard Casey gasp behind her and echoed the sound.

She recognized Luke immediately and Greg from the spa, although it was surprising that she did, since they were both covered in watermelon juice. The other four men were also covered in juice, their faces and chests pink from it.

All six were bare-chested, sitting around the long dining table stuffing watermelon into their mouths while the crowd around them—a bedraggled mixture of women and children—cheered them on.

Ms. Ruth was at the front of the crowd, cheering and shouting with the best of them. No one seemed to notice their arrival.

"Which one's Luke?" Casey asked, whispering in Lydia's ear.

Lydia turned her head slightly without taking her eyes off the surreal vision to whisper back, "How did you know?"

"Because I know they're not the Chippendale guys—although they could definitely qualify—so they have to be from Mr. Complete. *Which one is Luke?*"

"To our right, second one down." The moment the words left her mouth, Luke looked up and saw her, as if he sensed her intense regard. A quiver shot through Lydia, right into her belly, where it kept on quivering. Her breath quickened. He was covered in watermelon juice, and his hair was dark, as if it were wet. The juice on his chest and arms made his skin glisten, intensifying the rippling motion of his muscles as he set the huge slice of watermelon on the splattered table.

He was one big, hunky, sticky mess, and the sight of him made Lydia feel faint with a need so fierce it shocked her to the core.

She wanted him, right then and there, watermelon juice and all.

"Ah," Casey said. "He would have to be the sexiest one."

Lydia didn't have the breath or the presence of

mind to disagree. As far as she was concerned, the other men didn't exist.

Only Luke, and he was rising from his chair, his gaze locked with hers. His khaki shorts hung low on his hips, revealing a sexy line of dark hair that disappeared into territory Lydia itched to explore. He wiped his mouth with the back of his hand, his eyes still on her. Even that barbaric move jolted her libido.

Why? Why did this watermelon-soaked gigolo turn her on?

Vaguely, she realized the shouting and cheering was beginning to die down as the rest of the crowd noticed them. One by one the men looked up and saw them.

They grinned sheepishly, as if they'd been caught doing something naughty. So that naughty smile *was* a job requirement, Lydia thought dazedly.

"Shit," Casey said, her voice curiously hoarse. "Why can't Brett look like this? He'd never get to work, because I'd tie him to the bedpost and—"

"Lydia! Casey!" Ms. Ruth cried, rushing over to them. Her face was flushed red and she was smiling from ear to ear. "Did you see the playground? Wasn't that the sweetest thing you've ever seen? We can't thank the boys enough for doing this for Hope House."

Boys? Lydia almost laughed. Boys? Ruth saw these spectacular men as boys?

"Someone donated a truckload of watermelons yesterday, and I knew we'd never eat them all, so Luke suggested we have a watermelon-eating contest to celebrate getting the playground equipment together."

The only thing Lydia could think of to say was, "I thought someone needed a manicure."

Ms. Ruth laughed. "Yes, someone does. In fact, I believe Greg needs one as well as Jet and Tyler. They all have important dates tonight. Isn't that a coincidence? And with all that rough work they did putting the equipment together, well, it just ruined their fingernails. I told them you and Casey wouldn't mind, not after what they did for us."

Lydia swallowed hard, feeling lightheaded for no apparent reason. "You—you said something about a sunburn?"

"Luke kept his shirt off a little too long, and so did Collin. Collin's so fair, you can see why he burned easily. I knew you'd have just the right remedy for it."

So they weren't just pink from the watermelon juice, Lydia realized. They were sunburned from putting together playground equipment for Hope House.

A ploy on Luke's part to manipulate her into believing he was a good guy? Or . . . a genuine, honest-to-God gesture of goodwill? Lydia knew she shouldn't have been hesitant to make her choice.

But she was, and she immediately warned her hesitant heart that keeping her confused was also Luke's ploy. She doubted he did anything without a hidden motive. Men like Luke were trained in the art of conning women, making them believe they cared when they didn't.

Casey poked her in the back. "I'll take care of Collin," she whispered, sounding shamelessly breathless.

Her friend's apparent breathing problem—and the familiarity of it—alarmed Lydia to the point of recklessness. She turned around and grabbed Casey's shoulders, startling her. "Stay away from him," she whispered. "Stay away from all of them, Casey. They're . . . they're . . ." *What were they?* Dangerous? Lethal? Mesmerizing?

But Casey laughed and brushed her hands away. "Don't be silly. You know I love Brett, but there's no harm in looking, is there? Especially when my own man is hardly ever around for me to look at."

Before she could answer, big, strong hands landed on her shoulders and spun her around. She stared into Luke's handsome, smiling face, her heart flip-flopping around in her chest. In a flash, his hot intimate gaze resurrected their erotic little dance last night in her doorway.

"Lydia? Would you mind taking a look at my back?"

Yes, Casey, Lydia thought as weakness flooded her knees, there is harm in looking.

Chapter Eleven

"God, that feels good. You've got the hands of an angel, Lydia."

She could have done without him including her name in his husky, appreciative comment. In fact, she could have gone the rest of her life without ever knowing what an absolute, erotic, breath-stealing pleasure it was to smear aloe gel on Luke's broad, gorgeous, sunburned back.

Her slow strokes were designed to keep from hurting him, she told herself, not to prolong her own pleasure.

Yeah, right.

Meanwhile, Greg was on the love seat, and Casey sitting in a kitchen chair parked in front of him. The two were chatting away as she filed, shaped, and buffed Greg's blunt nails. Lydia kept a wary eye on them.

More than once she caught Greg looking at her with something akin to horror, as if *she* had been solely responsible for his pain and suffering the day he came in for a wax job. Okay, yes, she might have ripped the muslin cloth a little too quickly, and she might have smiled when he screamed, but a hot wax job was never a painless procedure.

"I would gladly pay you to do this to me all night," Luke said, arching his back as she trailed the gel along his reddened spine.

Lydia forced herself to stop when her fingers reached the top of his shorts. She hoped she didn't sound as shaky as she felt when she said, "Imagine that. *You* paying *me*."

"Ouch."

She stopped. "Did I hurt you?"

"Only with your words, Lydia."

She resumed her doctoring, if one could call such a pleasure doctoring. She had covered every inch of his skin at least twice, but she hoped he hadn't noticed. "So I injured your ego."

Before he could answer, Bart's mother, Sandra, came into the room and handed Luke a wet towel so he could wipe the sticky melon juice from his chest and arms. She was a petite blonde with sad blue eyes, but she had a special smile for Luke. "I want to thank you again for what you did for Bart last night, Luke."

Luke? Did everyone at Hope House know his name? Lydia was surprised at the possessive feeling that swamped her. Was she crazy? Luke wasn't hers!

He was a useful tool in her plan to close Mr. Complete.

"I only did what anyone would have done, Sandra. Don't mention it."

The moment Sandra was out of earshot, Lydia couldn't stop her wayward tongue. "There. Ego all better now?"

Luke startled her by turning around until he straddled the chair, facing her. Slightly alarmed, Lydia stepped back, gel-smeared fingers raised in the air. He took his time looking at her, from the tips of the painted toes revealed by her sandals, to the top of her upswept hair, heating her skin with his hot gaze.

"If I told you no, would you kiss it and make it better?" Without taking his eyes from hers, he offered her the towel.

Without thinking, Lydia reached for it.

He snagged her wrist and tugged her to him. Lydia sucked in a sharp breath as his thighs brushed her legs. The back of the chair stood between them. Her face grew hot at the thought of Casey and Greg watching them. Thank God the others were busy cleaning up after the contest and the children were outside enjoying the new playground.

She tried not to move her lips as she hissed, "Let me go. Casey knows we're not a real couple, so you can stop acting."

Abruptly, Luke let her go, his expression one of mocking disappointment. "Spoil sport."

"Show off," she countered—but not before she was safely out of reach.

Casey talked nonstop on the way back to Atlanta.

Lydia listened halfheartedly, her mind straying constantly to Luke and his motives for what he'd done for Hope House. It was almost as if he was trying to prove something to her, as if he knew what she really thought of him. But he couldn't possibly, she assured herself.

"Greg gave me some interesting tips on how to interest Brett in sex again," Casey said, capturing Lydia's attention. "He's been with the same person for ten years now."

"Person? Don't you mean woman?" Lydia's face burned as Casey burst into laughter. "What's so funny?"

"You don't know? Greg's gay! Man, I can't believe you didn't guess that when he came in for a waxing."

Stiffly, Lydia said, "Muscle builders get their bodies waxed and so do wrestlers."

Casey shot her a knowing look. "Ah . . . I get it. You just can't accept the fact that Greg can't be one of *them.*"

"You're being ridiculous."

"Just consider it, Lydia. Isn't it possible that not all the guys who work for Mr. Complete sell sex? That maybe—just maybe—some are hard-working, decent guys like Greg?"

Lydia turned her face to the window. She didn't

want Casey to see her doubt and gloat. "Even if by some slim chance you turn out to be right, it doesn't change the fact that Mr. Complete needs to be shut down. It only takes one bad apple to spoil the whole bunch."

"What if Anthony was that bad apple?"

"Don't forget the other leech, Graham Somebody, whom Detective Parker told me about."

Casey fell silent for a long moment. Finally, she ventured, "It's just that they all seem so nice. Did you know that Tyler, Collin, and Ivan are married and that they all have kids? I just can't picture them prostituting themselves, knowing their wives and kids are waiting for them at home."

"They've brainwashed you, Case, plain and simple. Luke tries to do the same thing to me." *And damned near succeeds.* "They're trained to be convincing."

"I don't know."

"I do." Lydia let out an aggravated sigh. "Casey, you're a perfect example. You were in their company less than two hours and you're ready and willing to believe they're nothing but perfect angels." She hesitated before adding, "Luke's already hinted at a price."

The car swerved. Casey shot Lydia a shocked look. "No! Has he? What did he say?"

"I asked him if he ever got involved with his assignments, and he said yes. Then he said that everything had a price."

Casey flipped her blinker on and veered onto an exit ramp. "You could have taken that totally wrong,

Lydia! What if he was talking about emotions? Maybe he's gotten involved with someone and *he* got hurt? Isn't that possible?"

It was just impossible for Lydia to imagine self-assured, conceited, Mr. Perfect putting himself in the line of emotional fire. No, she couldn't. Not in a million years.

Now to convince Casey before she totally defected on her. It meant she would have to get personal, but during war sacrifices had to be made. "He's also been, um, very forward."

"Define forward. I don't think they've used that term since the latter part of the nineteenth century."

"Well, he, um, kissed me last night." *And I kissed him back, and we both nearly went up in flames.*

"Oh . . . my . . . God!"

Lydia sniffed. "Don't be sarcastic, Casey. I don't think seducing a woman in an open doorway is part of his job . . . if he's the angel you think he is."

"Seducing? What? You didn't say anything about seducing, Lydia! You said kissing. And aren't you supposed to be the one doing the seducing?"

"I never get the chance. It's almost as if he anticipates my every move before I can make it." Not that she would have had the courage to do to him what Luke had done to her. At least not so fast. Okay, maybe not ever.

She was a plodder.

Luke was a jumper, and boy could he jump!

"I don't see what the problem is, then," Casey said.

"If he's already showing signs of willingness, why don't you just make him a deal, do it, and get it over with?"

It was a damned good question.

"Are you afraid you might enjoy it?"

Bingo. "No," Lydia lied. "How could I enjoy having sex with a man who's probably thinking about the size of my checking account?"

"Oh, I don't know. Maybe paying a man to perform is a secret fantasy of yours."

"It certainly isn't!" Was it? Lydia bit her lip. What if it wasn't Luke that turned her on, but the *idea* of Luke? Now Casey had succeeded in making her question herself! It was nuts. The entire idea was nuts.

Wasn't it?

"Some women get off on that, you know," Casey said, swinging the car into the tree-lined driveway leading to Tempera's house.

"Obviously, or Luke would be driving a Honda instead of a luxury SUV."

"Maybe he's independently wealthy?"

Lydia shot her a candid look as Casey stopped the car in front of the mansion. "Maybe. Or maybe he's a gigolo and a woman bought the SUV for services rendered."

"You've got a one-track mind," Casey said with slight exasperation.

"Before you met Mr. Complete's harem of men," Lydia shot back, "our minds were on the same track." She hated to fight with Casey, but she couldn't allow

Casey to become another gullible victim. Pausing as she opened the car door, she looked back at Casey, lifting a taunting brow. "Care to come in and visit with Aunt Tempera? Maybe you could compliment her on her weight loss, or give her some tips on how to deal with those dark circles under her eyes. Oh, and while you're at it, maybe you could also give her some pointers on how to mend a broken heart and a badly shattered ego."

Casey lifted a stubborn chin. "Two wrongs don't make a right. I think you should call this whole thing off before someone else gets hurt, Lydia."

Lydia's fingers tightened on the door handle. Very softly, she said, "You're afraid that someone is going to be me, aren't you?"

Luke eased carefully back against his office chair. His back still burned and he ached in places he hadn't known existed, but it had all been worth it.

Seeing those kids' faces light up, hearing their laughter as they played on the newly assembled equipment was enough to make a grown man choke up.

Greg had openly cried.

And, yes, he had to admit that the confused look on Lydia's face when she realized what they'd done had definitely added to his feeling of accomplishment. Imagine, a pack of womanizing gigolos sweating it out beneath a hot sun, ruining their manicures and blotching their complexions, all for a bunch of homeless people . . .

He pushed back the sleeve of his crisp white shirt to check the time. One hour until he saw Lydia again. One whole hour before he could see for himself if she'd softened at all toward him and his crew.

The door to his office creaked open. Luke glanced up, surprised to find Tyler standing in the doorway. He was dressed in a dark conservative business suit—one of their many attires for the many roles they played. "Tyler. What brings you to the office on a Saturday evening? I thought you had an assignment."

"I do." Tyler came on into the room and flopped down in a chair. He stared at Luke for a long moment. "I came to warn you about Lydia Carmichael."

"Oh?" This should be good, Luke thought, folding his arms. "You've met her before yesterday at Hope House?"

Tyler nodded, his expression serious. "Anthony pointed her out to me one night at some charity function we both had to attend. She's Tempera Foster's niece."

"I know." Luke knew Tyler was waiting for him to explain further, but he forced himself to keep quiet. He had decided in the beginning to trust no one but Greg until this business with Lydia was safely handled. Thanks to his blabbermouth secretary, Jet knew more than he should, but Luke hoped it would go no further.

"Rumor has it Tempera Foster hasn't left her house since Anthony dumped her."

Luke clenched his jaw, recalling the deep sorrow in

Tempera's lovely eyes. "I think 'scammed' her would be a more appropriate description," he said, his voice clipped.

"Yeah, which brings me to my next question. After what happened to her aunt, why would Lydia Carmichael hire an escort from Mr. Complete?"

Tensing, Luke sat forward in his chair. "How do you know she did?"

Tyler sighed and shook his head, as if he couldn't believe Luke would ask such an obvious question. "Because like the rest of us, you're not a man women easily forget, and women talk. You weren't hard to recognize from their detailed description—and there was the fact that you called yourself Luke. You're lucky that most people know you only as L. J."

"Yeah, I'm lucky." Luke relaxed slightly. Tyler's explanation sounded logical. It also told Luke that Tyler was aware *something* was going on, and if Tyler suspected, the others likely did as well. And why wouldn't they? He had asked them to refer to him as Luke yesterday at Hope House, instead of using their typical good-natured handle of *boss* or *boss man.* His men had brains as well as charm and good looks, and he was ashamed that he had forgotten that important fact, even for a moment.

"I don't know what you're up to, but whatever it is, I think you should be careful."

"Thanks for your vote of confidence," Luke said dryly. "It's good to know my employees believe I can be so easily fooled by a pretty face."

"Hey, you're not just my boss, you're my friend." Tyler stood, carefully brushing the front of his dress pants. "I wouldn't have been able to sleep a wink tonight if I hadn't talked to you."

"You're a good man, Tyler, and I really appreciate your concern."

When he'd gone, Luke drummed his fingers restlessly on the desk top. What had started out as a little lesson had turned into a much more complicated affair. The more people who knew of his involvement with Lydia, the riskier it became. If she found out that he was L. J. Reynolds before he could sway her opinion of him and his company, then all was lost.

She would not only detest him for his part in the charade, she would never believe that Mr. Complete was a reputable escort company that operated with strict moral codes. Understandably, his bad-boy actions to date would strengthen that belief.

Yet Luke had no trouble justifying those actions. He *had* to give her reason to believe he was easy. If he suddenly became the model escort, Lydia might give up on trying to get him into bed and find a way to hire another escort from his company. Eventually even the enterprising Mrs. Scuttle would run out of excuses.

The thought of Lydia coming on to another man in that innocent, yet highly erotic way she had made Luke mutter a curse and head for the door. She had no idea of her seductive powers, and he had no intention of letting another man enlighten her.

Chapter Twelve

"Learning computer skills will not only benefit the adults, it will help the children by providing them with access to research materials, furthering their education and giving them a head start in the ever-tightening economy."

Holding aloft two elegant flutes of champagne, Lydia stopped behind Luke, immobilized by his passionate and winning speech to a group of potential funders. In helping her convince them they should give their money to Hope House instead of a dozen other competing charities milling about the room, he was going above and beyond the call of duty.

He was an escort, there to provide silent support—emphasis on *silent*. He was required to dance when she needed a partner, eat beside her at the banquet table, and generally give everyone the impression that she was stable and respectable. Lydia thought it was ridiculous that in this day and age there were still people who thought of women as the weaker sex.

But then, pleasing the wealthy society of Atlanta hadn't exactly been on her agenda when she hired Luke in the first place.

"The obvious choice is Hope House, ladies and gentlemen," Luke concluded.

Okay. It was official. Luke was trying to impress her. Why? To soften her up before he tried to sell her his body? Was this just another tried-and-true ploy of his?

"Here she is now." Luke took her elbow and pulled Lydia into the circle. He dropped his arm to her waist and tugged her against him as if he had every right.

Lydia stifled her annoyance. Hadn't she told him she didn't like public displays? Obviously he needed to be reminded . . . later. She handed him a glass of champagne and took advantage of the whispered argument that broke out between two elderly sisters who owned a chain of dry cleaning stores. "Why do I get the impression that you've done this before?"

Luke smiled at her. "I have. My foster mother was an animal activist. If you lived in her house, you believed what she believed."

"Or . . . ?"

His smile twisted cynically. "Or she took away your toys."

She shifted, her hip brushing his. She moved hastily away, but not before she felt a vibration coming from his pocket. "I think your beeper's vibrating." At least she hoped it was a beeper. She fought a blush and ducked her head, sipping her champagne.

"I was trying to ignore it."

"Don't on my account. I don't expect your exclusive attention." The bald fact was that she was curious. Did Luke have a girlfriend? A dog? A cat? A friendly neighbor who looked after his pet if he had one? She knew personal things about his past, but nothing about his present. Did he live in a condo? A house? Have a roommate? Did he leave the cap off the toothpaste?

She tried not to stare as he took out his beeper and read the message scrolling across the tiny screen.

"Hmm," he said, frowning. "It's an SOS from Jet. Will you excuse me?"

While he was gone, Lydia tried to focus on the conversation around her, but she couldn't concentrate. She remembered Luke introducing Jet to her at Hope House, and she wondered what could be wrong.

She didn't have to wonder long. Luke returned a few moments later, still frowning.

Taking her aside, he told her in a low voice, "I have to leave. Jet's in trouble."

Lydia found herself responding to the urgency in his voice with genuine concern. "I'll go with you. We'll take the limo."

Luke looked surprised. "What about your work here?"

Instead of answering, Lydia fished in her purse and brought out a stack of business cards. She quickly passed them out, smiling her apology. "I'm sorry, but I've got an unexpected emergency. You can mail your donations to the address on the card. Thanks so much."

"Oh, dear. I hope it has nothing to do with our darling Tempera?"

The question was posed by Beverly O'Nassa, widow of tycoon Marcus O'Nassa. A casual acquaintance of Tempera's, but not a close friend. Lydia's smile was strained as she shook her head. "No, nothing to do with my aunt. That nasty flu bug has left her weak, but she's rallying nicely. She should be back to her old self very soon."

Beverly's malevolent look told Lydia that she knew Tempera wasn't recovering from the flu. "Such a long time to recover from a . . . *flu.* Do give her my love, Lydia."

"I will." She had no intention of even mentioning Beverly's name to Aunt Tempera, but she held her smile and managed to get out of the room without telling Beverly where she could stick her insincere platitudes.

The moment they stepped into the warm night air, Luke said, "I wasn't aware that your aunt was sick."

Lydia was still seething over Beverly's evil digs. How did Aunt Tempera tolerate her? "She was having a good day when you met her."

"She seemed like a lovely woman." Luke waved Roger back into the limo and opened the door for Lydia.

"She is." She heard Luke give Roger directions before he joined her.

They sat facing each other in the limo. Lydia was staring out the window, but she could feel Luke's questioning eyes on her. It was uncanny the way his gaze seemed to generate heat wherever it touched.

"Would you like to talk about it?"

Lydia did her best to look confused. "Talk about what?"

"About why you're so mad."

"I'm not mad. There's nothing to talk about." Surprisingly, Lydia found herself wishing she *could* talk to Luke about her aunt. But that would be silly, all things considered.

"What you and your aunt do for the homeless is nothing short of saintly," Luke said, as if he felt the need to boost her confidence.

She couldn't suppress a snort. "If anyone's a saint, it's Aunt Tempera for keeping her temper around malicious, back-stabbing women like Beverly O'Nassa."

"Ah. Beverly O'Nassa's the reason why your eyes are throwing off flaming darts."

She shot him a couple of those darts as she said, "I get defensive when someone attempts to malign my aunt's character."

"That's putting it mildly," Luke drawled.

Lydia thought it was prudent to change the subject—before she confessed something she'd regret. "So where are we going?"

"A new club that just opened. Deep Impact, I believe it's called."

She remembered reading about it in thc paper yesterday morning. "Isn't Cameron Rose supposed to perform there tonight?"

"Yes, I believe she is." Luke shot her an enigmatic look before tapping on the closed partition. "Roger, can you get this monstrosity down an alley?"

"I can give it a try, sir."

"Good. Turn left into the alley just past this club and stop at the second door. Be ready to move fast."

"Yes, sir."

Her curiosity highly piqued, Lydia glanced out her window at the long line of people fighting to get into the club. Roger had to slow to a crawl to avoid a nasty accident as people pushed and jostled each other. Lydia's eyes widened as two girls fell to the ground, punching and pulling each other's hair. "Now I'm glad I didn't come," she said faintly.

"You were thinking about it?"

He sounded too surprised for Lydia to give him a simple answer. "Why wouldn't I? Contrary to what you might think, I do put my pants on one leg at a time, just like everyone else."

"I didn't mean—hold on." He punched a number into his cell phone and said, "We're just turning into the alley now."

Lydia waited until he hung up. She wasn't about to let him off the hook. "You were saying?" she prompted.

"I was saying that I wouldn't have pegged you for a rock 'n' roll lover. Classical music, maybe, but not rock."

"Actually, I'm very versatile when it comes to music," Lydia informed him coolly. "Cameron Rose has a fantastic voice—" She broke off as the car door opened abruptly. Before she could satisfy her curiosity, Luke grabbed her arm and hauled her onto his lap to make room for the couple piling into the car.

She was too shocked to move, or to notice who had joined them until Luke said, "Lydia, meet Cameron Rose. Cameron, I believe Lydia's a fan of yours."

Luke decided he definitely liked surprising Lydia. She not only let her guard down to express an almost childlike shock, she forgot important facts, like that her bottom was nestled intimately against his crotch.

She felt good in his arms. Damned good.

Squirming, however, wasn't a good idea.

"Be still," he whispered urgently in her ear.

"But, that's—that's Jet, with Cameron Rose." Her fingers closed over his forearms and tightened. "You—you could have told me."

"There wasn't time." She was soft and feminine and smelled heavenly. Luke pressed his nose against her neck and inhaled. Soon she'd come to her senses and scramble from his lap.

There wasn't a moment to waste. He flicked his tongue out, tasting her velvet skin. She was sweet.

Very sweet. A groan rose in his throat, but he managed to swallow it down.

"My God, Luke. You should have told me you were in the middle of something," Jet said. "I could have called Greg."

Luke sighed and lifted his head from Lydia's enticing neck. "Greg's working tonight. And I'm not in the middle of anything." Although he'd like to be. Oh, yeah.

"No, he isn't," Lydia added, sounding mortified for no good reason that Luke could think of. He'd only been nuzzling her neck. Okay, so he'd licked her neck, but he didn't think the other couple had seen him.

She struggled, and he reluctantly let her go. She scrambled to the opposite seat, looking from Jet to Cameron, as if she couldn't believe her eyes.

She completely ignored Luke. Was it Cameron who shocked her? Or was it the fact that *Jet* was with Cameron? Luke discovered he was dying to find out.

Before he could figure out a subtle way to accomplish this, Cameron spoke. "I'm so grateful for your help, Luke." Her powerful voice trembled slightly. "When I saw *him* in the crowd, I—I just panicked. My voice shut down and I just stood there looking stupid."

Jet caught her hand in his. "You didn't look stupid. The crowd just thought you were taunting them." He sounded frustrated and angry. "I just wish I could get my hands on that creep."

"There wasn't anything you could do, Jet. The fact

that you were there helps more than you could ever know."

"What happened to your driver?"

The performer looked stricken. "I don't know. I couldn't reach him by phone, and Eddie always keeps his phone on."

"Would someone mind telling me what's going on?" Lydia demanded, apparently over her shock.

Luke caught Cameron and Jet's worried exchange and said, "She can be trusted. Besides, she has a right to know; she not only left an important fund-raiser to come with me, this is her limo."

"Oh." Cameron offered Lydia a warm, if wan, smile. "Then I should thank you as well, for coming to my rescue. This man's been stalking me for the past few weeks, and tonight I saw him at the club." She shivered, causing the brilliant sequins adorning her gown to shimmer as if they were alive. "I've been trying to keep this out of the tabloids. The police seem to think that the spotlight might make him even bolder."

"How frightening for you!" Lydia's sincerity was obvious.

So was her curiosity about why Cameron was with Jet, Luke thought, wisely hiding his amusement. He took pity on her. "Jet once worked as a bodyguard for a politician."

"He's your bodyguard?" Lydia squeaked out.

"Yes, and my escort." Cameron smiled faintly. "I get two for the price of one."

"That's what *you* think," Jet teased. "Just wait until you get my bill."

"I'm sure it will be worth every penny." Her smile fading, Cameron dug her cell phone out of her purse. "I'm going to try to reach Eddie again," she said, biting her lip. "I hope nothing's happened to him."

Everyone sat in expectant silence as she waited for Eddie to answer her call. When her face lit up, Luke heard a collective sigh of relief.

"Eddie? Where on earth are you? What? Oh . . . my . . . God! Are you okay? Did you phone the police?" Cameron put a hand to her breast, her expression wide-eyed with shock. "You sit tight. I'm on my way. Yes, yes, I'm okay. Jet's with me." She hung up the phone, looking dazed. "After Eddie dropped us off at the club, he went back to get the stack of glossy photos I left lying on the hall table. I was going to autograph them for the club. Someone—someone was in the house. They clubbed him from behind and took some of my personal things."

She started to shake uncontrollably. Jet pulled her against him and tried to reassure her. Luke was beginning to understand Jet's frustration now, because he, too, wanted to get his hands on the creep terrorizing Cameron.

They rode in silence the rest of the way to Cameron's estate. When they stopped in front of her modern, sprawling house, Cameron turned to Luke. "Would you—you mind coming in with us? Just for a few moments?" She looked at Lydia, her gaze imploring. "Both of you?"

Luke lifted a questioning brow at Lydia. Without hesitation, she nodded.

What a woman.

Chapter Thirteen

Eddie turned out to be a surprisingly young black man with a wealth of glossy dreadlocks and a beautiful smile. But behind his smile Lydia saw strain and concern—not for himself, she sensed—but for Cameron.

He was waiting with two police officers in the living room of the spacious mansion. Lydia was surprised to find the decor homey and comfortable, with an oversized sofa and two matching chairs situated in front of a huge fireplace. A big flat-screen television hung from the ceiling, and to her delight, there was an impressive built-in aquarium filled with tropical fish dominating the back wall of the living room.

When Lydia spotted a pair of fuzzy pink slippers by one of the overstuffed chairs and photos of a young boy on the mantel, she began to relax. Cameron Rose might be a rising star, but at home she was a person just like everyone else, with comfy slippers and pictures of her son proudly displayed.

As Jet and Cameron talked to the officers, Lydia wandered over to the aquarium. A dog-faced blowfish gave her a toothy grin as he swam by. Lydia could see the outline of a child's hand on the glass, evidence that not long ago someone else had stood where she did, gazing at the fish. Someone much shorter, she mused.

"Thank God her son is with his father," Luke said, as if he'd read her mind. He reached out and traced the hand print. "Since this all began, she hasn't gotten to spend much time with him."

"She's probably wise to send him away," Lydia murmured, feeling sorry for the singer. She'd hate to be forced into sending her child away because of some disturbed maniac who should be locked up. "I guess there are a lot of disadvantages to being popular."

Luke nodded. "Even fame has its price."

A jolt of shock rocked Lydia. He was talking about prices again. Coincidence? Or a hint? Surely he wasn't thinking about sex at a time like this? Poor Cameron had just been burglarized!

She gasped as he reached out and grabbed her chin, forcing her to look at him. "Believe it or not, Lydia, I'm not *always* thinking about sex."

"My God," she whispered, closing her eyes to lessen her embarrassment, "you're a mind reader."

"No. Your face is just very expressive, babe."

Babe. Normally, Lydia would object to being called a "babe." Luke made it sound like an erotic nickname, something no sane woman would mind his whispering in the heat of the moment. *Now* who was thinking about sex? She was shameless . . . or hopeless. Probably both.

Cameron saved her.

"Lydia, would you mind coming with me? The policemen want me to take a good look at my bedroom . . . see if I can tell what's missing." She twisted her hands, looking pale. "They've checked to make sure he's gone, but I still don't want to go in there alone. Eddie says it's a mess, so I'd rather not take Jet with me."

Lydia instantly understood. Cameron felt violated, and she felt more comfortable around a woman while those feelings were still running high. "I don't mind at all." She was more than grateful to get away from Luke's all-too-knowing gaze.

The master bedroom was located at the end of a long hall. They passed an exercise room, a guest room, an office filled with computer equipment, and a child's room before they came to Cameron's spacious bedroom. Decorated in varying shades of green and white, it was far more opulent than the previous rooms Lydia had viewed. It was also obvious that Cameron favored velvet. There was a dark green velvet bedspread and matching curtains, and dozens of velvet pillows in lime green, hunter, and white, stacked neatly on the king-size four-poster bed.

Lydia followed Cameron to a walk-in closet, admiring the singer's bold decorating style. It gave Lydia the impression that Cameron was largely untouched by her rising fame.

Cameron stopped abruptly in the doorway of her closet, her hand over her mouth.

"What is it?" Lydia asked sharply, sensing her distress. She moved past her to see for herself what had upset Cameron.

The closet was much like her own, with space-saving dividers and drawers and built-in shoe shelves.

But there the similarities ended. Unless Cameron was a slob—and the rest of her house didn't indicate she was—the intruder had spent a lot of time in the closet, going through Cameron's lingerie. Bras and panties, silk stockings and satin teddies . . . everything that Lydia suspected had been neatly folded and put away now lay scattered everywhere.

With a strangled cry, Cameron backed hastily out of the closet. She was breathing hard, her eyes wide with horror and disgust. "I can't stay here tonight. I can't stay here alone. I can't. I just can't!" She stumbled, turned, and ran into Jet, who had come rushing down the hall at her cry. "Oh, God, Jet! He was in my closet! He was—he was touching my *underwear!*" Her breath hitched on a sob. "Stay with me. Stay here with me tonight. I can't stay here alone!"

Luke appeared behind Jet, his concerned gaze clashing with Lydia's. He lifted a questioning brow. Lydia waved a hand behind her, indicating the strewn underclothes.

"Stay with me, Jet!" Cameron clutched his shoulders, sobbing her heart out.

Lydia caught an odd exchange between Jet and Luke. Before she could fathom its meaning, Jet said, "We'll take you to a hotel. You'll be safe there."

Cameron took a deep shuddering breath and wiped her streaming eyes. "I don't want to be alone. Please stay with me?"

Jet shot Luke an angry, frustrated look before he reluctantly shook his head. "I—"

"You can stay with me," Lydia cut in, unable to bear Cameron's disappointment. It was obvious Jet had been about to tell her that he couldn't—or wouldn't—stay with the distraught woman. What was wrong with him? How could he be so callous, so unfeeling? Cameron just didn't want to be alone, and Lydia didn't blame her.

"Oh, I couldn't," Cameron said. "You hardly know me, and—"

"My aunt has dozens of guest rooms, and we could get to know each other over a double chocolate fudge brownie." Lydia smiled encouragingly. "Deal?"

For a long moment, Cameron remained indecisive. Finally, she summoned a tiny smile and said, "Can I get ice cream with that?"

"You bet. Your choice of five flavors. I'm an ice cream nut, and so is Aunt Tempera. I think we're about the same size, too, and I've got tons of wacky nightshirts to choose from."

Cameron glanced around the closet, the horror returning. She clasped her hands over her arms and shivered. "I'll have to have everything cleaned." She shook her head, tears still shimmering in her beautiful brown eyes. "No, I think I'll just throw everything away."

Lydia didn't blame her; she was certain she would do the same thing, no matter how much it strapped her budget.

"Can you tell if anything's missing?" Luke asked, his face dark with anger as he looked around.

"It's . . . no, I can't tell. Everything's such a mess." Cameron walked into the bedroom, taking her time looking the room over. Suddenly, she gasped and covered her mouth.

"What is it?" Jet demanded, instantly by her side. He turned her to face him, holding her by her shoulders. "Cameron, what is it? What's wrong?"

Between her shaking fingers, Cameron said, "I—I had a small framed picture of Byron and me together, over there by the bed. It was taken at Disneyland last year." Her voice dropped to a whisper. "It's gone. He took it. That creep has a picture of me and my son."

The moment Lydia and Cameron were safely inside the mansion and out of earshot, Jet exploded. "I can't believe you, Luke! Didn't you see how scared she was? I didn't know you were such an insensitive jerk."

Mindful of Roger listening, Luke waited until the limo was in motion before closing the partition. He understood Jet's anger, but Jet didn't know all the details. "We were followed from the club," Luke said the moment they were guaranteed privacy.

"All the more reason for me to—"

"Not by Cameron's stalker," Luke cut in. "By Detective Parker. If you had spent the night with Cameron Rose, Parker would have been knocking on the door at daylight. He'd probably be holding a warrant for your arrest."

Jet looked murderous. "Wouldn't the sneaky bastard have to prove we'd had sex? Because I'm not that stupid, Luke. I was there when you warned us about Burgess and his nasty tricks, and about Parker and his threats, and I wouldn't do anything to jeopardize my job or your company."

"I never insinuated that you would, Jet. All Parker needs is for a client with Cameron's clout to swear you slept with her, whether you did or didn't."

This time Jet sputtered. "You think Cameron would lie? Why in hell would she do that? Look, you're way off base if you think that Cameron—"

"She used Rhew's escort service before she came to us," Luke reminded him quietly. "I know you hate to think Cameron might be influenced by Rhew, but—"

"I *don't* think it," Jet said coldly. "Just because you see your foster brother behind every bush doesn't mean that the rest of us do, Luke. Cameron's a warm, sensitive, loving *mother*, and I won't have you talking badly about her."

Luke felt a cold chill steal over him. He hated this part of his job, but he was the boss. "Jet, if you're thinking about dating Cameron, I'll have to let you go. You know the rules."

"What about *you?*" Jet challenged. "You were all over Ms. Carmichael tonight. Are you exempt just because you own the company? Will Parker see it that way, you think?"

"You don't know what's going on."

"You're right. I don't. And I don't know how you could be more obvious about not trusting your own employees."

"It's not about trust." When Jet stared at him, Luke sighed. He not only valued Jet as an employee, he valued his friendship, as well. He suspected that friendship would be in jeopardy if he didn't tell him the truth. "Ms. Carmichael's not officially a client; she just doesn't know it. Mrs. Scuttle's been instructed to immediately shred her checks, and there will be no record of her payment anywhere for Parker to get his eager little hands on." He saw that he'd shocked Jet. The realization made him flush. Putting his sneaky game into words made it sound . . . devious. Wrong. Fiendish.

"I'm assuming there's a reason behind this?"

Luke told him about eavesdropping on Lydia's conversation with her business partner.

Jet looked dazed. "Wow. Talk about a case of serendipity! You've either got a guardian angel, or you're just plain lucky."

"I was thinking the same thing when I realized what she was planning, and to whom she was planning to do it." Luke's chuckle was dry and short-lived. "If I hadn't been there at that place and time, I probably wouldn't have figured it out until it was too late. She and Tempera have different last names, and I doubt Mrs. Scuttle would have noticed that they live at the same address."

"You're assuming Lydia would have succeeded with her plan," Jet pointed out, his anger apparently deflating now that he knew the reason behind Luke's earlier insensitivity. "I've escorted women ten times more beautiful and managed to restrain myself. I'm sure the others could say the same." His lips twisted with wry amusement as he added, "With the exception of Greg."

"I don't know. Lydia gives temptation a whole new meaning," Luke blurted out. He jumped as Jet clapped his hands on both knees.

"My God!" he exclaimed. "You're falling for her!"

Luke scowled at the grinning fool. "Don't be ridiculous. I'm merely having a little fun while I teach Ms. Vengeful a lesson."

But Jet wasn't convinced. "You must be planning on sleeping with her. Otherwise there would be no need to get rid of the evidence, right?"

Luke wasn't accustomed to squirming, but he found himself doing just that. "Nothing wrong with using a little precaution, just in case," he muttered lamely.

"Just in case . . . what? You get carried away with Ms. Temptation? Luke, why don't you just tell her that you know her game?"

"Because I . . . well . . ." Luke closed his eyes and imagined his fingers around Jet's thick neck. "Because I like her, and I wanted her to realize that she's wrong about Mr. Complete."

"And snacking on her neck is going to convince her?"

Smug, irritating bastard. "It's complicated. I have to give her reason to believe she's going to succeed in buying me for sex, or she'll go after you or someone else at Mr. Complete."

"Well, we can't have that, can we?" Jet drawled sarcastically. "God knows she's irresistible."

Luke ignored him. "She's stubborn, so I don't think just telling her will work. I need to show her."

"Hmm."

Okay, now he was imagining squeezing his fingers, making Jet's smug-ass eyes bulge in their sockets. "In the meantime, she's sexy and mysterious and tempting . . . and I want her." Badly. More than he'd wanted anything in a long, long while.

"There. That wasn't so hard, was it?"

Luke opened his eyes. He glared at Jet's grinning, triumphant expression. "All of which doesn't change the fact that she's out to ruin me, Rhew's out to ruin me, and Detective Parker would like nothing better than to see either one of them succeed so *he* can get a piece of me as well." Luke paused deliberately before he added, "And if I go down, you and the others will be gathering at the unemployment office."

"Well, that's not going to happen," Jet said with

absolute conviction. "Because you're the smartest man I know, not to mention the damned *luckiest.*"

"Thanks," Luke said dryly. "I hope I can live up to your expectations."

"Me and my Jaguar hope you can, too."

He said it with such feeling, Luke had to laugh. "Back to this thing with Cameron Rose . . ."

Jet let out a wistful sigh and waved his hand, as if it didn't matter when it obviously did. "Don't worry. She just feels safe with me. I don't think she thinks of me in a romantic way."

Luke hoped Jet was right; the last thing Mr. Complete needed was another Tempera situation—with or without sex involved.

"I just don't understand it." Cameron, dressed in one of Lydia's novelty nightshirts decorated with a huge yellow Tweety Bird on the front, stared morosely into her bowl of double ripple fudge ice cream. "It's not like he hasn't spent the night before."

Lydia spewed a mouthful of Rocky Road onto the counter of the breakfast bar. Mortified, she slid off the bar stool and grabbed a handful of paper towels. Her hands shook as she mopped at the melting ice cream. "You—you mean you and Jet have—he's—" She threw the soggy paper towels in the trash bin, struggling to sound casual, instead of disgusted. "I'm sorry, it's really none of my business, but isn't that sort of unethical?" Maybe, Lydia thought, she wouldn't have to sleep with Luke after all.

She ignored the disturbing, traitorous stab of disappointment she felt.

Cameron shrugged. "I pay him to be my escort. I'm not paying him to have sex with me."

Now Lydia was totally confused. "You and Jet didn't sleep together?"

"I didn't say that. I said I didn't pay him to do it."

Lydia returned to her ice cream, wondering how far she could push the enlightening conversation. "So you justify it in your mind by telling yourself that the two have nothing to do with one another?"

The singer finally looked up. Her brow wrinkled in thought. "Yeah, I guess I do. How do *you* handle it? I mean, with Luke?"

This time Lydia didn't spew her ice cream onto the breakfast bar; she nearly choked to death on it. By the time she caught her breath, her face was flaming. "Luke and I haven't—we're not—" She swallowed hard. "Luke's just an escort."

For the moment.

Cameron smiled knowingly. "At least if you're paying a man, he's less likely to kiss and tell. In my profession, that's a big bonus."

"Aren't you afraid you'll get serious about him?"

"Oh, I already am."

Her smile turned dreamy, making Lydia's stomach churn. She recognized that expression from watching her aunt's face when she talked about Tony.

"Jet's not only a fantastic lover, he's sophisticated, romantic, sensitive, strong, courteous, and a great

dancer, and that's just the tip of the iceberg."

Lydia tried biting her tongue, but it didn't work. Her wayward lips moved anyway. "Um, I think you just described the job requirements of a male escort. I've met the others, and they all seem to be just as perfect." Too perfect for Lydia's taste, although Luke definitely had his flaws.

He was dangerously, painfully clumsy with zippers.

He seemed to attract excitement—the bad kind.

He was overly confident of his effect on women, which, perversely, made the flaw endearing, rather than disgusting.

"Oh, no," Cameron argued with alarming conviction. "Jet's different."

How many times had she heard Aunt Tempera say those exact same words—even after the jerk's defection? Tempera was still convinced that something had happened to scare Tony away.

It frightened Lydia to realize how close she'd been to believing Jet was genuinely concerned about Cameron. Now she saw the true picture; Jet was concerned about his investment. Cameron just happened to be that investment.

"You should see him with Byron. They're already crazy about one another."

Lydia put a hand over her churning stomach and pushed the melting ice cream out of reach. Could it get any worse? And what could she do about it? Could she save Cameron in time, or was it already too late? Cameron didn't deserve the heartbreak that Lydia was convinced she would suffer if she stayed on her present course.

She had to try.

Which meant she had to step things up with Luke.

The burst of adrenaline that shot into her system was a normal reaction, Lydia told herself, and had nothing to do with anticipation or desire.

Chapter Fourteen

Lydia suppressed a yawn as she sipped coffee with one hand, and reached for the spa's appointment book with the other. It was seven-thirty in the morning, a full hour earlier than the spa's normal opening time. Casey had called her late last night to let her know that Bridget, one of their part-time helpers, had a family emergency and wouldn't be in today. Then Casey had gone on to explain that she had booked a party of first-timers before she found out about Bridget.

Today was supposed to be Lydia's "boss" day, but she had found out a long time ago that anything could happen when it came to running your own business, and being the owner meant absolutely nothing when you had a budget as tight as theirs.

She and Casey scrubbed the floors instead of hiring a cleaning service, along with a hundred-and-one other chores that went along with owning a business. They had talked about raising the prices so they could afford more help, or at the very least a cleaning service to do the grub by work, but in the end she and Casey had decided not to.

The satisfaction of making an affordable spa available to the working middle class was the reason they'd opened the business in the first place. Take that away and they became just another spa.

Lydia yawned again, flipping open the appointment book. She'd taken yesterday off to run some personal errands for Aunt Tempera, so she had yet to familiarize herself with today's appointments. Casey had mentioned a party . . . Lydia ran her finger down the list of appointments to read the name heading the group. She reached it just as Casey came rushing into the office, precariously juggling a foaming latte, her purse, and an armful of magazines.

The dropping of Lydia's jaw coincided with Casey's hasty explanation.

"I should have told you, I know, but I was afraid you'd try to reschedule the party."

"I would have." Lydia's shock receded to a dull ache behind her eyes. She rubbed her temples. "I would have given them the entire spa for the day, just to avoid the headache I'm getting right now. Have you forgotten the chaos just *one* of these guys caused the last time?"

Casey dumped her purse and the magazines in a chair and hopped onto a corner of the desk with her latte. "Yeah, but can you deny they were good for business?"

"We have more than enough business. In fact, we're booked two weeks ahead right now, and *you've* got vacation time coming up." The reminder didn't seem to phase Casey, and Lydia wondered if her lack of interest over pending vacation time had anything to do with Brett's recent neglect.

"We're wasting time arguing a moot point, aren't we?" Casey checked her watch. "They'll be here at ten. Our first appointment arrives at eight. With any luck, we'll have our regular clients out of here by the time our party of hunks arrive."

Lydia belatedly noticed that Casey wore a very feminine-looking calf-length dress rather than her customary attire of faded jeans and silk blouse. She narrowed her eyes in speculation. "Do you have something up your dress—er—sleeve?"

With practiced nonchalance, Casey examined her blunt fingernails. "I don't know what you're talking about . . . unless you mean the fact that Brett's supposed to take me to lunch today."

"But we won't have time for lunch, thanks to you."

Casey grinned. "Guess I'll have to tell him when he comes by to get me."

"Casey! You're trying to make Brett jealous?"

"Could there be any harm in that? Greg says—"

"Greg's a gigolo!"

Her friend wagged a finger at her. "I thought we

established that Greg is exempt from your list of suspects."

"If he's knowingly working for a corrupt company, that makes him guilty by association or an accomplice or something."

"Your desperation is showing," Casey remarked dryly. "Anyway, Greg was telling me about the time he helped a client win her husband back. She made her husband so jealous by hiring Greg, he dumped his mistress and came back to her."

Lydia tried and failed to see the upside to her story. "Greg must thrive on living dangerously, and if the husband had a mistress, why on earth would she want him back?"

"Because she *loved* him, goofus!" Casey slid from the desk and leaned over to peruse the appointment book, her tongue caught between her teeth. "We should get started. Why don't you take Mr. Burgess and Mrs. Riley, and I'll do Mrs. Schooner and Mrs. Brandt? With any luck we'll have them done and out the door before the guys from Mr. Complete arrive."

"Mr. Burgess? We have another man coming in today?"

Casey nodded. "Fifth one since Greg's unforgettable appointment. Word of mouth, my dear. Best advertisement in the world."

Lydia's sigh was tinged with exasperation. "Fine, but I thought we opened this spa so that working middle-class *women* would have a chance to get pampered for a change."

"Watch it, Lydia. You're asking for a discrimination suit. There are plenty of working middle-class *men* out there in need of pampering, too. Besides, the reason the guys are coming today is because the women of Hope House gave them their gift certificates as a thank you for putting together the playground equipment. Wasn't that sweet of them?"

"Great," Lydia muttered ungraciously. "We're not even going to get *paid* for this headache."

Casey laughed. "Well, look on the bright side; you get to see Luke today. In fact, you get to massage those hard muscles and lubricate that gorgeous skin of his with essential oils." She paused, her eyes glinting with unmistakable mischief. "It's been four days since you've seen him, and I've noticed you've been a bear."

"I have not!" Lydia could do nothing about the guilty blush that suffused her face, but damned if she would admit the truth to Casey. "And I wasn't even here yesterday, so there."

"No, but I spoke to Tempera and she agreed that you've been uncharacteristically irritable."

With that disturbing, parting shot, Casey flounced from the office, leaving Lydia fuming. If she *had* been irritable, it had nothing to do with missing Luke. If anything, she was dreading seeing him again, having made the decision to accelerate their relationship in the hope of saving Cameron Rose from becoming another victim.

The plain, awful truth was she *liked* Luke, apart from his distasteful occupation. She tried very hard to *dis*like him, but she kept finding out things about him that aroused her admiration and respect for him. Of course, there was still the very real possibility that all Luke had done in the way of gallantry had been a deliberate manipulation on his part.

Admittedly, he couldn't have staged Bart's fall from the crate, but he could have taken advantage of the crisis. As for Cameron's rescue, Luke could have easily planned the entire episode.

Lydia bit her lip, wondering if Luke always went to such great lengths to soften a prospective victim, or if she had become paranoid beyond even *Casey's* wildest dreams.

Paranoia . . . or perception?

Safer to stick with perception, Lydia decided. That way she wouldn't look like a fool when it was all said and done.

The only fool would be Luke when they put the cuffs on him and charged him with prostitution, giving Detective Parker the final ammunition he needed to close down Mr. Complete.

So why didn't the prospect lift her spirits and fill her with righteous joy?

She was jarred from her unsettling thoughts as Casey raced into the office and slammed the door. She leaned against it, breathing hard, her expression incredulous.

"If I didn't know better," she muttered, hands over her heart as if she feared it would fly away, "I'd be convinced Brett was going to an awful lot of trouble to test my loyalty. Either that, or God is sending me a sign."

"What is it now, Casey?" Lydia arched an exasperated eyebrow. "Our Mr. Burgess is actually Brad Pitt in disguise?"

Wide-eyed, Casey shook her head. "No. Worse. I mean, better. Ten times better. A definite *ten* on the scales. Make that a ten plus." She gave a dramatic shudder and approached the desk. Her grave expression was comical. "Brace yourself, Lydia. He's better looking than your Luke."

"He's not *my* Luke," Lydia automatically protested. "And for goodness sake, Case, will you please get your hormones checked? You say *I've* been acting strange! You're drooling over guys left and right—"

"That's because," Casey interrupted, slapping her hands on the desk, "I'm running into good-looking guys left and right. *This* guy will definitely appeal to you. He looks like a pirate, right down to his ink-black ponytail. And get this; he's got green eyes. Moss green, not that murky blue-green, but moss green, and I don't think he's wearing contacts."

"Looks aren't everything, Casey."

"A strong, sexy square jaw, with a five-o'clock shadow." Casey rambled on as if Lydia hadn't spoken. "And just to make things interesting—as if he needed it—he's got a cleft in the middle of his chin, like Michael Douglas."

"Case—"

"I'm guessing six-foot-two or maybe -three, with

broad shoulders and a trim waist—probably hiding a six-pack to die for—and thighs that look as hard as rocks." Casey's eyes had glazed over. "He's wearing a diamond heart in his right ear."

"And I suppose he has a mysterious scar?" Lydia's sarcasm sailed right over Casey's head. She nodded emphatically.

"Yeah, right along the edge of his jaw. Can I do him, Lydia? Please?"

Lydia closed the appointment book and rose. "No, Casey, you can't. Drool and oil doesn't mix."

Someone, Lydia mused, more than a little worried about her friend, needed to have a heart to heart with Brett about his husbandly neglect.

Apparently, Greg's helpful tips hadn't worked.

Two hours later, after giving Mr. Ten-on-Casey's-scale a manicure, pedicure, and full-body massage, Lydia took Mr. Burgess's check, his outrageously large tip, scarcely heard his compliments on her spa, mumbled a thank you and have a good day, and stumbled into her office.

She closed the door and went to her desk. In a daze, she sat and covered her face, her entire body thrumming with shock.

She was doomed with a capital *D*.

Doomed.

Doomed.

Doomed.

The word boomed over and over inside her head,

increasing the ache. There was no other explanation, no more excuses. Mr. Burgess was everything and more that Casey had said he was. On top of that, he had a deep, sexy voice and he was charming and cultured. His hard, perfect body would have been a delight for any masseuse.

Lydia doubted he would have had to drop his drawers to make Mrs. Solton swoon.

Yet . . . yet . . . he had left Lydia completely unmoved. Not a ripple of interest, not a spark of ignition, not even a tiny flame of desire. *Not even a smidgen of admiration for his superb physique.*

Nothing.

Nada.

Doomed.

The door to the office sprang open. Lydia slowly lowered her hands, dread settling like a stone in her belly. What next?

A flushed, disgustingly happy Casey appeared in the doorway. "Get ready to party hearty! The guys are here!"

And just like that, the stone in her belly turned into a dozen full-winged butterflies.

Definitely doomed.

The frightened look on Lydia's face told Luke everything he needed to know. His jaw locked tight with disappointment and growing fury as a tight-lipped Lydia led him into a small room and instructed him to disrobe down to his *black silk boxers.*

Luke wondered if she heard his teeth grinding as he did exactly as she asked, right down to those boxers she had been so smugly certain he was wearing.

Which he was, of course.

Before he saw Rhew Burgess coming out of the spa, he'd been beside himself with anticipation at seeing Lydia. He'd bought a dozen silk boxers in a variety of flashy colors.

Before he saw Rhew Burgess, he'd been clear on his plan of action. Jet was right; he was making things hard—no pun intended—when he could make things easy. He was going to come clean with Lydia and get the ugly misunderstanding out of the way so they could make a fresh start. He would, if it took him the rest of his life, convince her that his company had earned its place in the respectable business world.

Before Rhew Burgess, he'd been on the verge of admitting that he'd fallen for the tempting brunette.

Now he knew that Lydia didn't work alone.

Now he knew that his worst nightmare had come true.

His evil foster brother, his fiercest competitor, the proverbial rock in his shoe, had sent him a Trojan horse in the shape of a tempting, refreshingly shy, sexy-as-hell woman named Lydia Carmichael.

He knew, but his mind was slow to accept the fact because he didn't want to.

Rhew and Lydia were working together to bring him down.

Lydia. Sweet, sexy, mouth-watering Lydia. Not just

understandably misguided in her attempt at justice, but working with a devious, dirty-fighting snake like Rhew Burgess.

And now that he knew, he also had to face several more ugly facts. The entire time that Lydia was playing him like a puppet, she'd probably known how Rhew had stolen his fiancée just days before their wedding. She probably knew that Rhew had made certain Luke caught them in bed, doing the nasty on *his* satin sheets, his fiancée's throaty moans of passion slicing through his heart like razor sharp knives.

She probably knew, all right, that his loving fiancée had chosen Rhew over Luke because in the end, money *did* matter, and Rhew had it. Luke had never been able to shake the stigma of poverty, no matter how many suits he owned or how many women lined up to sleep in his bed. He was *not* a member of the family, just a poor homeless charity boy the family had taken in to impress their friends.

Luke stared at the closed door, waiting for Lydia to return. Every muscle in his body was tense, tight, angry.

Women had flocked to Luke, attracted by his good looks and body. They'd had no qualms, no hesitation about sleeping with him, but when it came right down to the wire, they preferred the rich pretty boy over the poor pretty boy.

When it came to the spotlight, they wanted to be on Rhew's arm. The one with the money.

Even his fiancée.

After that unforgettable night when he'd walked in on her and Rhew, he'd made some drastic changes in his life. No longer did he feel flattered when a woman noticed him. No longer did he look for the one woman who would love *him*, not who he was or wasn't, or what he had and didn't have. He had outgrown his boyish yearning for acceptance.

Until Lydia, which made the humiliating blow that much harder to bear.

A knock came at the door, followed by Lydia's muffled voice inquiring if he was ready.

Luke's smile was totally devoid of humor as he drawled, "Come in. I'm ready."

Ms. Temptation was in for one hell of a shock. He'd make her rue the day she thought to make a fool out of *him*.

The only fools would be Lydia and Rhew, after he proceeded to break every single rule in his own little book.

Chapter Fifteen

"Lock the door."

Lydia froze at Luke's growled command. The butterflies in her stomach tried to take flight, beating relentlessly against the walls of her belly. Her voice was hoarse as she asked, "Um, is there a reason you want the door locked?" He was lying on the table on his stomach, with his head positioned facedown in the cradle so she couldn't see his expression.

"I don't want to be responsible for some woman fainting."

"You—you heard about Greg's visit?"

"Yes."

She swallowed hard as she locked the door. There was an intensity about Luke's voice that stimulated her already raw nerves. Something different. A hard edge that hadn't been there before. A purposefulness. "You have a tattoo, also?"

"No. I'm expecting something to come up that would be a lot more shocking."

Lydia's knees almost buckled at his blatantly sexual statement. She forced her shaky legs to carry her to the counter where the array of oils and lotions waited. How did Luke always seem to know when she was ready to make a move, and beat her to it? She poured warm scented oil into her palms and rubbed them together, her heart beating like a jackhammer. Excitement and anticipation streaked through her like lightning.

She approached the table, trying to peer beneath the towel he'd draped over his waist and butt without actually touching it. Was he completely naked? Or had she guessed right when she'd told him to undress down to his black silk boxers? Gathering her courage, she reached for his broad, tanned shoulders.

The moment she made contact with his incredibly tight muscles, a shaft of pure pleasure shot through her, just as it had when she'd rubbed his sunburned back with aloe. She dug her fingers in, rolling the pads of her fingers in circles, loosening the muscles, working his skin. She was faintly aware that she was breathing hard and fast, lost in the feel of him, in the joy of touching him.

She moved her hands lower on his back, joyfully working the tight muscles. He moaned, and liquid heat pooled between her legs. She was panting helplessly, frightened and exhilarated by the way her body came alive just from touching him. Moving closer to the table, she leaned against him, working her hands to his far side.

He groaned again, this time a low, agonized sound that made her freeze. He brought his arm from his side and thrust it between her legs, up high, his hand splaying over the back of her thigh and right butt cheek to hold her to the table.

The position left her straddling his forearm.

He began to flex his forearm muscle in a steady, erotic rhythm, making it pulse against her core, leaving her to gasp in shock. His voice was rough and sexy as he ordered, "Keep going."

Lydia bit back a moan and leaned forward to continue her massage, steadily working her way to the curve of his buttocks. The movement intensified the pressure of his arm between her legs.

The towel slipped lower, exposing a provocative tan line. Lydia caught her lip between her teeth. He wasn't wearing boxers. He wasn't wearing *anything*.

"Lower," he growled, taking the words right out of her mouth.

Without stopping to question the unethical ramifications of what she was doing, Lydia obeyed, letting out a blissful sigh as she refamiliarized herself with his incredibly hard butt. Shamelessly, she began to move against his arm, increasing the friction, her breath catching in her throat each time he flexed his muscle against her throbbing core. The most intense pleasure began to build inside her, in rippling waves that grew bigger and bigger.

When he slipped his arm from between her legs, she let out an involuntary protest.

"Shh," he whispered, his breathing ragged. He turned onto his back, allowing the towel to slip to the floor.

Lydia stared, mesmerized, at his full, thrusting arousal. Like the rest of him, it was proud and beautiful. She made no protest when he grabbed her by the waist and lifted her on top of him. He positioned her legs so that she straddled him on the narrow massage table, her jeans the only barrier between his rock-hard erection and her throbbing center.

She dug her fingers into his chest for balance, biting her lip to hold back a moan as he took her hips and moved her until she formed a tight cradle around his erection.

Then he began to slide her back and forth.

"Open your eyes."

Until he spoke, Lydia hadn't been aware they were closed. She opened them, staring into his beautiful, desire-hardened face.

"Look down, Lydia," he instructed hoarsely. "See what I'd like to put inside you. Deep inside you, so that I can feel you when you come. Feel you tighten around me. Hear you cry out my name."

She looked. She gasped.

He cupped her generous, aching breasts through her tucked-in cotton blouse with both his big hands, flicking his thumb over her rigid nipples. She sensed his frustration because he couldn't touch her skin.

She shared his frustration, her hand going to the button fastened just above her cleavage with every intention of helping clear up the problem.

"Lydia?"

Her gaze flew upward in shock. It wasn't Luke who had spoken.

The doorknob rattled. There was a puzzling pause before Casey's muffled voice came again. "Lydia? I need to get the sea salt from beneath the counter. Collin's skin is peeling from that sunburn, and I need to exfoliate."

In her haste to get off of Luke, Lydia landed on the floor on her rump. Her face felt as if it would burst into flames, it was so hot. "Turn over!" she hissed frantically from her undignified position on the floor.

Luke propped his arms behind his head and stared at the ceiling. "No."

Lydia's eyes bugged. "What? Luke, you have to turn over! She'll see . . . she'll—" Her gaze riveted on his impressive erection, Lydia grabbed the edge of the table and hoisted herself up. She scrambled for the fallen towel and draped it hastily over him. It covered him, but emphasized his swollen arousal to a cartoonish degree.

Dear God.

Her legs felt like rubber, and the throbbing between her thighs felt permanent. She bumped her head on the counter as she pulled out the jar of sea salt and stumbled to the door. She hesitated, cradling the jar in one arm, her fingers on the lock.

Her face was beet red. She knew it, could feel the tremendous heat scorching her skin. Would Casey believe it was from the physical demands of massaging?

She looked behind her.

Luke was still in the same position. All of him, his erection making a tent of the towel. Why wouldn't he turn over? Did he *want* to embarrass her? Or maybe he couldn't turn over because of . . . because of . . . Best she not think about that at the moment, if she had any hope of convincing Casey everything was just peachy.

Blocking the doorway as best she could, Lydia unlocked the door and pulled it open—just enough to shove the jar of sea salt through. "Here you go!"

Oh God. Her voice. It was an audition for a nine-hundred number!

Casey automatically grabbed the jar, but left it wedged in the door space, preventing Lydia from slamming it as she intended. "You okay? Why did you lock the door? Why is your face so red?"

Lydia closed her eyes and took a deep breath. Or tried to. She couldn't seem to find enough air to suck into her lungs. She looked at Casey, trying to convey a message with her eyes. *Leave me alone. I'll explain later.*

It didn't work.

"Will you be much longer with Luke? I'm nearly finished with Collin, but the other guys are getting impatient. Well, everyone except Greg. He keeps inching toward the door like he's trying to escape."

"I'll—I'll be out in a moment." *Or however long it will take to dig a hole in the floor and crawl into it.*

"Oh, I almost forgot." Casey had the good sense to remember to lower her voice to a conspiratorial whisper as she continued. "Detective Parker called. I told him that you were busy. He said he was going to be in the neighborhood, so he'd just drop by."

"You—you—" Panic wiped out the last lingering remnants of desire. Lydia felt as if she were suffocating. "Casey! What if one of the guys recognizes Parker?"

Casey's eyes widened in sudden realization. "Oh. I didn't think about that. Man, I'm sorry, Lydia."

"Don't be sorry," Lydia hissed, praying Luke couldn't hear them. "Just get on the phone and tell him not to come around today!" She gave the jar a good shove and closed the door.

She locked it again, just as a precaution.

Then she leaned her burning forehead against the door. This had to be the worst day of her life. Luke lay on the massage table behind her with a raging, unfulfilled erection in *her* place of business, and Detective Parker was stopping by. If one of the guys recognized Parker and reported their suspicions to L. J. Reynolds, her cover could be blown to smithereens.

She gave a start as the table behind her creaked. She turned around, watching with a confusing mixture of relief and acute disappointment as Luke began to get dressed.

He started by slipping black silk boxers over his erection.

Lydia licked her lips, valiantly ignoring the shameless need that still gnawed at her insides. "I—this shouldn't have happened," she choked out. "I don't know what got into me."

Luke darted a quick, hot glance at her before reaching for his shirt. "Nothing got into you . . . more's the pity."

His crude comment should have offended her.

Instead, it brought to mind an instant, highly arousing image of his erection sliding in and out of sight with every forward and backward motion of her hips. If she had worn a dress today . . .

Her nipples peaked and hardened; liquid pooled between her already damp thighs. She had heard of the phenomenon, but she hadn't believed it.

Now she had physical proof.

Physical proof. The thought reminded her of something she should never have forgotten in the first place.

Her plan to get Luke into her bed. Or his. Technically, anywhere would suffice as long as it happened on *his* time card.

Oh God. Lydia felt faint as the full realization of what she'd nearly done hit her. She had nearly had sex with Luke on *her* time card. She had broken every moral and ethical rule in the spa handbook the moment she allowed Luke to touch her intimately.

The fact that he was using a gift certificate to pay for her services made little difference.

The word *doomed* took on a whole new, terrifying meaning for Lydia.

She stood frozen in place as Luke approached her. He tilted her face, his hungry gaze roaming over her features. "Thank you," he whispered, "for making my first massage unforgettable. Maybe next time we won't be interrupted and we'll get to experience . . . *complete* satisfaction."

Lydia felt the blood drain from her face, wondering how Luke could possibly have mistaken her horrified expression for one of sexual disappointment.

"See you Saturday night."

He placed a rough, scorching kiss on her mouth before moving her aside so that he could unlock and open the door.

As if he sensed her need to recover, he closed it behind him.

Luke knew that he had every right to feel vindicated for turning the tables on Lydia. What he'd done was no more or less than what Lydia was planning to do to *him*.

He *knew* it. So why did he feel the urge to go home and take a shower, wash the slime from his body? She, apparently, was suffering no qualms over her devious plot to frame him for prostitution. Before he'd realized she was collaborating with Rhew, Luke had understood her reasoning, even if he hadn't totally agreed with her.

He had believed that *she* believed she was doing the right thing.

Not now. Not any longer.

The gloves were off, the rose tint removed from his glasses. If Lydia Carmichael wanted to fight dirty, then he could get down and dirty with the best of them.

He hadn't forgotten how.

Gone was his silly, romantic desire to prove to Lydia that his company—his escorts—were respectable working men with honor and values, not the slimy, womanizing gigolos Lydia believed them to be.

By the time Luke reached his office, his anger had cooled enough to consider that Lydia's beliefs had been fueled by his foster brother's smooth-tongued lies . . . and by his own less-than-pristine actions. But that realization didn't change a thing, as far as Luke was concerned.

Once upon a time he'd competed with Rhew Burgess for acceptance and love from his foster parents, and finally, for the love of a woman. He'd outgrown that stage in his life and possessed no desire to go back.

If Lydia couldn't see that Rhew Burgess was a wolf in pretty sheep's clothing, then she wasn't the woman he'd thought she was in the first place.

He still desired her, but now that his silly, romantic

notions had been blown away, Luke could call it by its real name.

Lust.

He lusted for Lydia, and that reckless, if not brilliant, stunt he'd pulled in the massage room had only fueled his desire to an almost painful degree. Why shouldn't he satisfy that lust? She was offering, and now that he knew the true extent of her deceitful motives, he could take what she offered with a clear conscience.

And just to make things interesting, he'd force her to do the seducing. So far he'd been reacting like a hormonal teenager to her hesitant come-ons.

It was time Lydia Carmichael did her own dirty work.

Chapter Sixteen

Lydia was furious with Luke for more than one reason.

Not only had he left her jittery and aching beyond belief, but he'd also forced her to consider the possibility that she was being too harsh in her judgment of Mr. Complete.

Maybe there were extenuating circumstances surrounding Anthony and Tempera's relationship. Maybe . . . maybe Tony had gotten carried away in the heat of the moment.

As she had with Luke.

As Luke had with her.

Possibly Tony had been so enamored of Tempera that he'd forgotten he was on the clock, that Tempera was paying him to be her escort, not her lover.

Yet . . . Lydia bit her lip. If that were the case, then

why did Tony dump Tempera and take off in Uncle Theo's car? Admittedly, Tempera had given Tony the car free and clear, but it seemed wrong, somehow, that he would keep it after deciding that what he felt for Tempera wasn't love, but lust.

If that were the case.

Lydia sat abruptly in front of her vanity mirror, staring at her reflection. Luke would be picking her up in ten minutes, and she still didn't know what she was going to do. Tempera wasn't any better, but closing the escort service was beginning to feel more like an act of spite, rather than justifiable vengeance.

But what about Cameron Rose, and the other woman who had been wronged by one of Mr. Complete's escorts? Was she going to just forget about them?

Cameron Rose wasn't beyond saving. At least, Lydia didn't *think* she was. What if she went to L. J. Reynolds and talked to him about Jet and his unethical relationship with the singer? Would Mr. Reynolds care? Would he do anything to rectify the situation?

He could fire Jet, but that wouldn't necessarily make the situation better for Cameron Rose. More ethical, but not safe as far as her heart and her money were concerned. Jet could continue to pursue her.

With her aunt, Lydia never had the chance to stop the inevitable from happening. With Cameron Rose, she did.

The doorbell rang. With her heart and her brain locked in battle, Lydia grabbed her lace shawl and made her way downstairs. Maybe seeing Luke again would help her decide what to do.

Only it wasn't Luke standing in the foyer chatting with Sweeney.

It was Greg, looking gorgeous in jeans and a burgundy polo shirt. Lydia had specified casual because the fundraiser they were going to was an outdoor barbecue at the home of a millionaire.

Greg was dressed casually, but Lydia ruefully admitted there was nothing casual about his looks. She went to meet him, sternly reminding her disappointed heart that it hadn't been long ago when she'd requested someone different.

The moment Greg spotted her, he launched into an explanation. "I was just telling Sweeney that I'll be your escort to the barbecue tonight."

Lydia summoned a carefree smile. "Wonderful! Shall we get going?"

"Do you want to take the limo, or should we go in my car?"

"Your car," Lydia said, linking her arm through his. She felt him flinch, and she bit back a sigh. The moment they were outside, Lydia dropped her arm. "If I said I was sorry, would you stop looking at me as if I were the devil incarnate?"

Greg's fair skin made his blush all the more visible. "Sorry. I'm not very good with pain, as you've probably guessed."

"You didn't know waxing would be painful?" Lydia lifted a questioning brow as he opened the passenger door of a beautiful red Mazda. She got in, inhaling the scent of real leather. Greg got in and buckled up before answering her question.

"No, I didn't. Ramon's always playing jokes on me."

"Ramon?"

"My boyfriend." Greg flashed her a purely wicked smile as he started the car and gunned the engine. "I'll let you in on a little secret, if you'll promise not to tell."

"I promise."

"I told him that it didn't hurt at all, so when he comes in for a waxing next week, you be sure and give him the same treatment that you gave me, okay?"

Lydia burst out laughing. "Okay, but I really am sorry about that."

"I forgive you. Luke thinks you're an angel. He can't be *all* wrong."

This time it was Lydia's turn to blush. "I'm sure you're exaggerating." Please be exaggerating! She was feeling enough confusion without Greg making it worse with his obviously imaginary perceptions.

Expertly, Greg eased into the expressway traffic and set his cruise control. "I'm not exaggerating, and Luke doesn't say that about just anybody."

"Speaking of the devil . . ." Lydia refused to take Greg seriously. "He was supposed to be my escort tonight."

"Oh. That. Well, our secretary sort of double-booked him tonight, so you're stuck with me."

Before Lydia could think, she blurted out, "He's

with another woman?" She suspected her face came close to matching Greg's shirt, but the damage was done. She had sounded jealous because she *was* jealous, which was totally ridiculous. Of course Luke was with another woman. It was his job to escort women.

Greg shot her a mysterious glance. "He'd kill me if I told you the truth."

Lydia clenched her hands until her short nails bit into her palms. "You have to tell me now." She braced herself for the impact.

"He'll kill me—"

"Greg!"

"Okay, okay. He got the short straw, which means he had to take the secretary, Mrs. Scuttle, out to dinner for her birthday."

For a stunned moment, Lydia's mind was blank. Then relief rushed through her as she remembered the strange conversation she'd had with Mrs. Scuttle on the phone. The woman was obviously harmless, possibly even delusional. She had implied to Lydia that Luke often made passes at her. "Oh," she said, following her exclamation with a shaky laugh. "I met her over the phone. She seemed very charming."

Greg snorted. "About as charming as a rattlesnake."

"Do I detect a note of affection in there?"

"Yeah, I guess. She can be scary, though. Last week, she bit Jet on the hand."

"Excuse me?"

"That's what I said. She bit him on the hand. He thought she was dead, you see, when she was really taking a nap sitting straight up, so—what's so funny?"

Lydia gave up trying to contain her mirth. "A secretary who bites? What does your boss think about this?"

"He's more scared of her than we are." Greg sounded amused. "She throws things at him when she gets mad."

"Why doesn't he just fire her and hire someone else?"

"Because she's seventy-eight, widowed, and draws a small social security check. If she didn't have this job, she'd be in a nursing home like most of her friends." Greg shrugged. "And she's a good secretary, I guess."

Hmm. Lydia had a hard time reevaluating the evil L. J. Reynolds in her mind. Could a man who kept a seventy-eight-year-old woman employed just to keep her out of a nursing home be as bad as she'd first assumed? And what would become of the feisty Mrs. Scuttle if Lydia managed to close Mr. Complete?

"Tell me more about your boss," she said. To her frustration, Greg shook his head.

"I've already told you more than I should have. He's a very private person, and he wouldn't like it if he knew that I was talking to you about him."

"A man of mystery," Lydia murmured. Or a man who was hiding something.

"Not really," Greg said. "Nothing mysterious about him. He's just really dedicated to giving his clients their money's worth and protecting their privacy."

Lydia prudently kept her mouth shut. She was, after

all, one of those clients, who had almost gotten *more* than her money's worth.

And she definitely wanted to keep that private.

"May I take your plate, ma'am?" the waiter asked politely.

Luke hastily reached across the table under the pretense of helping the waiter. He gathered his secretary's utensils, water glass, coffee cup, and anything else he thought she might try using as a weapon, and piled them onto her empty plate.

When he reached for the crystal salt and pepper shaker, Mrs. Scuttle slapped his hand away. "What's gotten into you, Luke? He doesn't want the salt and pepper shakers, and I'm not finished with my coffee, thank you!"

The coffee cup was made of heavy stoneware, Luke noted gloomily. Heavy enough to blacken his eye or bust his lip if his secretary decided to throw it at him.

He could wait . . . but in the end he knew that it wouldn't make any difference. If Mrs. Scuttle blew a gasket, she would find something to throw at him, even if it came from another table. Bracing himself, he handed her the envelope.

She blinked at the envelope. "What's this? Another present? Oh, you shouldn't have, Luke!" Clearly, she was moved.

Luke winced inwardly.

Mrs. Scuttle took her time admiring the blank envelope before pulling out the card tucked inside.

The gift certificate fluttered to the table.

She blinked several more times, then ignored the fallen paper to peruse the card. His entire crew had signed the card, so it took her a few moments to read all the names and accompanying birthday wishes.

Finally, she set the card aside and picked up the gift certificate.

For one insane moment, Luke considered snatching it from her hands before she had time to—

"What?" Mrs. Scuttle screeched out. "What is this? A gift certificate to Lydia's Affordable Spa? What would an old woman like me . . ." Her voice trailed into silence. She sat staring at Luke with open suspicion. "I'm not going to throw anything at you, Luke. I'm not a child, you know."

He tensed as she took a sip of her coffee. He didn't relax until she'd let go of the handle and put her hands back into her lap.

"Tell me what this is about. I know that you know I don't have any use for spa treatment. For Pete's sake, I haven't shaved my legs in twenty years. I don't want some stranger smearing mud on me, and I'm not about to get naked and let some strange man or woman rub me in spots *I* haven't touched in more years than I can count."

Luke began to roll his napkin. "What about the hot stone massage?" he suggested hopefully. "I've heard it does wonders for arthritic muscles."

"Hmm. What else?"

"There's electrolysis." Luke glanced around to ascertain their neighbors weren't listening. "I noticed you had a nasty razor cut on your chin a few weeks ago."

"Is that right?" Mrs. Scuttle's expression never changed as she calmly got up and shuffled to the nearest table. "Excuse me," she said to the surprised woman as she picked up the bowl of soup the waiter had just placed before her. "I need to borrow this."

Just as calmly, she shuffled over to Luke, dumped the soup in his lap, returned the empty bowl to the astonished woman, and shuffled back to her seat. She folded her arms, apparently appeased by Luke's agonized expression. "I saw a shrink once, but it didn't do any good. Sorry about that, Luke. Those pants looked new."

Luke swallowed hard as the hot soup seeped into his lap. He was painfully aware that their neighbors were staring at them in shock. "Yeah, they are. Were."

"So you want me to spy on this woman who's out to ruin you."

"Us. She's out to ruin *us*," Luke corrected. He took his cloth napkin and laid it gently on his scalded lap. "If she manages to close Mr. Complete, you'll be out of a job, too."

"I don't see how I can help."

"You could keep your eyes and ears open."

Mrs. Scuttle blinked her owlish eyes. "Huh?"

"I said you could keep your eyes and ears open. I need to know how often my foster brother goes into the spa, and any other pertinent information you can glean."

For a long moment, his secretary's eyes disappeared behind her pale lids. Luke was beginning to think she'd gone to sleep when she suddenly snapped them back open.

"He's in on this?" she barked.

"Yes, I believe he is." Luke swallowed a ball of disgust. "You *are* shredding her checks as I instructed, aren't you?"

"Of course not! I wouldn't throw good money away like that, Luke. I'm putting those checks into my private checking account."

Luke choked.

Mrs. Scuttle flashed her false teeth in a wicked grin. "Gotcha, and you flat deserved it. By the way, she sent a big bonus with her last check, and it was made out to you. Mind telling me what you did to deserve that?"

"If I told you," Luke said with a deadpan expression, "I'd have to kill you."

"Not if I kill you first," was her swift response. "Ever been clobbered with a heavy stoneware coffee cup?"

"Um—"

"Start talking." She peered at her oversized watch, then back at Luke. "Considering the sacrifices I make for this company, I deserve to know."

There were some things not worth arguing about, Luke thought with an inward sigh.

* * *

It was official; Luke was a magnet for the bizarre.

In direct contrast, the night with Greg had gone smoothly. No stuck zippers, no kids jumping off crates, and no damsels in distress. Greg had been the perfect gentleman—charming, courteous, and always right beside her.

No running off to the bathroom every few seconds. No mysterious phone calls to his co-workers. No innuendos, no rattling of her libido. No shocking groin grinding in the doorway when Greg said goodnight.

All in all, it had been a fruitful evening for Hope House, and a much-needed *calm* evening for Lydia. Unfortunately, not being around Luke gave her unfuddled mind too much time to think.

Now here she was at two in the morning, sitting in the dark living room sipping a cup of hot cocoa that tasted like burned chocolate. She had weighed the pros and cons of continuing on the path she'd taken.

The pros were obvious, of course. Closing the escort service would ensure that some other unsuspecting woman in the future wouldn't be wasting away from a broken heart, like Tempera. The guys, as Casey was so fond of calling them, would have to strike out on their own instead of using the camouflage of a legitimate business.

That was the good part.

The cons list was bigger, which bothered Lydia. Greg, whom Lydia was now convinced wasn't like the other gigolos, would lose his job. So would the feisty and endearing Mrs. Scuttle, who would then most likely be shipped off to a nursing home. And what of the others she knew next to nothing about? Those escorts with families? What would she be doing to *them?* Assuming they were innocent . . .

Lydia set her cup on an end table and tucked her feet beneath her. She sighed, reluctantly admitting to herself that to be fair to Greg and Mrs. Scuttle, she should try talking to Mr. Reynolds first. If she could convince him to enforce stricter guidelines on the rest of his staff, and agree to keep a closer watch on them, then maybe she could drop her plan of action. L. J. Reynolds was a shrewd businessman, according to Greg. Surely he would realize the benefits of her advice? The company already had two strikes against it, and Luke strongly indicated that he was ready to plunge into the next phase of their relationship.

She was certain that phase involved an exchange of money or gifts.

If they hadn't been interrupted, strike three would have been a reality. Was it possible L. J. Reynolds wasn't aware that some of his escorts were breaking the law? According to Detective Parker, Reynolds knew about Anthony and Graham, but denied any previous knowledge of their intentions. Was he denying it only because a complaint had been filed against them? Did he turn a blind eye otherwise?

It was obvious to Lydia that she had been so blinded by righteous indignation that she'd failed to consider the possible consequences of her plan. Casey, in her blunt wisdom, had tried to point this flaw out to her, but Lydia hadn't been ready to listen at the time.

It was settled, then. Lydia felt a weight lift from her shoulders. She would call and make an appointment to have a heart-to-heart with L. J. Reynolds. If nothing else, he would at least be aware that he was in danger of losing his business by turning a blind eye to what his staff was doing.

And if he didn't know what was going on, then she would be most happy to enlighten him.

Lydia ignored—or tried to—the acute feeling of loss that came over her when she realized what this would mean.

She wouldn't be seeing Luke again.

Chapter Seventeen

"I'm sorry, Ms. Carmichael, but I'm afraid it isn't possible for you to see Mr. Reynolds."

At the mention of Lydia's name, followed by his own, Luke came to an abrupt halt in the foyer outside the office door. Why would Lydia want to talk to L. J. Reynolds? Was it a ploy to convince Luke that she didn't know *he* was L. J. Reynolds?

"Why not? Well, um, I'm not really supposed to give out that information . . . but, since you're such a good client, I'm sure he won't mind."

Luke stifled a groan and closed his eyes. He felt an enormous headache coming on.

"The truth is . . . he's having some liposuction done. No matter what the poor man does, he can't seem to get rid of those love handles. You probably read about the lip job he had done last year? No? Well, it was all over the tabloids, not that you can believe what they say, mind you. Had the fat pulled right out of his butt and pumped into his lips. You think Goldie Hawn has fat lips, you should see *his*. I have to bite my own lips to keep from grinning every time he talks to me."

The phone line had to be running somewhere along the wall, Luke thought, desperately searching for it. He got down on his knees and looked beneath the fax machine.

No such luck.

"And you'll never guess what he's thinking about doing next. Have you heard about those hair plugs?"

He crawled across the floor, peering behind a potted fern.

Bingo!

"They say they can take the hair from any part of your body, including the—"

Luke jerked the cord from the wall in the nick of time. Breathing hard from his undignified efforts, he sat back on his haunches and listened.

"Hello? Hello? Ms. Carmichael? Hmm. Must have gotten disconnected."

Mrs. Scuttle let out a shriek as Luke appeared in the doorway, holding the phone cord. Her eyes widened to twice their already enormous size.

"I couldn't be on safari in Africa?" Luke bit out through gritted teeth. "Or on a cruise? How about feeding the starving kids in Cambodia, or chaperoning terminally ill kids at Disneyland?"

His secretary looked like a defiant child caught operating on the neighbor's cat. "It's the first thing that came to my mind, Luke. I was reading in *Star* magazine where Robert De Niro—"

"Mrs. Scuttle."

"—had his thighs suctioned. And instead of glaring at me like I did something wrong, you should be thanking me for my quick-witted thinking."

"Liposuction and hair plugs?"

"Well, it's not like she knows who you are, Luke." Mrs. Scuttle tossed her head of tightly permed blue curls. "So I don't see what all the fuss is about."

"I think she knows *exactly* who I am," Luke said, tossing the phone cord aside. "If she didn't know before, Rhew would certainly have told her by now."

"Oh, goodness. What will you do now?"

Luke's jaw tightened until he heard an ominous popping noise. "Go on like nothing has changed. See how far she's going to take this nutty plan of hers. As long as she doesn't know that *I* know, then I've still got the advantage."

"Luke, you *will* be a gentleman about this, won't you?"

"Not on your life," Luke growled. Could it get any more complicated? Did she or didn't she know he was L. J. Reynolds?

He needed to talk to Greg. Greg had escorted Lydia Saturday night in his place, so maybe he could shed some light on the subject.

He picked up the phone, realized it didn't have a dial tone, and slammed it back down.

"See where that temper gets you?" Mrs. Scuttle said smugly.

Liposuction? Hair plugs? Lydia stared at the dead receiver for a dazed moment before putting it back in the cradle. Either Mr. Complete's secretary was insane, or L. J. Reynolds had one hell of an ego problem.

Not that it mattered. If he couldn't be reached, then she couldn't confront him. Her plans, either way, were on hold. Since she'd made the decision to try talking to Reynolds before moving forward with her plan, Lydia felt it would be wrong to make another move until she could.

So what should she do? Continue using Luke as an escort while trying to keep things cool between them? Lydia almost laughed out loud at the absurdity of her thoughts.

Keep things cool between her and Luke? That would be paramount to pouring a glass of ice water on an active volcano.

Yet she had to try. To sleep with him when it might not be necessary smacked of self-gratification, not to mention hypocrisy.

"Ms. Lydia?"

Lydia gave a start as Sweeney handed her a gold-embossed envelope. It looked like an invitation of some kind. Nothing out of the ordinary, except that it was addressed to *her*, not Aunt Tempera.

Sweeney cleared his throat to get her attention. "I

thought you might want to know that Ms. Tempera received a postcard today."

"A postcard?"

The butler nodded. "It wasn't signed, but I think it was from *him*."

"Anthony?" When Sweeney nodded again, Lydia smothered a groan. "How did she react?"

"She was happy, ma'am." Sweeney said the words gravely. Like Lydia, he knew exactly how damaging something like this could be for Tempera.

Lydia hissed between her teeth, so angry she couldn't speak for a moment. Finally, she ground out, "Why doesn't he just leave her alone? Hasn't he done enough damage?"

"I don't know, ma'am. Maybe you should check on her. After I gave her the postcard, she closed herself up in her room."

"I'll go right now. Thank you, Sweeney." The unopened invitation in her hand momentarily forgotten, Lydia went upstairs to assess the damage.

She found Aunt Tempera sitting on her balcony overlooking her rose garden.

She was humming lightly to herself.

Before the postcard, Lydia would have taken it as a good sign.

Now, Lydia wasn't so sure how to take it.

"Aunt Tempera?" Lydia joined her on the balcony, sinking into a lounge chair next to her aunt's. "How are you today?"

"I'm wonderful, just wonderful." Tempera turned a

bright smile her way. Her eyes were strangely shiny. “He still loves me, you know. I knew that he did.”

Lydia floundered. Her stomach lurched with dread as she chose her words carefully. “Is that what the postcard said? That he still loves you?”

“No, but I know he does. Why else would he send me a postcard?”

To taunt you with your foolishness? Lydia thought, but didn’t say. She could never say anything so hurtful to her beloved aunt. “How . . . how do you know it’s really from Tony?”

“Because it’s from Barbados. That’s where Tony’s best friend lives.” Tempera glanced at the invitation in Lydia’s hand. “Anything I should know about?”

“Um, I don’t know,” Lydia said. She opened the envelope and withdrew the card, reading it quickly. “It’s an invitation to a pool party at the home of Cameron Rose.” Lydia felt a burst of excitement—before she remembered that Cameron Rose was being taken in by Jet just like Aunt Tempera had been taken in by Tony.

Her balloon of excitement quickly burst.

“You should go,” Tempera said. “You’ve been working too hard lately.”

“I suppose there will be a lot of wealthy people there,” Lydia said reluctantly, thinking about Hope House and the funds she could probably generate.

Tempera surprised her by protesting. “No. You should just go and enjoy yourself for a change. Take Luke. I like him. He seems like a very decent man.”

Decent. Lydia bit her lip. She couldn't deny that she admired Luke in a lot of ways, but *decent?* Not exactly a word she would use in association with someone who sold sex for a living. "Um, I just might do that, Aunt Tempera."

But she'd be going alone. No way did she trust herself enough to be with Luke when neither of them would be working. His seductive charm was too potent and her willpower too weak.

The combination spelled disaster for Lydia.

Going would, however, give her an opportunity to talk to Cameron again about her unhealthy relationship with Jet. Maybe this time the singer would listen to reason.

"How do *you* know that she's going to this party?" Luke asked Greg over lunch.

Greg picked up his double-bacon cheeseburger with both hands and took a huge bite. He chewed and swallowed before answering. "Casey told me. I asked Casey to go with me and she said Lydia had already asked her."

Luke suddenly lost his appetite. He figured he would regret it, but he had to ask. "Why would you ask Casey to go with you to Cameron Rose's party? You're gay and she's married."

"Oh my God!" Greg dropped his burger and feigned shock. "I'm gay? Hey, man, thanks for telling me!"

"Very funny. Seriously, Greg. What are you up to?"

Greg found his french fries fascinating as he mumbled, "That husband of hers needs a little wake-up call, that's all."

"And you're just the guy to give it to him," Luke drawled, not bothering to hide his exasperation. Sometimes, like now, he felt as if he were the head mistress of a boys' school. "Greg, just because you didn't get shot the first time, doesn't mean it won't happen this time. Jealous husbands can be unpredictable."

"But I'm gay. I'm no threat to her husband."

"And he knows this?"

"Well, no, but just before he hits me, I'll tell him." He popped four fries into his mouth and chewed. "Hey, what do you care? I'm not going to be on the clock for this one."

"Unlike the last time," Luke muttered.

"Yeah, unlike the last time. I knew you'd understand. So are you going? This would be a good time for you and Lydia to spend some quality time together, without all that red tape in the way."

Luke threw up his hands in disgust. "Have you heard a word that I've been saying?"

Greg blinked innocently. "Sure, boss, sure. You said that Lydia's hooked up with that Rhew Burgess snake, and she knows who you really are. I heard you, but I just don't agree with you."

"What?"

"I think you're being paranoid. Lydia was asking about L. J. Reynolds, and believe me, I could tell she didn't have a clue that you and he are the same person. As far as her hooking up with Burgess . . ." He frowned, then shook his head. "Nope. I don't think she's the type to be taken in by the likes of him. She's too smart. Besides, she's got her own agenda."

"Yeah, taking me out."

"I don't think she's capable of murder, Luke."

"And I don't think you're as dumb as you look, Greg. You know I wasn't talking about murder. I was talking about Lydia's determination to ruin me."

"If you'd stop *acting* like a gigolo, maybe she'd stop *thinking* you were a gigolo." He shook a fry at Luke, his expression stern. "You can't say you blame her, can you? Tony did a number on her aunt. I can't say I wouldn't feel the same way if it had been my aunt."

"Your aunt's a lesbian."

"*Now* who's acting dumb?" Greg dipped a few fries in some ketchup and stuffed them in his mouth. "And she's never really admitted she's a lesbian. I just know that she is."

"Speaking of assumptions," Luke said dryly, "let's assume, just for the sake of assuming, that Lydia and Rhew aren't in this together. What other reason can you give me for seeing him at the spa?"

"Oh, I don't know. Let's go down the list on that brochure Casey gave me. There's micro abrasion, good for getting rid of old, wrinkled skin and uncovering the fresh new you; and there's the self-tanning treatment, for those who fear skin cancer. Then there's electrolysis, for those irritating nose hairs that just won't stay away; and there's always waxing, which I don't recommend for the faint of heart." Greg's eyes twinkled. "I don't know him personally, but from what you've told me, he's more vain than Michael Jackson. Could be any or all of the above."

Luke folded his arms, his brows arched. "Just a big fat coincidence, right?"

"Hey, it happened to you, didn't it? You just happened to be sitting behind Lydia and Casey in that booth. I don't think you can get more coincidental than that, Luke."

Forcing himself to give it some thought, Luke finally shook his head. "No, I just can't believe it was a coincidence that Rhew was at the spa."

"Okay, then, picture this. Rhew saw the two of you together somewhere, and now he's snooping around, trying to find out what's going on, maybe trying to figure out how he can work this to his advantage. If he knows Lydia's connection to Tempera—and he probably does—then he would naturally wonder why she's using Mr. Complete after what happened with Tony, something he would definitely know about since he sent Tony in to do the damage. Maybe he's got your office bugged and knows what's going on."

"Or maybe he's really Spiderman, and he's been hanging outside the office window, listening."

"Don't mock me, Luke. Stranger things have happened. Not the Spiderman bit, but I wouldn't put it past that weasel to bug your office. We know he's already planted two moles, Anthony and Graham, and we all know how *that* turned out. It stands to reason he's looking for another way to bring you down." Greg took a long drink of his iced tea. "All I'm saying is, don't underestimate this guy. He's obsessed with having what *you've* got, especially since he got disinherited and lost his wife—your ex-fiancée."

"Jet thinks I'm too paranoid as it is."

Greg frowned. "Yeah, well, Jet's led a sheltered life. He doesn't know just how mean the world can get." Suddenly, Greg's handsome face brightened. "Cameron's party would be an excellent opportunity for you to do a little investigating. Ask Lydia some subtle questions and watch her expression. Unless she's a first-rate actress, she'll trip up sooner or later."

Luke had to admit that Greg's idea held merit. And of course his approval didn't have a thing to do with wanting to see Lydia again. How could he after thinking what he'd been thinking? How could he want her in any way?

But he did.

Damned if he didn't.

Chapter Eighteen

"I cannot believe we're actually at a party at Cameron Rose's house!"

Casey's awed tone made Lydia smile. She had felt that same awe the first time she'd been inside Cameron's house. What she felt now had little to do with awe, though.

It was a nauseating mixture of dread, anticipation, and confusion.

Apparently Cameron had invited the entire crew of Mr. Complete to her party, and many of them had brought their wives and/or partners.

"Look!" Casey elbowed her in the side. "There's Ivan's wife. Isn't she a cute little thing? Doesn't look old enough to be pregnant, much less already have a three-year-old!"

Lydia had to agree. She knew from Casey that

Ivan's wife's name was Diane and that she was twenty-four years old. Ivan was twenty-nine and a freelance photographer during the day.

Escort by night. But was that all he was?

"Oh, and there's Greg and Ramon. Would you get a look at Ramon? Isn't he a hottie? It almost hurts to look at both of them at the same time!"

Again, Casey wasn't exaggerating. Ramon was every bit as sumptuous as Greg, although he was dark where Greg was fair. Casey had informed Lydia that Greg had quit his day job as manager of a steak house to stay home and take care of the house. He was also an excellent cook.

"Lydia—look, there's Luke. But who's that bombshell he's with?"

Casey's expression suddenly cleared—just as Lydia's heart started beating again.

"Oh, that's Collin's wife," Casey said. "He told me that she was a model and showed me her picture in a magazine. They've been married for fifteen years."

"You told me." Lydia tried to hide her exasperation. In her opinion, Casey had become too involved in the lives of the escorts. Brett was not only slacking in his husbandly duties, he was slacking in his social duties.

Meanwhile, under the pretense of observing Collin's gorgeous wife, Lydia got a much-needed eyeful of Luke, who was dressed casually in jeans and a dark blue cotton shirt that snapped down the front.

He looked, as always, downright mouth-watering.

Lydia nearly jumped out of her skin as Casey

grabbed her arm in a death grip. She looked around for the reason and spotted Cameron and Jet making their way around the pool in their direction.

"She's coming," Casey said faintly, still gripping her arm. "I hope I don't do something stupid."

"You won't. Just remember that she's a person, Casey. Like you and me."

"Like you and me," Casey repeated. But her grip tightened—if that were possible—as Cameron and Jet reached them.

Cameron hugged Lydia, looking happy to see her. "I'm so glad you came! I still have those clothes you loaned me. Why don't we go inside so I can give them to you before I forget?" She smiled at Casey's star-struck expression. "You can come, too."

Belatedly, Lydia introduced them. "Cameron, this is my friend and business partner, Casey Winters. She's a fan of yours, too."

Casey shook hands with Cameron, apparently speechless for the first time in her life.

"Do you know Jet, Casey?" Cameron asked.

Lydia suspected the singer was trying to put Casey at ease.

"Um, yeah," Casey blurted out. "I gave him a massage." When Cameron's brows rose, Casey looked horrified. "Oh, no! It—it isn't what you think. I meant that he came into the spa and I gave him a massage. A professional one. With the door open."

If Lydia could have figured out a way to pinch her friend, she would have. She was afraid that in her nervousness, Casey was going to blurt out that *Lydia*, on the other hand, had locked the door when she had Luke in the room. A fact that Cameron Rose did not need to know, especially in light of the talk she was hoping to have with Cameron later.

"She's very good at it," Jet offered, grinning at the way Casey was stumbling over her words. "Chill, Casey. Cameron told me that she goes for days without shaving her legs, just like the rest of you ladies."

Laughing her protest, Cameron swatted at Jet's shoulder. "More than she probably wanted to know, Jet. Thanks a lot!" She grabbed Lydia's hand and began to pull her toward the patio doors. "Come on, let's get those clothes."

Lydia caught Casey by the hand and dragged her along with them. She wondered if Cameron had experienced any further problems with her stalker, but didn't want to ask in front of Casey, knowing how Cameron valued her privacy.

Casey didn't have much of an opportunity to gawk as they raced down the long hall and into Cameron's bedroom. Cameron was still laughing when she let go of Lydia's hand and twirled around in the middle of the room.

"Whew! Jet's fantastic, but sometimes I feel as if I can't breathe properly around him." She fanned her face. "Do you know what I mean?"

"I felt that way when my husband and I first met," Casey said, looking around at the opulent bedroom with awe. "This is a great room."

"Thanks. I decorated it myself. Oh, here we are! I had them washed for you."

As Lydia took the neatly folded clothes, her gaze landed on the small framed photograph on Cameron's nightstand. It was a picture of Cameron with her son, Byron. A man-sized Mickey Mouse had an arm around each of them. "Oh, did you find the picture? I remember you thought . . . someone had taken it." She glanced at Cameron just in time to see an odd expression flicker over her face.

Cameron blinked and it was gone. "Um, yeah, yeah. I found it beneath the bed. He—he must have knocked it off." She clapped her hands, her smile brighter than ever. "We should get back to the party. I don't want Jet getting *too* drunk, if you know what I mean."

She winked as she breezed by Casey and Lydia. Lydia started to follow, but Casey grabbed her by the arm. "I've got to go to the john. Wait for me?"

The singer threw a careless wave over her shoulder. "Come along when you're ready. My home is your home!"

The moment Cameron was out of ear shot, Casey stunned her by saying, "I don't trust that woman."

"Casey!" Lydia didn't bother hiding her shock. "How can you say that? You've only just met her."

Casey thrust out a stubborn chin. "She's lying about Jet. Jet never gets drunk, and he hasn't slept with a woman in six months. She made it sound as if they were already lovers."

Lydia's jaw dropped. "How do *you* know all of this?"

"Because Jet told me . . . when I was giving him a massage."

"He could have been lying." Lydia hated to disillusion her friend, but her obsession with the staff of Mr. Complete was getting out of hand. "In fact, he probably *was* lying, Casey. Lying comes as naturally to them as—"

The look on Casey's face stopped her cold.

Casey wasn't looking at her, but behind her.

Slowly, Lydia turned.

Luke stood in the doorway.

Luke didn't try to stop Casey as she did a remarkable disappearing act.

He wanted to be alone with Lydia.

It was time they got something straight between them, and he wasn't talking about words.

"Luke."

"Lydia." He closed and locked the door behind him, his actions deliberate.

She licked her lips, the only sign that she was nervous about being alone with him in a bedroom behind a locked door. "You—you have a thing for locked doors," she said, her words just short of taunting.

He lifted a brow. "You would rather risk someone walking in on us while we're having hot, frenzied sex?"

She sucked in a sharp gasp. The pupils of her eyes disappeared altogether. "This is Cameron's bedroom. I'm not going to have sex with you here."

Luke noted with satisfaction that she hadn't said

"anywhere." He took it as a good sign, and completely ignored the self-reminder that he was going to let Lydia do the seducing. He had good intentions, until he saw her again. Then he was lucky if he remembered his middle name. "But you do agree that we have unfinished business?"

Her chin shot up a fraction of an inch. She was wearing a red satin halter dress and four-inch heels. The flimsy material molded to her curvy figure like a glove, emphasizing her glorious bust line to a gut-clenching degree.

She looked sexy as hell, and he couldn't wait to feel her hard, ripe nipples against his tongue.

He wondered—for a brief, agonizing moment—if Rhew had already had her. The possibility made him reckless. He crossed the distance in three strides, catching her gasp of surprise in his mouth. His hand tunneled through her thick, soft hair. He tightened his fist and pulled her head back for better access.

It was a kiss meant to conquer, to subdue.

To seduce her with its sheer intensity, and to rid his mind of the rage he felt at the thought of another man kissing her like he was kissing her.

And it worked. She pressed her delectable body against him, giving him back as good as he gave, her tongue frantically dueling with his own. She grabbed his hair and tightened her fist, letting him know she wasn't submissive, letting him know that two could play rough.

He nearly came on the spot.

Mustering his willpower—he had precious little of it—he forced himself to slow down. Lydia was right; this wasn't the place, even if it was thc time.

He broke the kiss, but kept his hand anchored in her hair so that she had no choice but to look into his heated gaze. "Just for tonight, I want you to forget everything you think you know about me, and pretend we just met. Can you do that?"

Locked into his gaze, she gave a slight nod.

Luke felt a savage jolt of joy rush through him. He tempered it, unwilling to let her see his weakness. "And just for tonight, I'm going to forget that you're a client and I'm not supposed to touch you."

She nodded again.

"We'll go to my place."

Her swollen, luscious lips moved, drawing his fascinated gaze. "What about Casey?"

"Greg and Ramon can take her home. From what I hear, her husband could use the shock. Might as well make it a double."

"What—what will we tell Cameron?"

"That we're going to my place to get something straight between us," he said, his voice thick with desire. "Any objections?" He didn't realize he was holding his breath until she nodded. "Good, then we'll call her from the car."

As Luke pulled her along the hallway, he was reminded of a wild beast dragging its prey into the bushes so that it could consume its kill in private. He felt that primitive, that wild, and that hungry.

Only Lydia wasn't prey and he wasn't hungry for food. She was a sexy, consenting adult, and she was about to get exactly what she wanted. What both of them wanted.

What they both needed.

They left through the front door without being seen. Luke didn't really care if anyone saw them, he just didn't want to be slowed down.

He'd never been so hard for a woman in his life.

The inside of the car was a torture room. He could hear her erratic breathing and smell her arousing perfume. From the corner of his eye, he could see the twin peaks of her exquisite nipples defined by the thin fabric.

As a result, his lust had in no way abated by the time they reached his apartment door.

He couldn't wait another moment.

Luke planted her in front of his door, which was relatively secluded thanks to a few hanging potted plants, and swiftly unfastened the top of her halter dress. His hips pressed into her, his arousal soaking up the heat of her body. Her frantic hands slipped beneath his shirt and set fire to his skin.

He pulled away the halter top and raked down her strapless red bra, exposing her hard, thrusting nipples to his hungry eyes and mouth. With a groan, he locked on to one, savoring the rigid texture with his tongue, then sucking hard, sucking until she cried out his name and clutched his head with both hands, pressing his face tightly against her.

She opened her legs, her hands sliding down to clutch his butt, and pulled him hard against her.

With a snarl of frustration, Luke picked her up and set her aside to unlock the door. He left the key in the lock as he pushed the door open and pulled her inside.

There was a sturdy table in the hall where he normally threw his keys and wallet.

It was small, but it would do. It would *have* to do.

With a careless swipe of his hand, Luke rid the table of the glass catch-all Mrs. Scuttle had gotten him for Christmas one year. It bounced to the carpet, but didn't break.

He pulled Lydia into his arms again, kissing her neck, cupping her soft breasts and cursing the restrictions of her outfit.

He wanted to touch her. He wanted to feel how hot she was. He wanted to find out if she was wet for him.

Finally, he managed to get the garment unbuttoned far enough to slide it down over her hips, to see that she was wearing a sexy red thong bikini.

She kicked her clothes away, grabbed his shirt in both hands, and jerked the snaps free. Then her mouth was on his chest, her teeth nipping, her lips sucking, and her tongue swirling around his flat nipples until they puckered in response.

As her fingers popped open the top button of his jeans, Luke ran his finger along the edge of her panties. He was torturing himself and her, prolonging the moment when he would touch her secret place for the first time.

She whimpered and pushed her hips against his hand. His zipper rolled carefully downward, releasing his raging erection into her hot little hands. She curled her fingers around him, testing his thickness, making little sounds of approval in her throat.

Luke's knees tried to buckle. He braced himself against the wall, scrambling in his pocket for the condom he'd put there earlier. All the while she was squeezing him, stroking him, inflating his ego with those sexy little noises she made in her throat. Whimpers of need.

He managed to get the condom and stuff it into her hand so that he could get back to the business of exploring her. While she unwrapped the condom, Luke sent his fingers seeking her hot, damp spot.

He found it.

A white-hot flame of desire knocked another inch into his arousal.

She murmured her surprise and pleasure, and Luke groaned against her neck, his finger slipping into her tight tunnel. Her muscles instantly tightened around him, hinting at the pleasure to come. Promising him an unforgettable journey. "You are so hot, baby," he whispered. He hooked his finger in her panties and took them down, down, along legs that seemed to go on forever.

And since he was already down, he couldn't resist burying his tongue inside her.

Her choked scream made his heart leap with excitement. She grabbed his hair, trying to pull him up, to make him stop his torture.

Luke was glad to know that she wanted what he wanted.

To be inside her, filling her, stroking her over and over again.

He lifted her hips and placed her bottom on the edge of the table. Panting, she reached down and guided him into position.

Together, they watched as he slowly sank into her. The beautiful sight reminded Luke of their encounter in the massage room, and he wondered if she was remembering it, too.

When he was buried to the hilt, Luke cupped her breasts in both hands and brought her nipples together. He laved them with his tongue, then suckled first one and then the other. He scraped his teeth gently over the surface and was pleased when she moaned her pleasure.

Finally, as he began to move in a slow, teasing rhythm, he took her mouth again. She sucked his tongue until he had to either make her stop, or risk losing control.

So he sucked hers, swallowing her smothered cries as he stoked the fire, sinking into her again and again, mimicking the act with his tongue. He could feel her spasms beginning, could feel her surprise and joy as the climax caught her up and swept her away.

"Luke! Oh, God, Luke!"

Her sweet cry pushed him over the edge into the most earth-shattering orgasm he'd ever experienced.

Chapter Nineteen

"Luke, you there? Listen, I hate to interrupt . . . but Ramon and I need a ride home."

Lying in bed after a slower, more thorough bout of lovemaking, Luke tightened his arms around Lydia. He could tell by the sound of her shallow, even breathing that she was asleep. He'd been on the verge of sleep, too, until the phone rang, followed by Greg's disgruntled voice on his answering machine.

Why would Greg need a ride home? He'd brought his own car to the party, and he was supposed to take Casey home.

"I guess you're probably wondering what happened to my car." There was a pregnant pause before Greg continued. "And I know you're going to gloat because you always do. The thing is . . . Ramon seems to think it's against the law to drive without a windshield."

With a muffled curse, Luke relinquished his hold on Lydia and lunged for the phone. "What the hell happened to your windshield?"

"So you *are* there? Did you get the cash up front?"

"Go to hell. What happened to your car?" Luke glanced at Lydia. Her eyes were still closed. The satin sheet had fallen from her shoulders, revealing her full breasts to the moonlight shining in through the bedroom window.

His breathing immediately accelerated. He took a few deep breaths in an effort to slow it down.

"Well, we were parked in Casey's driveway, and Ramon was just finishing up telling her about the time he and I dressed up as women and went to a straight bar—"

"Would you get to the point?" Luke growled. He'd heard the story several times.

"Fine. Casey's husband came out to investigate. When he saw Casey in the car with us, he grabbed up a rake and went berserk on my car."

"I take it you never got the chance to tell him that you and Ramon are a couple," Luke said dryly.

"You got *that* right." Greg sounded on the verge of tears. "Before anyone could say anything, he'd busted my windshield, both my headlights, and left a sizeable dent in my hood. Casey forgot to mention that her husband was a psychopath."

Luke didn't have to say 'I told you so.' "Why don't you call a cab?"

"Because Ramon has this phobia about cab drivers,

and don't ask, because he's giving me a murderous look just for telling you that much."

There were some things, Luke mused wryly, that a body didn't need to know. Sighing, he said, "I've got to get dressed."

"Ahhh."

"Shut up, Greg."

"Hey! All I said was—"

"I'll be there in twenty minutes. Have you called a tow truck?"

"Done. Can you hurry? People are staring at us from their windows. I think there should be a homophobia sign posted at the street corner."

"Just don't get within shooting distance of Casey's husband."

Greg made a choking sound. "Wouldn't dream of it, but I don't think we have anything to worry about. When macho man finished bashing my car, he picked Casey up and carried her inside like he was Rhett Butler or something. They were sucking each other's faces before the door closed."

"Mission accomplished . . . at the cost of how many thousands of dollars' worth of damage to your car?"

"Go to hell, Luke, *after* you take us home."

Luke was still chuckling as he hung up the phone and began to get dressed.

"Trouble in paradise again?"

Lydia's sleepy, sex-roughened voice halted his movements. He thought very seriously about letting Greg and Ramon find their own damned ride home and jumping back into bed with the surprisingly uninhibited Lydia. With a grim smile, he said, "Yeah. Maybe this time Greg's learned his lesson." He hesitated, deliberately turning his head when she stretched her voluptuous body like a cat after a long nap in the sun. She was too tempting. Too distracting.

Irresistible.

"We need to talk," he said gruffly. "Will you wait for me here?" It was time he laid his cards on the table.

And found out if she'd fold or call his bluff.

Lydia froze in the act of stretching, suddenly, sharply aware that the upper half of her body was exposed.

But Luke wasn't looking at her. He had turned his face away, as if he were embarrassed.

"We need to talk."

So the moment had arrived, she thought, as her stomach lurched and her heart cracked. What a fool she'd been to think for one moment—one *instant*—that their feverish desire for each other might have made Luke forget that he wore an invisible price tag.

Somehow, she forced her lips to move.

Somehow, she managed to find her voice.

And somehow, she was able to lie convincingly.

"Of course. I wouldn't think of running out on you." She quickly lowered her lashes over her lying eyes as he turned sharply to look at her.

A long, tense moment passed. Lydia remained frozen, wondering if he'd read between the lines. Wondering if he knew how badly she wanted to curl into a ball and cry.

"Good," he finally said. "I'll be back as soon as I can. There's food in the fridge, if you're hungry, and clean towels in the dryer if you want a shower." His voice held a trace of wry amusement as he added, "I never can seem to get around to folding them."

Her eyes were still downcast as he planted a warm, lingering kiss on her mouth.

She didn't move until she heard the door open and close.

The moisture that flooded her eyes made her furious. She jerked the covers aside and rose, ignoring the tears scalding her cheeks and burning her eyes as she went in search of her clothes.

Clothes Luke had impatiently taken off her just seconds before he showed her those marvelous fireworks she'd previously only dreamed about.

Maybe she would have been okay if fireworks had been the only thing she'd experienced. Maybe she could have held her head high and walked away with only minor discomfort.

But that wasn't the case. The case was . . . she had experienced more than intense sexual satisfaction. She'd felt *connected* to Luke in a way she'd never felt with any other man. He not only aroused her physically, he aroused her emotionally.

Doomed.

Like Aunt Tempera.

She'd fallen for a gigolo.

And now it was time to pay.

Lydia found all her clothes, but the matching purse was nowhere in sight. Her heart sank as she realized that she must have left it in Luke's car, along with her credit cards, checkbook, and some cash.

Not the brightest move she'd ever made, she thought, mentally kicking herself. She picked up the phone and called Roger. When he answered, she gave him Luke's address, then hesitated, biting her lip.

"Was there something else, Miss Lydia?"

Yes. Can you bash every mirror in the house before I get home so that I don't have to look at myself? "Um, yes. Do—do you happen to have any cash on you? I, um, misplaced my purse." Her face got hot, which was ridiculous, really. Roger couldn't possibly know why she needed the cash.

He couldn't know that she had to pay her gigolo.

"How much were you needing, ma'am?"

The ingrained politeness in Roger's voice didn't quite mask his curiosity. Lydia gnawed on her thumbnail. She didn't have the slightest idea what Luke charged for four hours of wild, incredible sex. They had made love twice, but in the interim, he'd made her scream with pleasure so many times she'd lost count.

Luke was no slacker in bed, and that was a bald fact.

So how much would he have demanded had she waited until he returned? Would he have given her a verbal invoice? Lydia slammed her eyes closed and bit hard on her bottom lip.

She couldn't believe she was paying a man for sex.

But most of all, she couldn't believe that she had willingly and wantonly pursued Luke for sex, knowing what he was. Knowing what it would make her if she slept with him.

If it had been premeditated, like she'd planned, maybe she wouldn't be feeling like such an awful hypocrite. If it had been something she'd had to grit her teeth to get through, maybe she wouldn't be tingling all over from the aftermath, and hating herself for it.

"Miss Lydia?"

Roger's patient prompting forced Lydia to make a decision. If she were the type of woman to gladly pay a man for sex, what would she be willing to pay the enormously talented Luke? A hundred dollars for each orgasm?

"Five hundred dollars," Lydia blurted out. Although Roger couldn't see her, she covered her burning face with her hands. Roger was a model employee, but even *he* would surely be shocked by her outrageous request.

But she underestimated Roger's training.

"Shouldn't be a problem, miss. I always keep a bit of cash lying around for emergencies."

Hysterical laughter bubbled inside Lydia. She covered her mouth, imagining Roger's shock if she told him that her emergency involved paying a gigolo for his time and talent. "Thank you, Roger. Can you hurry, please?"

"Yes ma'am. I'll be there before you know it."

Even shame and self-disgust couldn't completely wipe out the last magical four hours as Lydia finished dressing and went to stand by the window to watch for the limo.

She didn't want to be there when Luke returned.

"Stubborn, self-righteous, hypocritical . . ." Luke swore, long and loudly. He snatched up the stack of bills from the nightstand and tore them in half, then into thirds. Every muscle quivering with a mixture of mortification and anger, he strode into the kitchen and shoved the shredded money into the garbage disposal.

He turned on the water, then the disposal, gaining some gratification from the sound of the money disintegrating into a noisy gurgle.

It was only after he'd shut off the disposal that he began to feel foolish. He could have given that money to the homeless, or donated it to Hope House or any number of charities.

Or . . . he could at least have counted it, found out how much Lydia thought he was worth in bed. Maybe knowing would have lessened the injury to his ego.

Damn.

Why hadn't she waited for him to return? Why had she run out like a scared rabbit? Luke yanked his shirt over his head, his movements slowing as he caught a whiff of her unforgettable perfume. He buried his nose in the shirt and allowed himself a full moment to remember what it had been like to make love to Lydia, arouse her to a fever pitch.

Give her not only her first orgasm, but the next four as well. He'd definitely been on a roll, but then, he'd had a great incentive. There wasn't an inch of her curvy body that he hadn't licked, nibbled, sucked, or kissed.

His own body still tingled from her retribution.

The woman was dynamite in bed.

His jaw tightened as he again thought about the money she'd left him on the nightstand. When he'd said they needed to talk, had she actually assumed he was going to tell her how much he charged? Or was leaving the money her cowardly way of denying what was between them?

Or what he'd *thought* was between them, Luke corrected with a mental curse. Damn the woman! He'd never met a more stubborn, narrow-minded person so hell-bent on vengeance. And it hurt, he admitted—with another harsh curse—to know that what they'd experienced tonight hadn't changed a damned thing.

Not a *damned* thing.

She obviously still believed he was a gigolo, and she obviously still intended to do what she could to shut Mr. Complete down.

Luke turned on the shower and shucked his jeans, frowning. She'd paid in cash. She was bright enough to realize she couldn't catch him without evidence that he had accepted payment, and he'd bet Detective Parker had explained that much to her, and probably a whole lot more. Like how she couldn't bring up the subject of payment; he had to do it. Otherwise, it would be entrapment.

If she had waited around, she would have found out

that he was the owner of Mr. Complete, and that neither he nor his current escorts were guilty of prostituting themselves. He would have explained to her about Rhew Burgess and how he suspected the weasel bastard had tried to sabotage his business by planting Graham Potter and Anthony Cuff.

He would have apologized for not realizing what Rhew was up to before his moles had time to do damage. She would have had to see that he was sincere, to realize that he was still kicking himself for not suspecting after the first bad apple. He had assumed that Graham had been a fluke. In Luke's line of business, he knew there was always the chance that eventually one of his men would succumb to greed or temptation.

And now, because of Lydia, he had a better understanding of the willpower involved in resisting the temptations of this particular job. The greed part he would not tolerate no matter how much he understood the lure of wealth.

Did that make him a hypocrite? Luke gave his head a wry shake as he lathered his body. He suspected he and Lydia would be eating from the same crow entree after tonight.

The question that remained was whether she planned to pursue her plans to close his business.

Luke cursed softly, realizing he wasn't too thrilled with the alternative, if it meant he wouldn't be seeing Lydia again.

Chapter Twenty

Casey stared at Lydia, dumbfounded. "You're saying you just *assumed* Luke was going to talk to you about money?"

Lydia flushed at Casey's incredulous tone. "Come on, Casey. What else could it be?"

"Oh, I don't know," Casey drawled sarcastically. "Maybe he wanted to talk to you about his *feelings?* Is that so unbelievable?"

"Actually, yes." When Lydia realized how badly she wanted to believe Casey, it made her more determined than ever not to. How could she even think it, living with the proof of such foolishness? Aunt Tempera was a constant reminder.

"I see that you've made up your mind to believe the worst," Casey said, not bothering to hide her disappointment. "I hope for your sake that you're right, and you're not missing an opportunity to be happy."

"I *am* happy. I don't need a man to make me happier, especially one as distracting and as complicated as Luke. Do you realize I don't even know his last name?"

"Does it matter?"

"Yes! It matters! I had wild, crazy sex with a man I don't even know!"

Casey grinned. "At least now you know there's nothing physically wrong with you." She propped her feet on the desk and leaned back in her chair, her expression one of smug satisfaction. "As for not knowing his last name, why don't you just ask him?"

Lydia pushed her half-eaten sandwich away. It had been two days since the party, and she hadn't been able to eat or sleep.

Just like Aunt Tempera.

The thought terrified her. How could Casey be so blind?

"Because I don't want to know. In fact, I don't want to see him ever again." *Liar*. Lydia ignored the taunting voice. "Under the circumstances, I think that would be best."

"So does this mean you're not going through with your plans to close Mr. Complete?" Casey asked hopefully.

Lydia hesitated. "I was thinking about going to Cameron Rose. If I can convince her that Jet is just using her, then maybe I can get her to testify that he took money from her for sex."

But Casey was shaking her head before Lydia finished. "I'm telling you, Lydia, Jet hasn't slept with Cameron Rose. She's lying."

"Why would she lie?" Lydia was exasperated with Casey's misplaced loyalty.

"I don't know. I haven't figured that one out."

"Casey—" Lydia broke off as the ringing phone interrupted them. She picked it up, checking her watch at the same instant. They had been taking an afternoon break and their next appointment wasn't for another twenty minutes. "Lydia's Affordable Spa. Can I help you?"

"Miss Lydia, I think you should come home right away."

It was Sweeney, his voice hushed with concern. Lydia tensed, her imagination taking flight. "Has something happened to Aunt Tempera?"

"I'm not sure. She's—she's acting strangely. I'm afraid she may have taken too many of those sedatives the doctor prescribed for her."

Raw terror shot through Lydia. "I'll be right there." She replaced the phone and shot out of her chair, her heart pounding and her stomach rolling.

"What is it?" Casey demanded, alarmed by Lydia's pale expression.

Lydia explained briefly, grabbing her purse and her keys as she raced to the door. "I'll call you later," she promised.

The drive seemed endless. Lydia forced herself to concentrate on her driving, mentally lashing herself for not realizing just how serious her aunt's condition was.

Before the party—before Luke—she hadn't known that heartbreak could affect someone physically as well as mentally.

The last two sleepless, appetite-free days and nights should have clued her in.

She just hoped she wasn't too late.

"Come on, Aunt Tempera, keeping walking," Lydia coaxed, her arm firmly around Tempera's waist. They made it to the patio, then turned to make another trek across the bedroom.

"Just let me sleep. I'll be okay if I can just get some sleep."

The weakness in Tempera's voice alarmed Lydia. She forced her to keep walking. "We have to walk for another half hour, at least. The doctor said that you should be okay if we keep you awake until ten o'clock."

Tempera stumbled. "I just took a couple of extra pills to help me sleep," she protested faintly. "And drank a glass of wine. I wasn't trying to do myself in."

"I know." Lydia bit her lip. "But you drank three glasses of wine, Aunt Tempera. The pills made you forget. Mixing wine and tranquilizers is dangerous."

"I just need to get some . . . sleep," Tempera whispered. She leaned her head on Lydia's shoulder and sighed. "Every time I try to close my eyes, I start thinking about Tony. Did you know he was an orphan?"

Lydia didn't know and certainly didn't care, but if it helped Tempera stay awake, then she would encourage her to talk about the devil himself. They made it to the far wall and turned, heading back to the patio. This time, Lydia thought, she'd take her aunt outside onto the patio. Maybe the fresh air would help revive her. "Tell me about him," she said gently.

"It's a terrible story. He and his parents were living in their car when the accident happened."

If her aunt hadn't been so out of it, she would surely have felt Lydia tense. The story was all too familiar.

"A garbage truck backed over the car. Tony was asleep in the backseat, covered with blankets and clothes. It was the only thing that saved him." Tempera sniffled. "He said what he remembers most was the sound of his dog screaming. The poor thing was sleeping in the back window."

Nausea rose to burn Lydia's throat. So Luke had lied. Was it a generic story all gigolos told their prospective victims?

"His parents were killed instantly," Tempera added in a tearful whisper. "Isn't it just an awful story?"

"Just awful," Lydia managed to choke out. To think she had felt sorry for Luke! And Bart . . . poor unsuspecting Bart had believed him as well. Her aunt's next words jolted her even more.

"Tony called today."

Lydia stopped dead in her tracks, supporting her

aunt's slight figure. Her vision clouded over with a misty red rage. How dare he? How dare he call her aunt after what he'd done to her?

She was so furious she couldn't speak.

Aunt Tempera didn't seem to notice her silence—or that they had stopped walking. She went on in a dreamy tone.

"He didn't say anything, but I know it was him."

Lydia caught herself just before relief buckled her knees. Maybe it was just a wrong number. "How—how do you know it was Tony?"

"I just do." Tempera tilted her head, staring up at Lydia. Her eyes were full of grief and a heart-wrenching sadness. "Do you think I'll ever get over him, Lydia? Because I don't think I can go on much longer this way."

Her whispered words scared Lydia speechless. She started them walking again, taking Tempera out onto the patio. The warm, fragrant night air enveloped them. Finally, she found her voice, but it was shaky. "You *will* get over him, and you *will* go on." She steered her back into the bedroom and over to the nightstand. "And we're going to start by getting rid of these." Lydia picked up the bottle of sleeping pills and took Tempera with her into the bathroom.

The pills went into the toilet. Tempera surprised Lydia by reaching out and pushing the handle to flush them down.

Her aunt's eyes flooded with tears. They rolled down her chin and plopped into the toilet water. After a moment of silence, she took a deep, shuddering breath and straightened her slumping shoulders. "I'm sorry I worried you, sweetheart."

Lydia felt tears flood her own eyes. She hugged her aunt tightly, her heart aching for her. "Will you see someone?" she pleaded.

Tempera hugged her back, her strength encouraging. "If you think it will help."

"Are you absolutely positive you heard her correctly?" Luke hated to doubt his secretary, but the woman *was* hearing impaired. And her accusation was serious.

Very, very serious.

Mrs. Scuttle narrowed her owlish eyes, her fingers inching toward the plastic pen holder. "I wouldn't repeat something so disturbing, Luke, if I wasn't certain I heard it *correctly*. The woman—Casey, I think her name was—was a chatterbox from the moment I arrived."

"And you're certain she didn't know who you were?"

"How could she? She's never seen me, and I gave my maiden name of Richards over the phone when I made the appointment. When I saw what a long face she was wearing, I asked her if she wanted to talk about it." Mrs. Scuttle looked smug. "She said I looked like her grandmother, God rest her soul, and launched into the story as if she'd never heard of the word confidential." The secretary's eyes brightened. "By the way, you were right about that warm stone massage and its benefits. I feel ten years younger."

Luke thought briefly about his own erotic experience with massage and Lydia's talented hands. Sweat popped out above his lip. He cleared his throat, forcing the memory aside. "I'll have to try it sometime. Tell me again everything Casey said."

With her fingers curled contentedly around the pencil holder, Mrs. Scuttle went over the conversation again. "She asked me if I knew Cameron Rose, and I said no, I didn't believe that I did. She said good, because she needed to talk about her or she was going to burst. She said the woman was lying about a friend of hers, saying her friend slept with Cameron when she—Casey—knew that he hadn't done any such thing."

"How did you know Casey was talking about Jet?"

Mrs. Scuttle's gnarled fingers tightened on the pencil holder. "You're not *listening*, Luke. I was getting to that, although I've already told you. Now, if I didn't already know some of what's going on, I probably wouldn't have made any sense out of her story. She was talking in circles, mostly mumbling to herself as she laid out the stones on my back and legs. God, it felt heavenly!"

Luke tapped his fingers on his knee.

His secretary hefted the pencil holder in her hand, then set it down again. "She said her friend worked for an escort service, but that he was strictly on the up and up. She said she knew that some of those escort services had shady reputations, but she didn't believe this one did, although her business partner had different beliefs." Mrs. Scuttle paused, squinting at Luke. "Don't frown, Luke. It will make you old before your time. You know what Miss Carmichael thinks, and you know why. Now, getting on with my story . . . since I have to tell it *twice*, Casey then said her business partner and friend was determined to get Cameron Rose to testify that Jet slept with her for money. It was obvious to me that Casey didn't agree with her friend, and that's when she said for the third or fourth time that she believed Cameron Rose was lying about Jet. She said she just couldn't figure out a motive."

"Hmm. And she said all of this without telling you Lydia's reasons for wanting Cameron Rose to testify?"

"I told you, Luke. Casey wasn't really talking *to* me. She was getting something off her chest and I happened to be a good listener." She blinked. "I feel kinda bad for spying on her like that."

"I"m sure if she knew the whole story, she'd understand. Besides, it sounds like she's in our corner, doesn't it?"

His secretary nodded. "I got that impression, Luke, I surely did. Are you going to talk to Jet?"

"Yes. Wouldn't you if you were me?"

"I reckon I would, even if I *did* believe Casey."

"You don't?"

Mrs. Scuttle stared at the pencil holder for a long moment. Finally, she said slowly, "I like Jet and all, but he's not the best judge when it comes to women."

Luke sympathized with him. "See if you can track

him down. Tell him to meet me at Danny's in an hour."

Jet's spontaneous reaction to Luke's disturbing story convinced Luke that Jet was innocent.

"That's a lie, Luke! I told you before that I would never risk the company by getting involved with a client." When several customers at nearby booths turned to stare, Jet lowered his voice. "I'm not denying I'd like to be more than an escort to Cameron, but I swear to you that I've kept these fantasies to myself." He looked righteously perplexed. "I just can't imagine why she'd make up these lies about me."

"Well, at the risk of beating a dead horse, there's always the chance that Burgess has her in his pocket."

"I can't believe that."

But this time Jet's denial lacked conviction, and when his gaze suddenly veered from Luke's, Luke felt a chill scroll down his spine. "Jet? Is there something you want to tell me?" When Jet didn't immediately reply, Luke added with a hint of ruefulness, "I think you'll find me a bit more understanding now that I've come face to face with temptation." He didn't add that he'd lost; Jet already knew it.

"Well . . . I guess maybe I should tell you—just in case there's a slight chance that you're right about Cameron and Burgess—that I sort of talked to Cameron about the situation."

The air in Luke's lungs grew scarce. "The situation?"

Jet nodded, staring mutely at his water glass. "I know it's no excuse, but she's—she's real easy to talk to, and one night the subject just came up."

Very softly, Luke asked, "Do you remember who brought it up, Jet?" Luke had a pretty good idea. . . .

"I guess she did." He heaved a sigh and let it out on a low curse. "I'm an idiot when it comes to women."

Luke privately agreed with Jet's last comment. "Did you tell her everything?"

"Basically, yeah." Jet shot Luke a miserable look, tinged with a hint of defiance. "You could be wrong, you know."

He could be, but Luke didn't think he was. It made too much sense. "If Cameron knows what's been going on between myself and Lydia and she's on Rhew's payroll, then we're probably screwed." He was trying his very best not to be angry with Jet, but it wasn't easy. "Does Cameron also know what happened between Lydia and me the night of the party?"

When Jet nodded, a four-letter curse burst out of Luke. "He was probably hoping Lydia would do all his dirty work for him—going on the shaky assumption that Lydia isn't working for Rhew—and was keeping Cameron as a backup and using her to goad Lydia on. Now, if Lydia doesn't go through with her plans, my guess is he'll send Cameron forward to claim she paid you for sex. She's a celebrity. Her word against yours . . ." Luke didn't think he had to explain. "Either way, we're screwed."

"Maybe you could talk to Detective Parker, tell him what's going on."

Luke laughed without humor. "I'd need a translator to explain this mess. Who in his right mind would believe me?" How had he gotten to this point? He'd started out wanting to have a little fun, teach Lydia a lesson in life and love.

Now he was on the verge of losing his business, and Lydia believed more than ever that he was a gigolo. Even if he managed to slip out of this mess with his business and reputation intact, Rhew would simply come at him from a different angle.

The prospect made Luke feel very weary.

Chapter Twenty-one

"It was sweet of you to offer me a free treatment," Cameron told Lydia. Lounging on the reclining massage chair, the singer was unrecognizable beneath a body wrap composed of seaweed.

Lydia felt a pang of guilt. She had an ulterior motive for offering the free session; Cameron just didn't know it yet. "Don't mention it. Casey and I have found out that word of mouth is the best advertisement." She held her arms beneath the water faucet to wash away the seaweed, then dried herself on a clean towel.

Finally, she could put it off no longer. She turned to face Cameron. "Besides, I wanted to talk to you about Jet."

Cameron carefully opened her eyes. One seaweed-smeared eyebrow rose in question. "Oh? What about

Jet?" Her laughter echoed in the room. "Don't tell me—he's married?"

"No. At least, not that I know of." Lydia busied her nervous hands with straightening the counter. "I wanted to tell you what happened to my aunt." Keeping it as simple as she could, Lydia told the sad tale, ending with, "Aunt Tempera believes something scared him away. I believe he was scamming her all along. When he got what he wanted, he dumped her and disappeared."

The singer was quiet for a long moment. Her voice was subdued when she finally spoke. "I'm sorry that happened to your aunt, but I don't see what it has to do with me . . . and Jet. Jet's nothing like this Anthony person."

"Isn't he?" Lydia challenged. "How do *you* know he isn't? You said yourself that you've slept together. If he can break one big rule, then why can't he break a million small ones?" She waved her hand in a helpless gesture. "I just don't want to see you get hurt, like Aunt Tempera." *Like me.*

"You think I should stop seeing him?"

Lydia sucked in a fortifying breath before blurting out, "Not only that, but I think you should report his unethical actions to the police."

Cameron sat up abruptly, the whites of her eyes pronounced against the dark backdrop of the seaweed. "I can't do that! If he's doing something illegal, I'm just as guilty."

Wincing inwardly, Lydia said, "You can say you

were seduced. These guys are professionals. They know exactly what they're doing."

The singer slowly lay back against the massage chair, frowning. "I probably shouldn't tell you this. It's rather embarrassing, in light of what you've told me, and if you *are* right about Jet . . ." Cameron fell silent, biting her lip. She made a face, grabbing a tissue and spitting out a mouthful of seaweed. "I loaned Jet some money."

Lydia closed her eyes and groaned. She didn't realize how badly she'd been hoping she was wrong until that moment. "How much?"

"Ten thousand. He—he said he needed to pay off a loan before they repossessed his car."

"Did you get a receipt?"

Cameron shook her head, looking ashamed. "I didn't want him to think that I didn't trust him."

"He asked for cash?"

"Yes."

"And you didn't think his request was strange?" Lydia prompted gently.

"I guess I just wasn't thinking." Cameron grabbed another tissue and dabbed at her eyes, smearing seaweed in the process. "Maybe we're wrong. Maybe Jet's nothing like—"

"Anthony wasn't the first," Lydia inserted. "There was another escort who conned a client, just a month before Anthony. *Now* will you report Jet to the police?"

"What about Luke?" Cameron asked, glaring at

Lydia as if she were the enemy. "Why don't you report *him?*"

Lydia turned her back to Cameron before the woman could notice her guilty flush. "I don't have any proof."

"Neither do I."

"You're a celebrity. Chances are the police will believe you." She couldn't explain to Cameron that she had been trying to set Luke up from the beginning. And she certainly wasn't going to humiliate herself by confessing that her plans had backfired. Big time. Composing herself, she turned back to Cameron, who was shaking her head.

"I can't, Lydia. The publicity would be awful. I have a son to think about."

"You're a victim. Detective Parker would be discreet."

"I can't take that chance." Cameron sounded definite. "If you want a complaint filed, you'll have to do it yourself."

Unable to hide her frustration, Lydia said, "Will you at least stop seeing Jet before it's too late?"

Cameron's expression crumpled. Tears flooded her eyes. "It's already too late, Lydia. I'm in love with him."

Back to square one.

"Can you finish the massage, Lydia? My limo will be picking me up soon. I'm—I'm sorry I couldn't be more helpful."

Lydia was sorry, too.

Twenty minutes later, Lydia stood at the shop window watching the doomed woman get into her limo. She saw a flash of inky black hair, the hard edge of a shadowed, square jaw as a man leaned forward to take Cameron's arm and helped her into the limo.

But it wasn't Jet, Lydia realized with a start of surprise. It was the unforgettable Mr. Burgess. She sighed, turning away. Why couldn't Cameron be in love with *that* man, instead of Jet?

A slim brunette with the name tag of *Wendy* pinned to her breast led Lydia to Detective Parker's office at the back of the busy police station. His office was nothing more than a dark hole in the wall, but it was surprisingly neat.

Detective Parker sat behind his desk, a young, serious-faced man of about thirty. He kept his sandy blond hair cropped short and wore jeans and a pullover shirt.

Lydia had never seem him in uniform, and she wondered briefly if he had some kind of aversion to wearing one.

"Miss Carmichael." Parker rose politely until she was seated in the chair facing his desk. "Excuse the mess."

"I was expecting worse," Lydia said, mustering a smile. "Thanks for seeing me on such short notice."

Parker's brow rose. "I've been trying to get in touch with you."

"Oh." Lydia flushed. She'd forgotten about his inopportune visit the day the escorts came to her spa. "I was, um, in the middle of something very important." Lydia highly doubted Detective Parker would agree that straddling a man on a massage table was considered "highly important," but she wasn't about to reveal the truth.

"Well, the important thing is that you're here now. I'm hoping you've got good news for me?"

Lydia shook her head, feeling her face heat another five degrees. "I'm afraid that's what I came to talk to you about. My, um, plans to help you didn't work out."

"He didn't take the bait?"

Parker sounded so surprised that Lydia blushed on top of her flush. Luke had taken the bait all right . . . five times. But that was her little shameful secret. "I—I didn't really try." *Liar, liar, pants on fire.* "The fact is, I've changed my mind. Aunt Tempera seems to be getting better, so I thought it would be best to try to put this behind us."

The detective stared at Lydia long enough to make her squirm. He made a steeple out of his hands and continued to regard her thoughtfully. By the time he got around to speaking, Lydia's nerves were screaming.

"It's good that your aunt is getting over her ordeal," he said slowly. "But I was hoping you'd go ahead with your plans to help me get the dirt on Mr. Complete. In fact . . . I was certain that's why you were here, in light of the anonymous phone call I got a couple of days ago."

Lydia licked her suddenly dry lips. He knows, she thought. She didn't know how or why, but Detective Parker knew about her intimate meeting with Luke. Hoping and praying it was only a case of extreme paranoia, Lydia tried changing the subject. "Can't you use one of your own people for this?"

Parker shook his head, his gaze still intent on her face. "The chief doesn't think it's worth the manpower and expense it would take. I was really counting on you. Are you sure you don't have something to give me?"

She could give him Cameron . . . and Jet, but considering her own guilt, it would be the height of hypocrisy. In the end, she shook her head. "No, nothing."

Detective Parker's eyes narrowed. Something resembling regret flickered in their blue depths before they crystalized into hard orbs. "I'm sorry to hear that, Miss Carmichael, because you leave me no choice."

"P-pardon me?"

"The phone call I received was from a very reliable source. I was told you left a party with one of the escorts from Mr. Complete, and that you went to his apartment and remained there a total of four hours." There was a deliberate pause before he added, "Alone with him."

Lydia's jaw dropped. She had suspected, but hearing it put so baldly floored her. "That doesn't prove anything!" she blurted out in a high, squeaky voice. "And he wasn't my escort at the time. We just happened to be at the same party."

His expression never changed. "But you can see how someone in my position . . . knowing what I know, would be suspicious of these actions? A month ago, you were swearing vengeance on the company. Now it sounds as if you're defending it."

"I'm not defending it," Lydia sputtered, mortified that the detective would even think such a thing. "I'd like to see Mr. Complete shut down as much as you."

"He got to you, didn't he?"

He spoke softly, but he might as well have shouted the accusation. Lydia jumped to her feet, knocking her purse from her lap and scattering the contents onto the floor. Her cheeks flamed. "No, Detective Parker. He did not get to me. Do you really think I could be fooled after what happened to Aunt Tempera?" Oh, how bitter the lie! And how utterly foolish she felt.

"Then prove it," he challenged. He came around to help her retrieve her purse and its contents, handing it back to her. "Get Luke Reynolds to name a price, and write him a check. Then call me. You don't even have to sleep with him."

I already have. For one stupendous second, Lydia was afraid she'd blurted out the ugly, shameful truth.

Then Parker's words sank in.

Lydia felt the room tilt. She abruptly sat again.

"Don't tell me you didn't know?" Parker demanded. He brought her a cup of water from a grimy water cooler in the corner. "Here. Drink this. Are you okay?"

"No," Lydia said faintly. "I'm not. Luke is . . . L. J. Reynolds? Are you sure?"

Grim-faced, Parker nodded. "When I saw you with him, I just assumed you knew, that he was short on escorts or something and was filling in."

Lydia put a hand to her forehead, trying to make sense of this new information. "Why—why wouldn't he tell me?"

Parker shrugged. "I think Reynolds has issues about privacy."

But Lydia wasn't buying that flimsy excuse. No, there was a deeper motive for Luke keeping quiet about his identity. She had asked about L. J. Reynolds, giving both Luke and Greg the perfect opportunity to tell her the truth.

Luke obviously had his reasons for keeping the information from her. And she was going to find out what those reasons were.

"Don't beat yourself up, Miss Carmichael. Few people know what L. J. Reynolds looks like. He came here from West Virginia about five years ago to start his business. It wasn't until a few months ago that his company came under suspicion." Parker put a comforting hand on her shoulder. He squeezed. "Will you help me rid Atlanta of these parasites?"

Still reeling with shock, Lydia got clumsily to her feet. "I need some time to think about this," she said before stumbling to the door.

Luke was L. J. Reynolds.

Luke was L. J. Reynolds.

He wasn't getting liposuction, as his secretary so eagerly informed her.

By the time she reached her car, a startling realization had washed over her. Luke must have known all along who she was and what she had been trying to do. Now that she knew *who* he was, everything fell into place with crystal clarity.

But how? How had he known?

Luke was just stepping out of the shower when the doorbell rang. It coincided with the microwave timer announcing his dinner was ready.

What now? Another catastrophe? It seemed he'd been having nothing but catastrophies since he'd met Lydia.

Lydia.

He groaned as he flung his towel on the rack and grabbed his robe. He still hadn't decided what to do about Lydia, or Rhew. He wanted to tie Lydia to a chair—or better yet, the bed—and force her to listen as he unraveled this tremendous mess.

As for Rhew Burgess . . . Luke wanted to break his pretty fingers, one by one, until Rhew agreed to keep his miserable carcass out of Luke's business and his life. Atlanta was a big city. There was room for both of them.

With these two unpleasant thoughts careening through his mind, Luke opened the door.

The last person he had expected to find on his doorstep was Lydia. He wasn't prepared because he still didn't know what to do. Tying her to the bed, however, still remained a favorable option.

But that was his libido speaking.

His brain told him to close the door before he opened his mouth and allowed his pride to make an even bigger mess of things.

He ignored both and simply stared, waiting for her to speak first. He just soaked up the sight of her looking uncertain and desirable and, God help him, unforgettable.

She finally moved those luscious, tasty lips. "I wanted to apologize in person for the way I ran out on you."

Her husky voice was temptation with a capital *T*. Luke turned away sharply to hide the reaction his robe didn't completely cover. How could he be so angry with her yet desire her to the point of pain? And was she truly sorry, or was this another trick?

"Come on in," he all but growled. He stalked into the kitchen to get his dinner out of the microwave. Slamming it on the counter, he muttered a curse and stuck his burned fingers in his mouth. He was painfully aware of Lydia behind him. He could hear her breathing.

Smell her perfume.

Sense her body heat.

"Are you okay?"

Was he okay? Luke looked down at the sizable

bulge in his robe. Depends on what she considered "okay."

"Did—did I leave you enough money?"

Luke froze, his hands now braced on the counter, his back to her. So she wasn't ready to give up the game. Well, he was good for another shot . . . or two or three. From the size of his erection, he was good for one hell of a shot.

By clenching his teeth, he was able to say evenly, "Going by the number of times you screamed my name, I'd say you were about two hundred dollars short."

He heard her gasp, and it made him smile despite his irritation.

After a small silence, she said, "Okay. I'll just write you a check."

"A check would be fine." Luke's disappointment was acute. Obviously, Lydia was still determined to go through with her plan to trap him for prostitution.

He heard a rustling noise, then the slight sound of a pen scribbling. It would serve Miss Righteous right if he took her check and gave her exactly what she paid for. She wouldn't have to know that he'd do with the check what he'd done with the cash she'd left him.

How many times would she be willing to sacrifice her body in the name of justice? Luke felt a jolt in his groin at the possibilities. It would be terrible of him to take advantage of Lydia that way.

Terrible . . . but nothing more than she deserved.

He turned around just as she was tearing the check

from the book. She kept her gaze lowered as he reached out and took it, then stuffed it into the pocket of his robe without looking at it. "I changed my mind," he said. He didn't have to feign a husky voice, not in the condition he was in.

Her head popped up. She stared at him with wide, startled eyes. "W-what?"

"I've changed my mind," he repeated, slowly untying his robe. "You overpaid me, but don't bother writing a different check. I'm more than willing to make up the difference."

Luke dropped the robe to show her just *how* willing he was.

Chapter Twenty-two

Lydia backed up until she bumped against the breakfast bar, trying desperately not to look at Luke in all his splendid nakedness.

And he *was* splendid.

"We—we need to talk," she stammered. She held out a restraining hand until she realized it looked as if she were reaching for him, then she quickly put it down. Breathing hard with no apparent cause, she tried to reason with him again. "I didn't come over here for sex."

Luke lifted one brow and continued advancing.

"I didn't!" she insisted, panting shamelessly. "I came to talk to you."

"So start talking," he drawled, his gaze on her heaving breasts.

He stopped—thank God—when he was inches

away, the point of his erection hovering a scant inch from her quivering belly. Lydia tried to control her breathing, so she wouldn't continue to inhale the fresh scent of soap and male arousal. Already her knees were like useless putty. "I—I know who you are!" she blurted out.

His other brow rose to join the first. "I assumed Rhew told you."

"Rhew?" Who the hell was he talking about? Lydia wondered. He sounded as if he took it for granted that she would know this Rhew person.

"My not-so-loving foster brother, Rhew Burgess. As if you didn't know."

Shock widened her eyes for a telling second. Mr. Burgess was Luke's foster brother?

"Come on, Lydia. The game is up. You know and I know." His gaze dropped, moving slowly down her body, then up again, leaving her trembling and aching. "Let's get it out in the open and get on with . . . business."

She clutched the counter behind her and tried to keep her balance. Not an easy accomplishment with Luke standing boldly naked in front of her. "I don't know Rhew Burgess." Her chin came out and up. She eyed him with open defiance. "He came in for a massage one day, but that's the first and only time I've ever met him."

"Liar."

He didn't bite the word out, as one might expect

with a blunt accusation. He said it softly, with a hint of smile.

Lydia was more confused than ever. "I swear I don't know him. How—how long have you known that I—that I—"

"Planned to ruin me?" Luke supplied in a bone-melting, silky voice.

Why was he *doing* that—that seduction thing at a time like this? Lydia wanted to pound his chest and beg him to stop. It was difficult enough to think with him naked! He didn't have to turn on that killer charm along with it.

She licked her lips, inadvertently drawing his heated gaze to her mouth. "You've known all along?" The possibility mortified her. She hadn't thought the situation could get any worse.

Now she knew that it could, and Luke confirmed it.

"Of course. I was sitting behind you at Danny's Bar and Grill while you were discussing your little plot for revenge with your business partner."

No. It couldn't be true. Not even *she* was that unlucky! She shook her head, sending her hair flying around her face. "You expect me to believe—" She sucked in a sharp breath as he reached out and rubbed his thumb over her nipple. "Don't—"

"Don't?" Luke's beautiful, sensual mouth twisted. "Don't touch you? You've already paid, remember?"

"Don't be ridiculous," she snapped. "Now that everything's out in the open, we don't have to—"

"To what?" he asked softly, bringing his other hand up to stroke her nipple. "Are you saying playtime is over? And just when we were getting to know one another."

Lydia blushed deeply at his intimate tone. She tried to inch to the left, but Luke followed, his fingers torturing her, the musky scent of his arousal fogging her brain. "Luke, I came here to tell you that—well, I came here to tell you the truth. Then I was going to tell you that I've changed my mind about . . ." She sucked her bottom lip between her teeth as his teasing finger started a downward journey. "Getting revenge, I mean, *vengeance*," she hastily corrected.

"Ah, yes. Ridding the world of parasitic, conniving, cruel . . . gigolos."

She closed her eyes at his mocking tone, remembering herself uttering those exact words. "I'm sorry. That was before I met you and the others. I still don't approve of your lifestyle, and I think Jet's taking advantage of Cameron Rose, but I've decided she's a big girl and can take care of herself."

"Really?" Luke lifted her up and set her on the breakfast bar. He spread her legs and moved between them, his arousal bumping against her thigh, sending a jolt of lightning through her belly.

Lydia was getting the distinct impression he wasn't listening. She slapped weakly at his hands as he tried to unbutton her dress. "Stop that. I'm trying to explain my actions to you."

"And *I'm* trying to remind you that we have more than conversation in common."

"You don't have to remind me." Lydia clapped a hand over her wayward mouth. She hadn't meant to add fuel to the fire. "I mean, I already know. I mean, oh, you know what I mean! Would you *please* stop? I can't think straight with you touching me."

"That makes two of us," Luke murmured huskily, just seconds before his mouth claimed hers.

For all of thirty seconds, Lydia allowed herself the luxury of his kiss. At the end of that thirty seconds, she reluctantly moved her mouth aside. She framed his face with her hands, attempting to hold him back. "Luke, will you please listen?" Her voice sounded pathetically breathless even to her own ears. "I think someone else had the same idea that I had. Someone called the police station and told Detective Parker about the other night . . . when we were together here."

Luke nibbled the edge of her lips, his breath hot and exciting.

Distracting.

"Rhew Burgess," he mumbled absently. "I thought you two were working together." He clamped both hands on her spread knees, then ran his hands slowly upward, bunching her dress as he progressed.

Lydia's eyelids felt heavy, her nipples super sensitive as they brushed across his chest. She struggled to think clearly, but it wasn't easy with his hot lips trailing a path of fire along her neck to her breasts, and his hands inching closer to the throbbing junction of her thighs. "Why . . . didn't you tell me that you knew?"

His voice was muffled against her neck as he said, "Because I was having too much fun getting to know you."

At his confession, an unexpected jolt of pleasure shot through her. Lydia caught herself before she smiled, tensing with anticipation when his fingers tested the elastic of her panties. She was damp, and there wasn't a damned thing she could do about it, not as long as she was in the same room with Luke.

He closed his mouth over her thrusting nipple, his breath blasting easily through the thin material of her dress. Lydia gasped and tugged at his hair.

He ignored her.

"I'm—I'm not really rich," she ventured, just as his finger slipped inside her. She moaned and arched her back.

"I know." He caught her lips in his teeth, then swiped his tongue along her mouth as he whispered, "I'm not really a gigolo, so we're even."

She didn't believe him. He'd taken her check and he hadn't returned the cash she'd left the last time. Why was he lying to her? Was he telling her what he thought she wanted to hear? If only it *were* true.

"Luke . . ." She caught her breath as he ripped her panties off and threw them aside. The tip of his erection burned against her opening, teasing her. Tempting her. She reached down and closed her hand around him, holding him back. He pulsed and throbbed in her hand. "You don't have to lie to me."

He stilled.

She looked into his eyes. They burned intently into hers even as he continued to throb in her hand. She licked her lips, wondering what she'd said to put that look of resignation in his eyes. She took a wild guess. "What I mean is, I'm not exactly in a position to judge your . . . occupation."

"I'm overwhelmed by your understanding," he drawled with unmistakable asperity. "What would it take to convince you that I'm not a gigolo—and neither are my men?"

"It doesn't matter—"

He put a finger to her lips, shushing her. Lydia fell silent.

"At the risk of repeating myself, can I ask you to forget what you *think* I am until I love the living hell out of you? Because I'm about to burst."

This she believed. He was thick and hard and ready. When he surged forward, she tightened her fingers around him. Yes, she wanted him. She wouldn't bother denying the obvious. But she couldn't be reckless with her health, no matter how fogged her brain. "Wait. You forgot the condom."

He grabbed her wrist and brought her hand to his chest, his jaw tight, his eyes burning with exasperation and barely controlled passion. "Are you on birth control?"

"Yes."

"Then to hell with it. Whether you believe it or

not, I haven't had sex with anyone in almost a year—before you—and I've just had a physical. I don't have any diseases." He placed her hand on his naked butt, then took the other one and did the same. "I know from your conversation with Casey that you've been celibate for a while as well, so here comes the moment of truth."

Lydia gasped as he brought his arousal flush against her moist, ready opening. Her muscles quivered with anticipation of the pleasure to come. She'd never wanted anything so badly, she realized, more than a little shocked by her wild yearning.

He took her face in his hands, forcing her to look at him. "Do you trust me, Lydia? Because I'm leaving the rest up to you."

There was no mistaking his meaning. Either she trusted him and got what she wanted, or she told him no and went home empty and aching.

God help her, either way.

Luke could feel his heart pounding while he waited for Lydia to decide. It was true—and painfully obvious—that he wanted her, but he was startled to realize that he wanted her trust even more than he wanted to bury himself inside her tight, welcoming heat.

The moment of truth.

"Luke, I—"

Whatever Lydia had been about to say got drowned out by the sound of someone beating on his door. He growled a curse, reaching for his robe. He cast a warning look at her as he strode to the door, belting his robe along the way. "Don't move an inch. I'll be right back as soon as I get rid of the unfortunate person at my door."

The unfortunate person turned out to be Detective Parker.

"Mr. Reynolds, you're under arrest for prostitution."

Before Luke could close his dropped jaw, Detective Parker stepped inside and waved two uniformed men in after him.

"Search him," Detective Parker ordered.

As the two officers patted him down, Luke found his voice. "What the hell is this?" he demanded. Thank God he hadn't taken off Lydia's dress! Otherwise the men would be getting an eyeful of her sitting naked on the counter.

Realization hit Luke with the force of a blow.

He jerked his head in Lydia's direction. She was standing in the kitchen, her hand over her mouth, her eyes big and round.

Looking guilty as hell.

"Got something, detective." One of the officers held up the check Luke had stuffed into his pocket. "It's a check made out to Luke Reynolds from Lydia Carmichael."

"That's it!" Looking smug, Detective Parker snatched the check from the man's hand. "Cuff him and read him his rights." He glanced at Lydia, his voice tinged with regret as he added, "And cuff her too. Sorry, Miss Carmichael. You had the opportunity to do the right thing."

Not for a second did Luke believe the detective. He'd seen the look on Lydia's face, and it hadn't been shock. The detective was merely playing out a part, just as he would to protect a real undercover cop. They would cuff Lydia and book her, then let her go on some flimsy technicality.

While he rotted in jail and his business went to hell.

Not to mention his reputation.

She'd set him up, and he'd fallen into her trap like a gullible, trusting fool.

Two characteristics Luke thought he'd left behind when he'd left West Virginia and his fiancée in Rhew's bed.

"Detective Parker, this isn't what it seems," Lydia said.

Ruses and lies. Luke wasn't blind now, and he didn't believe her. There was no way the cop could have known unless Lydia had told them ahead of time what she was going to do.

Using the tip of his finger, Detective Parker held up her torn panties. "You were saying, Ms. Carmichael?"

Luke had to admit he was impressed with the way Lydia blushed a fiery red at the detective's taunt. He suspected the detective would pay hell for that one later, when they could drop their act and gloat over catching the bad guy.

Only he wasn't a bad guy.

He'd tried to tell her. He'd tried to show her.

She had refused to believe him.

After they let him dress, he was shoved into the backseat of a squad car with an almost convincingly chagrined and handcuffed Lydia. He was being charged with prostitution, and she was being charged—*as if*—with soliciting a prostitute.

Feeling her eyes on him, Luke deliberately looked away. He had nothing to say to her. At the moment, he was more furious with himself and his own foolish naïveté, but he knew the time would come when he would think about just how calculating and devious Lydia Carmichael had to be to catch him in a trap he'd been aware of since the beginning.

"I swear I didn't have anything to do with this."

She was good. But she wasn't *that* good. Luke didn't respond. He ground his teeth so hard it made his jaw ache. He welcomed the pain; it was no more than he deserved.

"You have to believe me, Luke! I saw Detective Parker earlier today and told him that I had changed my mind. I came over to tell you and to warn you that someone else was out to get you."

A snort of disbelief escaped before Luke could catch it back. He hated to give her even *that* much.

"Do you think he would arrest me if I was in on this?"

She was beginning to sound hysterical. Luke suppressed a sigh, wondering when she would get around to blaming *him*.

"Fine. Be mad, but you might want to remember that it wasn't *my* idea to have sex on the kitchen counter."

Bingo. He could almost admire her clever maneuver.

Too bad he'd seen it coming.

"And you could have torn up the check, if you're really not a gigolo."

She'd switched to taunting a response out of him. How original.

It wouldn't work.

He had nothing to say to her.

Chapter Twenty-three

The last person Lydia expected to see at the jail was Aunt Tempera.

In fact, Lydia was so overjoyed that her aunt had come to bail her out that she grabbed the cell bars and gave them a good old-fashioned shaking, momentarily forgetting her miserable state of mind. "Aunt Tempera! I've never been so glad to see you in my life!"

Tempera gave an injured sniff. "I find that hard to believe, Lydia, since you called Casey instead of me."

Some of Lydia's joy at seeing her aunt faded. "Oh. I take it Casey called you?"

"*After* you called *her*." Tempera obviously wasn't ready to let her off the hook. "Who do you think *I* would call if I got myself arrested?" She pressed her forefinger to her lips and pretended to contemplate the question. "Hmm. Let me see. Would I call my niece's best friend? No . . . I don't *think* so. Would I call Sweeney? Not before I'd call my niece. How about Roger?"

Lydia groaned. "Okay, okay! I get the point, and I'm sorry I didn't call you. It's just that I thought . . . well, I thought—"

"That I wouldn't come? That you shouldn't upset me?"

Tempera's eyes glimmered. She looked so stricken that Lydia wanted to kick herself. "I didn't mean—"

"Yes, you did, and you had every right to think it. I've been wallowing in self-pity to the point of selfishness, and it's time I stopped." She wiped at her eyes. "To think that my own niece didn't feel as if she could count on me at a time like this."

"Aunt Tempera, I love you more than anyone else in the world!" Lydia tried to reach her through the bars, but gave up. "I've been so worried about you." Lydia watched helplessly as her aunt tightly closed her eyes. When Tempera opened them again, the tears were gone. Looking back at her was the strong, independent woman Lydia had always admired and loved.

"This is my fault," Tempera said, her voice once again firm and strong, if not a little ashamed. "You wouldn't be in this mess if you hadn't been trying to right a wrong done to *me*."

Lydia tightened her fingers around the bars, imagining them around Casey's blabbermouth neck. "She told you everything?"

Tempera didn't have to ask who. "Yes, and I'm glad she did. I'm just sorry she waited so long to do it."

"This isn't your fault. I got myself in this mess, Aunt Tempera. How can you possibly blame yourself?"

"Would you have gone after the escort service if I hadn't fallen apart when Tony left?" Tempera challenged.

Hmm. Her aunt had her there. "Um, can we talk about this *after* you get me out of here?"

"No, we cannot." Tempera's expression softened. "Besides, the nice officer at the desk said it would take about twenty minutes to get the paperwork ready."

"They could at least bring you a chair."

"I don't need a chair." Tempera looked around at the dingy green walls of the hall as if contemplating a new decorating scheme. "I've been sitting, crying, and sleeping long enough. It's time I joined the land of the living again."

"Amen," Lydia mumbled. "If I'd known getting arrested would snap you out of it, I'd have done it a long time ago."

"Which reminds me . . . how *did* you manage to get arrested? Casey implied you were out to trap Luke and that Detective Parker knew about your plans."

Lydia's smile was grim. "Actually, I'd decided not to go through with it. That's why I was at Luke's apartment, to tell him."

Tempera frowned. "I don't understand. They can't arrest you for soliciting a prostitute without some sort of proof, can they?"

Heat scorched Lydia's face. She studied a wad of gum stuck to the grimy floor as she mumbled, "Well, they sort of had proof. I'd—I'd just written Luke a check for, um, his previous . . . services."

Instead of the shock she expected, Tempera sounded even more confused. "But how did the police know about the check?"

It was a damned good question, one Lydia had spent the last miserable four hours trying to answer. She knew Luke believed she had set him up, and why wouldn't he? If *she* was asking herself how they knew, then Luke had to be asking the same question.

And coming up with the same damning answer.

"Your stallions are here to bail you out, Reynolds."

Luke ignored the jailer's smirk and his smartass comment as he waited for him to unlock the cell door. It wasn't the first insult he'd suffered since being jailed, and he figured it wouldn't be the last.

Detective Parker had obviously wasted no time bragging about his coup to his co-workers. Like Lydia, they had been all too eager to believe the worst about Mr. Complete.

"Follow me," the jailer said, leading the way down the dingy hall.

Voices that had been muffled before, grew louder as they approached the main room. Luke frowned. It was two A.M. Apparently he was just in time for the drunks and riffraff of the city to crawl out of the woodwork.

But it wasn't riffraff making the fuss, Luke realized with an inward groan as they entered the main room.

It was Mrs. Scuttle, her blue hair pinned flat to her head with what appeared to be a thousand bobby pins. She was still wearing her night clothes, a mismatched ensemble that covered her from head to toe.

Luke immediately spotted the paperweight she held in her hand. He followed her purposeful gaze to the uniformed cop cowering behind the counter. Huddled in a nervous group several safe feet behind Mrs. Scuttle were his escorts.

He had little time to savor the warm feeling that swept over him at the sight.

"Mrs. Scuttle."

His secretary jerked her head around, her eyes curiously unfocused.

"You're in a police station," Luke explained calmly. "If you start throwing things, they'll put you in jail, and believe me, you won't care for the accommodations."

Mrs. Scuttle's thin lips tightened. "He was saying ugly things about you and my boys."

Her "boys" all nodded emphatically, as if they for once agreed with Mrs. Scuttle's violent method of punishment. Luke doubted they'd feel the same way if she directed her anger toward *them*.

"It's okay, Mrs. Scuttle. It's human nature for people to make fun of things they know nothing about." Luke speared the cowering cop with a pointed look.

"I'm sorry I had to get you out at this time of night. Let's all go home now, shall we?"

"Like I had a choice," Mrs. Scuttle muttered, lowering the paperweight by slow degrees. "I'm the only one—besides you—who can sign a company check. *Somebody* had to bail your worthless carcass out."

Very cautiously, Luke approached his secretary and removed the paperweight from her hand. He set it out of reach on the counter. The moment he did, the cop sprang from his crouch, sputtering with outrage.

"That old lady needs to be in a nut house!" he shouted, clutching his holstered gun.

As one, his escorts moved threateningly forward, fists curled and bristly jaws clenched. Collin was at the front of the group. His voice was calm but deadly as he told the humiliated officer, "I think you owe Mrs. Scuttle an apology."

Luke stared at his employees with a mixture of pride and exasperation. Yes, he was proud of their loyalty, but didn't they realize they were inside a police station? One touch of a button and the officer behind the counter could probably have a dozen guns drawn on his escorts, and each and every one of them thrown in jail for threatening a police officer.

Mrs. Scuttle included.

With a sigh, he took his secretary's elbow and positioned himself between the group and the nervous officer. "We were just leaving," he stated. Without looking at the guys, he added sternly, "Right, men?"

"I should throw you all in jail," the officer muttered,

his face a fiery red. "Bunch of whoring men wannabes."

Luke thrust out both arms to block Collin and Ivan's attempt to rush past him. After spending long hours in jail, he wasn't eager to return. "Get out of here," he growled. "And take Mrs. Scuttle with you."

When they had left, muttering and growling among themselves, Luke stepped up to the counter. "My lawyer will be getting in touch with you," he said in a deceptively pleasant voice.

The officer's gaze narrowed. "Why is that?"

"To sue you for slander."

Leaving the officer in open-mouthed shock, Luke stalked out of the police station. He wanted a stiff drink, a hot shower, and a comfortable bed—in that order.

But it was apparent the moment he stepped outside into the warm night air that his needs would have to wait.

Mrs. Scuttle and his escorts were waiting for him on the steps.

"What's going to happen now, Luke?" Ivan asked, looking bleary-eyed and unshaven.

Collin fired the next question before Luke had a chance to answer the first. "How could you let this happen? *You* were the one warning us to be careful, and then you go and get yourself caught prostituting—oof!" He grunted as Mrs. Scuttle planted a sharp elbow in his ribs.

"Mind your manners, Collin!" she screeched. "Luke

wasn't prostituting himself, you idiot! He was just teaching that Carmichael woman a little lesson by *pretending* to take her money. She believed he was a gigolo, so he was playing the part."

"Either way," Jet said morosely, "we're all out of work. Detective Parker said as much, pending a hearing before the judge."

"Oh, get over yourself," Mrs. Scuttle snapped, glaring at Jet. "Luke didn't get himself in trouble on purpose, now did he? Do you think he wants to lose his business? Well, do you?" When no one dared answer, she folded her arms smugly over her breast. "We'll sort this out, won't we, Luke?"

Luke gave her a weary nod, hoping she wouldn't notice there wasn't much conviction behind it. Short of begging Lydia for mercy, he was screwed.

They *all* were.

Lydia couldn't sleep.

The guilt over what she'd inadvertently done weighed upon her shoulders like an iron cape.

What would happen to Mrs. Scuttle?

What would happen to Greg and the others? She no longer cared what they'd done in the past or what they were doing in the present. She'd had no right to judge them. She didn't know their individual circumstances, had never stood in their shoes. Her concern for Tempera had blinded her.

With a sigh, she rose from her bed and went to the window to watch the sun rise. The only good thing that had come out of her clumsy attempt to right a wrong was Aunt Tempera's recovery.

She pulled the curtain aside, squinting as the sun peeked over the horizon. Luke's face rose to haunt her, that awful combination of disappointment and fury gleaming from his gorgeous eyes. How could she convince him that she'd changed her mind?

Parker had used her. That much was obvious, but how? How had he known about the check when she hadn't even known herself until the moment she wrote it? Did they have Luke's apartment bugged?

The possibility made Lydia's blood run cold, yet at the same time her face heated with mortification. If they truly had Luke's apartment bugged, then they had heard everything. . . .

"Oh, God," she muttered. She dropped the curtain and turned away, gnawing on her thumbnail. If she was right, was it legal? Parker wanted Luke badly.

Badly enough to bend the law to suit himself?

Brett would know.

Lydia snatched up the phone and quickly dialed Casey's number. It wasn't until Casey answered in a sleep-groggy voice that Lydia remembered the time.

"Sorry, Casey. I know it's early, but—"

"Not just early," Casey grumbled. "It's *insanely* early. Something wrong? You did get home okay?"

"Yeah, thanks to Aunt Tempera."

"I thought it was time she knew what you were up to."

Casey didn't sound at all repentant, Lydia noted

with a wry smile. "All right. I'll forgive you on one condition." She ignored Casey's groan. "Let me talk to Brett. I have a legal question for him."

There was a lot of grumbling and rustling; then Brett's sleepy, slightly irritated voice came on the line.

"What?"

Lydia clucked her tongue. "Grouch. I have an important question to ask."

Brett sighed. "I guess it can't wait until a decent hour?"

"Not really." Lydia grinned as she imagined Brett's sour expression. "Is it legal for the police to bug someone's apartment?"

"If they have probable cause and an affidavit signed by a judge. You talking local?"

"Yes."

"Hmm." Brett sounded fully awake now and a lot more compliant. "Casey told me what happened, Lydia. You know I'll be there for you if you need legal representation."

"Well, since I'm charged with soliciting a prostitute, there's a big chance I'll have to take you up on that offer." Lydia put a cooling hand to her hot face. Never in a million years would she have thought to be having this conversation with anyone.

If she felt this terrible and ashamed, how must Luke feel?

Chapter Twenty-four

"Did you get a warrant to bug Luke's apartment?" Lydia demanded before the detective could offer her a seat. She stood just inside the door to his little office, breathing hard and ready to do battle. "Is that how you knew that I had written him a check . . . and what it was for?"

Detective Parker remained seated. He didn't look surprised to see her, Lydia thought as she advanced into the office. She'd nearly driven herself insane waiting for the time to pass so that she could confront the cop.

She wasn't leaving until she'd gotten an answer.

"Of course," the detective finally said. He leaned back in his chair, totally at ease.

Lydia wanted to strangle him. "I want to see a copy of the affidavit." When he remained motionless, she plopped her purse on the desk and leaned forward. She wanted to make absolutely certain he realized how serious she was. "I said . . . I want to see the affidavit the judge had to sign in order for you to bug Luke's apartment. My lawyer said you would have had to get one."

After a long, tense moment, Detective Parker sighed. "I didn't bug Reynolds's apartment, Miss Carmichael."

"That's a crock of bull," Lydia said swiftly. After spending half the night in jail and the rest of the night worrying herself sick, she was pumped. "How else would you know about the check?"

The cop's gaze fell to her purse. "Maybe we can work out a deal."

Lydia's heart jumped into her throat. She remembered dropping her purse, remembered Detective Parker picking up her things and putting them back inside. Then, later, at the police station, they had taken her purse.

He'd had the opportunity to put something in her bag, and he'd had the opportunity to take it out.

If he hadn't bugged Luke's apartment, it was the only way he could have known.

Almost giddy with her realization, Lydia said, "The bug was in my purse, wasn't it?"

The detective's mouth thinned. "Sit down, Miss Carmichael. Let's work out a deal."

Lydia had no intention of working out anything

with the man, but she *was* curious about what he had to say.

So she sat, keeping a firm hold on her purse, wishing she'd had the cunning and foresight to bring a recorder.

Tit for tat.

"What kind of deal?" she demanded.

"I'll get the charges against you dropped . . . if you'll forget this little visit."

"That sounds suspiciously like blackmail, Detective Parker." Lydia felt like purring. "I take it putting that bug in my purse without my knowledge was illegal?"

Detective Parker slapped his hand against his desk, startling her. His eyes were hard and furious. "Three weeks ago, you were hell-bent on getting revenge on this company. Was he *that* good, Miss Carmichael?"

Before Lydia could think about the repercussions of her actions, she jumped up and slapped him. Her face was flaming, but now at least *one* side of his was flaming as well. She was trembling from head to toe as she said, "You used me to get to Luke. How does that make you different from him?" She stalked to the door. When she reached it, she took a deep breath, then faced him again.

She was smiling.

"See you in court, Detective Parker."

As Lydia wound her way through the crowded police station, she heard Parker cussing a blue streak.

* * *

Luke jerked open the door to his apartment just as Mrs. Scuttle punched the doorbell for the sixth time.

"Lydia told Casey and Casey told me that Detective Parker bugged her purse without her knowledge. Casey said her husband—he's a lawyer—will get the whole thing thrown out of court." She took a deep breath and surged on. "She says that her husband says the judge will be furious with the detective for using such backhanded methods. You weren't answering your phone, Luke." Her tone grew chiding. "What if I'd fallen and couldn't get up?"

Silently, Luke stepped aside so that his secretary could enter. Even in the dangerous state of mind he was in, he couldn't find the heart to tell Mrs. Scuttle that he already knew.

Casey had also told Jet, who had told Greg, Ivan, Collin, and Tyler. One by one they had called him to plead on Lydia's behalf, the traitors.

He had been forced to stop answering his phone.

He grunted as Mrs. Scuttle slammed her purse into his gut.

"Answer me, Luke! Have you lost your tongue?"

The shrill pitch of her voice wasn't helping his headache. Luke rubbed his temples and sighed. "I'm sorry I didn't answer the phone. I've got a headache." And a heartache, but that was definitely something he was keeping to himself.

As if.

"You don't believe Lydia?" Mrs. Scuttle demanded.

So it was Lydia now, was it? "I believe that she

might have had a change of heart when she realized the damage she'd done," Luke said carefully. When dealing with *his* group of people, each and every word could be used against him.

This time he managed to dodge her suitcase of a purse in the nick of time.

"Luke, you're not being fair."

Luke stared at her in sheer amazement. "*I'm* the one being charged with prostitution. *I'm* the one with a business on the rocks. And you say *I'm* not being fair? Whose side are you on, anyway?"

"Hers," Mrs. Scuttle said without hesitation. "At first I wasn't, but the more I thought about it, the more I decided you've been making an ass of yourself and it's your fault she believed you were a man-whore."

His face burned. "I prefer gigolo."

Mrs. Scuttle waved an impatient hand. "Gigolo, man-whore, prostitute, they all mean the same thing. The point is you carried your fun little game too far, and now you're sorry for it."

That was an understatement, Luke thought.

"And you seem to be forgetting that your evil foster brother was slithering in the shadows like the dirty snake he is, using that singer to goad poor, confused Lydia on."

"*Poor* Lydia?" Luke's headache increased its mad pounding. "Have you been drinking, Mrs. Scuttle?"

Wrong question.

Mrs. Scuttle clobbered the side of his head with her massive purse.

Luke saw stars . . . then black dots . . . He clutched his head and cussed like a sailor.

Silently, of course.

"*I'm* not the one who looks like a dirty old wino," Mrs. Scuttle screeched. She leaned toward him and sniffed. "And you need a bath, not to mention a shave." She shuffled back to the door. "I've got to go. The limo's waiting."

He stared at her. She had definitely clobbered him good, Luke decided, because he thought she'd said her *limo* was waiting.

But just in case . . . "Um, Mrs. Scuttle?"

She turned to glare back at him. "What?"

"Don't you mean that your *cab* is waiting?"

"No, I said the limo and I meant the limo. I'll be working for Miss Carmichael and Miss Foster until the charges are cleared and we can open the company again." She blinked her big owlish eyes and patted her tightly curled hair. "But don't you worry, Luke. My first loyalty is to you and that's not gonna change, no matter how much better I get treated by them."

Long after she'd gone, Luke stared at the closed door.

The world, he finally decided, had gone mad.

"Oh my God! You're that singer, Cameron Rose!"

Lydia jumped as Mrs. Donnelly followed this shrieked announcement with an ear-piercing scream.

She muttered a curse beneath her breath and raced to start damage control before she had naked, seaweed-covered women converging on the waiting room.

She grabbed Cameron's arm and pulled her inside the office, slamming the door on a wide-eyed Mrs. Donnelly. "Are you insane?" she asked Cameron, more sharply than she had intended.

Cameron shrugged. "I'm used to that kind of reaction. Are you busy?

Lydia glanced at the mountain of paperwork on her desk and sighed. "A little, but I can take a short break. What's up?" She indicated the chair in front of her desk before returning to her own.

The singer took her time crossing her legs and smoothing out her sleek silk dress before settling her troubled gaze on Lydia's expectant face. "I've been thinking about what you said, about talking to the cops about Jet. He—he says he loves me, but when I try to bring up the subject of commitment, he manages to wiggle out of it." She bit her bottom lip, lowering her gaze. "I heard about what happened to you, and I thought that if we both went before the judge together, we could—"

"Stop." Lydia stared at the singer with mounting suspicion. "Who told you what happened?"

"Jet, but please don't be mad at him. We have a very close relationship, you see. We tell each other everything."

"Oh." Lydia took out a pencil and tapped it on the desk thoughtfully. "So I guess he knows about your relationship with Mr. Burgess, Luke's foster brother and competitor?"

Cameron's eyes flared wide for a nanosecond.

It was enough to confirm what Lydia had suspected. "I saw him in your limo the last time you were here," she explained. "When Luke mentioned him, I remembered seeing you with him, but I didn't figure out the reason until just now."

"He'll ruin me," Cameron whispered tearfully.

Lydia wasn't so quick to believe her this time. "Like you tried to help me ruin Luke? Tell me the truth, Cameron. You and Jet have never slept together, have you?"

The singer slowly shook her head.

"And Jet didn't borrow any money from you?"

"No." Despite her tears, Cameron flashed her a defiant glance. "You don't understand, Lydia! Rhew's a monster. He has a video tape of me having sex with one of his escorts, and he's threatened to make it public."

"So he's blackmailing you into helping him ruin Mr. Complete?"

"Yes. The plan was to get Jet to sleep with me. He said that since I would be the victim my identity would be protected. Just when I was about to give up, Jet told me about you and Luke, and how you planned to get back at the company for what happened to your aunt."

"So I fell conveniently into Rhew's lap," Lydia concluded, feeling ill. "Why does he hate Luke so much?"

"A million reasons, but mainly because Luke's the better man and Rhew knows it. Rhew took Luke's fiancée from him, but Rhew couldn't make her happy. When his father disinherited him, she divorced him." Cameron's lip curled. "The bastard got a taste of his own medicine."

Lydia spoke slowly, the pieces of the puzzle falling into place. "Unfortunately, his hard knocks appear to have made him even more determined to outdo Luke. He must have been delirious with joy when Tony got involved with Aunt Tempera—" Cameron flinched, causing Lydia to come to a startling halt. She sucked in a sharp, disbelieving breath. "Did Rhew send Tony to Mr. Complete?"

"And Graham Prescott, too." Cameron closed her eyes. Tears squeezed between her lids. "He's going to be so furious with me. You just don't know what he's capable of, Lydia."

The door behind Cameron silently opened. Jet stuck a finger to his lips and eased the door shut. Lydia was tired of playing games, but she figured Jet deserved to know the truth about Cameron's feelings.

"And the break-in at your house?" Lydia prompted, recalling the photo Cameron had claimed was missing. She deliberately avoided eye-contact with Jet, not wanting to give him away.

"A ploy to get Jet to spend the night so that I could seduce him," Cameron admitted shamefully. She wiped angrily at her eyes. "Rhew would laugh if he knew how much I truly cared for Jet. I fell in love with him, not that Jet will care once he finds out about all this."

Lydia waited for Jet to announce his presence. When he remained still and silent, she blew out an exasperated sigh before she said to Cameron, "What are you going to do about Rhew and the tape?"

The singer looked at Lydia in helpless despair. "What *can* I do? He has the tape, and he's got the connections. He can and will ruin my career with this."

"I'm sorry." Lydia realized with some surprise that she meant it.

With a grain of an idea forming in her mind, Lydia said impulsively, "Don't tell him about our conversation just yet. Does he know that I changed my mind about helping Detective Parker?"

Jet pushed himself away from the door and stepped forward. "No. I just gave her enough information to hang herself."

Cameron let out a startled shriek and stumbled to her feet. She whirled around, her hand to her mouth. "Jet!"

"In the flesh." Jet sauntered closer, his gaze searching her dismayed expression.

Lydia wondered if Cameron saw beyond his obvious disappointment and hurt to the hope still lingering there.

"Jet!" Cameron's face crumpled. "I—I didn't mean to hurt you, I swear. Can—can you ever forgive me?"

Jet's eyes narrowed speculatively. "That depends . . . on what you do next."

"I'll do whatever you want me to do," Cameron declared passionately. She fell into his arms and sobbed against his shoulder, her blubbering barely intelligible. "I'm so sorry, Jet! So sorry. I love you. . . ."

The emotional scene put a lump in Lydia's throat. She wished it was that simple for her and Luke. If she thought for a second that it would work, she'd fall into Luke's arms and beg his—

Oh God.

Lydia's heart stumbled to an electrifying halt, then made a clumsy attempt to start again.

Tony and Graham had been sent by Rhew to sabotage Luke's business.

Jet had been slandered by Cameron, who was being blackmailed by Rhew, which meant that Jet—Jet wasn't a gigolo.

I'm not rich, she had confessed to Luke.

And I'm not a gigolo, so we're even, he'd answered, the fierce heat of his desire blazing a trail straight to her heart.

He'd claimed that he had played the part because that's what she believed, and he was having fun getting to know her better.

What if it were true? What if Luke wasn't a gigolo?

Her horrified gaze clashed with Jet's. His sudden, startling grin was supremely smug.

"It's about time you came to the right conclusion."

Yes, she knew the truth at last. Lydia groaned and put her face in her hands. But was it too late?

Chapter Twenty-five

Luke took his damp T-shirt from his belt loop and wiped his face again. He glared at the midday sun, then at his employees busily painting the huge plantation house.

They'd been at it since daylight and had hardly made a dent.

"Tell me again how we got roped into this?" he asked, itching for a fight. He knew where they all stood on the subject of Lydia versus Luke, and it stung. How could they side with her when she was the very reason they were painting a damned plantation house instead of sipping damned champagne and nibbling damned lobster hors d'oeuvres in a damned cool mansion?

Tyler, the brave one who answered, sounded too damned cheerful for Luke's peace of mind.

"Number one, we don't have anything else to do. Number two, it's for the homeless. Number three, *Greg* volunteered us." He lifted an accusing brow at Greg, who grinned sheepishly. Heedless of Luke's simmering anger, he added the last, but not least reason they were painting the house. "Number four, Mrs. Scuttle said we had to do it."

Luke slapped the paintbrush onto the faded boards and growled, "She doesn't even work for me anymore."

"*You* tell *her* that," Ivan challenged from a safe distance.

"And she's not my mother," Luke said a little louder.

"Amen!"

"You tell her, boss!"

They all burst out laughing.

Everyone except Luke, who kept on scowling. "Go to hell." He wasn't in the mood to graciously amuse them.

"Couldn't be much hotter there," Ivan muttered, causing another irritating round of laughter. "Hey, Collin! Have you finished the plans for the stage?"

"Nope. I don't lack much, though. Should finish them tonight—if I can hold a pencil after this." He groaned as he stretched to reach a spot he'd missed before he changed positions.

Luke clamped his jaw shut, painting in short, angry strokes that did nothing to relieve his tension. He didn't know what they were talking about, and he told himself he didn't care. They could all just kiss his ass.

Traitors. Every single one of them.

"Think we'll have enough wood left over from those crates the playground equipment came in?" Tyler asked. He leaned over as he spoke, stretching dangerously to reach an area to his left with the paintbrush.

Luke held his breath, pretending not to notice. He didn't let it out again until Tyler righted himself and decided to move his ladder.

Clumsy traitors. All of them.

Greg tapped Luke on the leg. "Here's a fresh can of paint, boss. I noticed you were almost out."

"You're so kind," Luke said between clenched teeth. He snagged the can ring with his finger and slammed it down on the board beside him.

To Tyler, Greg said, "What about that old tree house in your backyard? Your kids are too big for it now, aren't they?"

"Yeah, but did you forget? Amanda's pregnant again."

Which proved Luke's point, since Tyler hadn't bothered to tell *him* his joyous news. He was surprised they'd included him in the painting job.

Traitors. He bet Lydia knew all about the coming baby.

"Go, stud!" Collin teased. "Keep on and you'll have that baseball team."

Tyler made a crude gesture with his finger, making everyone laugh.

Everyone but Luke.

"Hey, I know!" Jet said from his precarious perch on an upturned barrel. "What about that unfinished room, Tyler? You know . . . the one you've been working on for three years?"

Tyler shook his head so violently, sweat smacked Luke's arm. Luke glared at him, but Tyler either ignored him or didn't see him.

"Why are you guys picking on me? That's Vicky's sewing room. She'd cut me off for a month if I took it apart for the lumber."

"We could always put it back," Collin said. "With all of us working, it wouldn't take long."

Luke wondered if they noticed that he wasn't volunteering. Hell, he hadn't volunteered for this job, either, but that hadn't seemed to matter.

Black-hearted traitors.

Fiends.

Disloyal brats.

"Did Ms. Foster find someone to donate the food?" Greg paused to wipe his forehead with the back of his forearm.

Luke took an unhealthy glee in noting he'd smeared paint on his handsome forehead. Was it impossible for them to work without chattering like a bunch of women at a Tupperware party?

"Yeah. She's got three choices. I think she's going to wait and ask Lydia's advice when she gets back from Barbados."

By some quirk of fate, Collin happened to be standing below Luke's ladder when Jet delivered this bombshell.

He landed on top of Collin, knocking the breath out of the other man and humiliating himself. His embarrassment heightened when he caught Tyler handing Jet a ten-dollar bill.

"Told you," Jet whispered gleefully.

"Whatever," was Tyler's sour, sore-loser response.

Immature traitors, Luke thought murderously as he got to his feet. He considered leaving Collin to his well-deserved pain, but in the end he decided it would just give them something else to laugh about.

So he ground his teeth and held out his hand.

Collin eyed it with open suspicion before taking it. The moment he was on his feet, he hastily pulled his hand free and put a safe distance between himself and a glowering Luke.

But he was grinning.

Luke closed his eyes and counted to ten.

Then twenty.

When he reached fifty, he took a deep breath and opened them.

Everyone scrambled back to work as if they hadn't been staring at him.

"What," he ground out, "is Lydia doing in Barbados?"

He wasn't picky about who answered, as long as someone did before he exploded. There were too many open cans of paint and too many easy targets for them *not* to answer, if they were wise.

Jet hugged the ladder as if his life depended on it. "Um, she's going to find Anthony Cuff."

When Jet was unwise enough to leave him hanging, Luke marched to his ladder. He grabbed it and gave it a threatening shake.

"Okay, okay! She—she's going to convince him to come back and testify against Burgess."

"Why?" Luke barked, poised to give the ladder another good shaking if needed.

"Because Burgess is blackmailing Cameron. Lydia's going to see if Burgess will trade Anthony's testimony for the tape."

Luke narrowed his eyes. "Tape?"

"He's got an incriminating video with Cameron and one of his escorts." Jet spat on the ground, his eyes now black as midnight, all trace of amusement gone. "The dirty bastard."

"Why is Lydia helping Cameron?"

"Because that's the kind of woman she is," Greg said before Jet could answer. "And you'd see that if you weren't so damned stubborn and blind."

But Luke wasn't listening to Greg's assessment of his character. All he could think about was Lydia alone with a creep like Anthony Cuff. He gripped the ladder so hard his knuckles turned white. Very softly, he asked, "Just how is she planning to convince Cuff to come back with her?"

Jet shrugged. "She didn't say. Maybe she's going to—"

"Shut up, Jet!" Greg said.

Collin waved his paint brush. "Yeah, shut up, man."

But Jet didn't cower easily. He stared down at Luke, and Luke realized that Jet had never been afraid of him in the first place. They had all been having a great big rousing good time at his expense.

Jet capped it by saying, "You said yourself that Lydia was tempting. *You* figure it out."

Luke swore loud and long, flinging the paintbrush against the house. "When did she leave?"

"This morning," Tyler said. He climbed down from his ladder and wiped his hands. He pulled out a folded, sweat-stained, paint-splattered envelope from his back pocket and held it out to Luke. "Here's your round-trip ticket. Call it an early birthday present from all of us."

Luke looked at the ticket and saw that his plane left in an hour. It would take twenty minutes to get to the airport from Hope House. No time to go home. No time for a shower. No time to pack.

No time to talk himself out of following her.

Someone smothered a snicker.

"I don't suppose you also packed me a bag?" he asked, hating the hopeful note in his voice.

This time someone didn't smother his snicker in time. It sounded like a donkey braying, and Luke had no trouble recognizing the ass behind it.

Ivan.

"Nope." Tyler shook his head, biting his lip to keep from grinning. "Didn't have a key to your apartment.

Besides, we weren't sure you'd take the—um, we weren't sure you'd go."

"The hell you weren't," Luke snarled. He turned his back on the laughing bunch of traitors and stalked to his truck.

Lydia was on her way to Barbados to find Anthony Cuff.

Had she lost her ever-lovin' mind?

Lydia was certain she had been to every hotel, bar, and restaurant in Barbados. She'd been pawed, clawed, smudged, yanked, and propositioned more times than she cared to count.

Still no sign of Anthony.

She had a picture of him she'd filched from Aunt Tempera's photo album, but so far nobody had recognized him.

She was hot, sweaty, tired, and downright disgusted by the time she returned to her hotel. Either Aunt Tempera had been wrong about the postcard and Anthony's location, or it was a habit for the natives to pretend they knew nothing.

Lydia suspected the latter, which made her shoulders sag even further. What was she doing anyway? Helping out someone who had deceived her by finding a man who had hurt Tempera? When would she learn her lesson?

The room, at least, was cool and dim, a welcome relief from the blazing sun and strength-sapping heat. She stripped on the way to the shower, leaving a trail of damp clothes. The water was cool, yet stimulating.

Soothing. Caressing.

It reminded her of Luke.

Everything reminded her of Luke, which in turn reminded her of how utterly blind she'd been. She'd never thought of herself as narrow-minded, but after Luke, she had to admit she had definitely been narrow-minded where Mr. Complete was concerned.

Why hadn't she believed him? Oh, she knew he wasn't without fault. He had admitted he'd intentionally led her to believe he truly was a gigolo.

But he'd gone too far in convincing her.

It hadn't stopped her from falling in love with him.

Just like Aunt Tempera.

So what if he *wasn't* a gigolo? Did that make it okay to fall helplessly, head over heels in love with a man who was virtually an expert on women?

Lydia shuddered, giving her hair one last rinse before reaching blindly for the towel she'd placed on the towel rack.

As her fingers closed over the towel, the back of her hand connected with warm skin.

She screamed and snatched the towel to her chest, her heart thundering. "Who—who's there?"

"Heard you've been looking for me."

It was Anthony. Lydia's knees buckled. She held on to the safety handle inside the shower until she felt they were steady enough to support her. Be nice, she told herself. *Don't hit him or scream or cuss unless he says he won't help.* "Can—can you give me some privacy?"

"Sure."

She heard the door click shut. Peeping cautiously around the shower curtain, Lydia saw that the coast was clear. She jumped out and hastily dried herself.

Then she realized her clothes were on the bed where she'd left them. Wrapping the towel around her as best she could, she eased the door open and poked her head out. She spotted Anthony at the mini bar trying to remove the seal from a miniature bottle of booze. Was he trying to drown a guilty conscience? she wondered. Striving for a neutral tone, she asked, "Can you bring me my clothes? They're on the bed."

Tony was striding to the bed to get them when someone knocked on the door. He glanced at her as he swept up the clothes. "Did you order room service?"

She shook her wet head, clutching the towel against her with one hand and holding down the short edges with the other. She wished he'd leave so that she could get dressed, but she was afraid he wouldn't come back. "Maybe—maybe it's the maid. Can you get it?"

With her clothes across his arm, Tony went to answer the door. Lydia couldn't see his expression, but she heard his muffled curse just seconds before he went flying backward.

"Tony?" She clutched the towel as she raced to him, kneeling on the carpet. "Are you okay?"

"He won't be when I'm finished with him," Luke growled from the doorway.

Lydia tripped over Tony in her haste to get up. She

stepped on the edge of her towel, dragging it from her body as she righted herself. Scrambling to cover herself, she was in no position to speak for some moments. By that time she was over the biggest part of her surprise at seeing him.

"What the hell are you doing here, Luke? And why did you hit Tony?"

Luke shut the door behind him, his mouth a grim slash in his tanned face. He smelled like sweat and paint, and looked like hell. "I came here looking for you, and I hit him because he deserved it." His gaze raked over her towel-clad figure, his eyes glinting with an unholy light. "Am I too late?"

Bewildered, Lydia blinked at him. "Too late for what? We haven't had a chance to talk—"

He swore explicitly, further confusing Lydia. Grabbing the unconscious Tony by the collar, he hauled him up and drew back his fist.

Lydia grabbed his arm, ignoring the thrill that hammered in her bloodstream just from touching him. "Don't, Luke! He's not even conscious." She held her breath, feeling the hard muscle beneath her palm as it slowly relaxed.

He let Tony fall with a thud to the floor. "You're right. I'd rather he be conscious when I knock his teeth out."

"Luke." Lydia shook his arm, forcing him to look at her. "What's gotten into you?" When he turned his blazing eyes her way, she flinched and dropped her hand. "What—what were you thinking, Luke?" She was afraid that she knew, and it hurt.

He clenched his jaw. "It doesn't matter. Get packed. We're leaving."

"I'm not going anywhere! I haven't had a chance to talk to Tony yet. I'm assuming—since you knew where to find me—that you also know why I'm here?"

"You're here to *convince* this scum to return with you so you can trade him for the tape Burgess has of Cameron."

It was the nasty emphasis he put on the word *convince* that helped clear the rest of Lydia's confusion and fuel her anger.

She'd been hoping she was wrong. No such luck.

"You—you really have a low opinion of women, don't you, Luke?" When he didn't answer, Lydia pointed to the door, her voice vibrating with outrage. "Get out of here before I call security."

He left without another word.

Lydia glanced at Tony on the floor. Her bra and panties clung to his jean-clad thighs, and the light summer dress she'd packed covered his groin area.

Then she looked down at her nearly naked state.

She closed her eyes and swore softly. Were she and Luke doomed always to assume the worst about each other?

Chapter Twenty-six

"I didn't set you up," Lydia stated for the second time. She stared at Tony's black eye, admitting that the sight of it gave her a vicious satisfaction. "But even if I *had*, it would have been nothing less than you deserved after what you put my aunt through."

They were seated in one of the many open restaurants eating dinner. Lydia, who discovered she was starving after her plane trip and subsequent sleuthing, had ordered the grilled salmon salad. Tony had decided on a thick steak seasoned with Cajun spices, although Lydia noticed he was doing more drinking than eating.

She squeezed a fresh lemon over a bite of the delicious grilled salmon as she asked baldly, "Why did you do it?" It was a question she had been burning to ask from the moment she realized it was Tony in her hotel room.

Tony took a long swallow of his rum and Coke. "I'm not proud of what I did."

"That wasn't what I asked you," Lydia said sharply. She sighed and shook her head, reminding herself that Tony could decide to get up and walk away and there wasn't a damned thing she could do about it.

She didn't want that to happen.

"Can you blame me for wanting to know? You broke my aunt's heart." She hesitated, uncertain just how much she should tell him. "For a while there, I was afraid she'd . . ." She left the sentence hanging, unable to put the ugly thought into words.

Tony apparently caught her unspoken meaning. "Oh, God."

Lydia looked up from her salad, catching Tony's agonized expression before he wiped it clean. So he was human, after all. The realization gave her hope that her mission wasn't in vain. "Did you care about Aunt Tempera at all, Tony?"

His hand shook as he brought the glass to his lips again. "I loved her."

"Then, why? Why did you leave?" Lydia put her fork down, her food forgotten. "Was Rhew blackmailing you, too?"

Tony shook his head. "No. I just needed the money. I'm behind on child support, and my ex-wife won't let me see my daughter until I catch up. I've been staying here in Bridgetown with my best friend, trying to get a job so I can pay my ex the rest of the money."

"Aunt Tempera would have helped you." Lydia was certain of this.

"I'd already taken the money from Rhew." Tony muttered something beneath his breath. "Believe me, if I had it to do all over again . . ."

"You'd what, Tony?" Lydia prompted. "You'd take *her* money, instead, then leave her?"

"No!" Tony shoved his plate away, his face flushed from too much rum and Coke and a good deal of shame. "I'd come clean with her and tell Rhew to go to hell."

Lydia felt a surge of triumph. Her initial plan had been to make him swear he wouldn't go near Aunt Tempera or try to contact her in any way when he returned to testify. Now it seemed that Tony truly had feelings for her aunt. "The story you told Tempera . . . the one about living in your car at the time your parents got—"

"It was a lie," Tony interrupted, flushing. "That happened to someone else. Rhew suggested I use it to gain Tempera's pity."

So it *was* Luke's story, Lydia thought with a surge of hope. "I want to give you a chance to make things right," she blurted, praying she was making the right choice.

"How? I've already spent most of the money Rhew paid me, and I . . . I had to sell the car."

"Aunt Tempera doesn't care about the car." Although Lydia suffered a pang at the thought of Uncle

Theo's classic in the hands of a stranger. "She believes you still love her."

"I do!"

His passionate declaration drew the curiosity of several diners. Still, Lydia hesitated. What if her instincts were wrong? If she brought Tony back into Tempera's life, and he walked out on her again? Lydia knew she would never forgive herself.

She had to be absolutely certain.

"I tried to make a deal with Rhew," Tony startled her by saying. "When I realized that I was in love with Tempera, I went to him and told him how I felt. I offered to pay him back the money in installments, after I found a job."

Lydia suspected she knew the conclusion. "He didn't agree?"

"Hell, no!" Tony's dark eyes flashed. "He said if I didn't carry it through he would tell Tempera everything." His gaze dropped, as if in shame. His Adam's apple bobbed as he swallowed hard. "I couldn't stand the thought of her knowing what I'd done."

"You thought she'd be better off thinking you had just gotten tired of her?" Lydia asked incredulously. When he didn't answer, she pressed on with her plan. "I want you to come back to Atlanta with me."

"I can't. You don't know Rhew. He'd never leave me alone."

"I think he will." Lydia wished she felt as confident as she sounded. "Because I've got an idea." She waved the waiter over, instructed him to take their plates, and ordered strong coffee for Tony.

When the waiter left, Lydia proceeded to tell Tony of her plans.

Luke sat on a stool in the restaurant's bar area near the door.

He had a clear view of Lydia and Tony.

After she'd thrown him out, he'd booked a room on the same floor, purchased a change of clothes from the downstairs boutique, and taken a much-needed shower.

His knuckles ached from where he'd hit Tony, but Luke knew he'd do it all over again, given the opportunity. The cold shower he'd taken hadn't cooled his temper.

Finding Tony in Lydia's hotel room had given him a taste for violence. He wanted—no, he *needed*—to do some convincing of his own.

He needed to beat Tony to a bloody pulp for even *thinking* about touching Lydia. As for Lydia . . . Luke tightened his hand around the glass. How could she blame him for thinking what he'd been thinking? When Tony opened the hotel door, he'd been clutching Lydia's underclothes, for Pete's sake! Luke hadn't taken the time to analyze; he'd just reacted on a primitive level.

Then Lydia herself had come into view wearing nothing but a skimpy little hotel towel around that luscious, tempting body of hers.

It was enough to drive a man insane.

Oh, he knew he'd goofed when he saw her expression. He knew then and there that there was a bizarre explanation for Tony being in her hotel room, holding her underclothes, with her wearing nothing but a towel.

But he hadn't been thinking straight at the time. Couldn't she see that? Didn't she know how much he loved her?

The moment the admission popped into his head, Luke let out a string of curses that made the bartender's eyebrows rise.

"Having woman problems, buddy?" the bartender asked, squirting another shot of straight Coke into Luke's glass without being asked.

Luke shot him a sour look. "You'd never believe me, so don't ask."

The bartender perked up at this challenge. "Wanna try me? I've heard some pretty fantastic stories in my day."

"What are you, all of thirty?"

"Close, but I've been bartending since I turned twenty-one." The bartender slapped his cleaning rag over his shoulder and leaned against the far wall. He folded his arms, revealing a tattoo of an island woman wearing a grass skirt. "Tell you what. You tell me your story, and if it's more fantastic than anything I've ever heard, I'll give you a free bottle of my best champagne. You can share it with your lady friend when you make up with her."

Although Luke liked the idea of making up with Lydia, he didn't see it happening anytime soon—especially in light of his earlier blunder. He should have realized the guys were just goading him when they insinuated that Lydia planned to use her considerable charms to convince Tony into returning with her.

Yep. He'd been ripe for the picking, and the guys—traitors, all of them—had glutted themselves on his helpless carcass.

What a laugh they must be having.

But payback was going to be a bitch, Luke mused as an idea came to him. God, he was brilliant! "You have a pay phone around here?" he asked the bartender. When the bartender nodded in the direction of the restrooms, Luke slid from the stool. "Add a shot of Jack Daniels to my Coke, and when I get back I'll give you that story and take your champagne."

The bartender laughed. "Whatever you say, buddy."

Luke found a pay phone in the hall leading to the restrooms. He used his calling card to make a call to Mrs. Scuttle. When she answered, he said, "Listen carefully. I'm only allowed one phone call. . . ."

Lydia couldn't sleep.

She was worried.

Was she doing the right thing by bringing Tony back to Atlanta? What if she wasn't? Was she setting Aunt Tempera up for more heartache?

She flung herself onto her back, staring at the ceiling. What if Rhew wouldn't make the exchange—

Tony's silence for the tape? Lydia bit her lip, thinking about Tony's startling confession when she mentioned Cameron and the tape.

"I've got reasons of my own for getting that tape back."

Tony was the escort on the tape with Cameron.

Could life get any more complicated?

Her thoughts turned to Luke. Why had he followed her? Did she dare hope he was jealous? Did he finally believe she was innocent? Mrs. Scuttle, Casey, Aunt Tempera, and the guys all urged her to go to him, explain to him in person what Detective Parker had done without her knowledge.

But Lydia's pride kept getting in the way. If he wouldn't believe them, why would he believe her? And besides, she had come so very close to being guilty. . . .

Lydia let out a frustrated sigh and turned onto her side. In some ways she regretted getting involved with Luke because once she'd experienced bliss in his arms, she had become instantly addicted.

To his hands, his mouth, his . . . everything.

His deep, sexy pillow talk.

That swaggering way he walked, as if he knew exactly how breathtaking he was. As if he knew he had the power to make her knees weak.

Those eyes . . . eyes that could set her on fire or make her shiver, depending on his mood.

The way he was roughly possessive one moment, and surprisingly tender the next, arousing her to the point of insanity, then rewarding her with the moon, the sun, and the stars.

All she had to do was think about him, think about *them*, making love. Laughing. Talking. Touching.

Lydia groaned, her body aroused and aching. She missed Luke, and she knew it wasn't just lust.

She loved him. Gigolo. Man. It didn't matter, and if that made her gullible and foolish like Aunt Tempera, then it was her cross to bear.

Because she realized that she *didn't* regret meeting Luke, or making love with Luke, or anything else she'd done with Luke.

The knock came softly, startling a gasp from Lydia. She slipped from the bed and threw on a thin wrapper over her nightshirt. Her heart began to pound with anticipation.

She wanted it to be Luke.

It was.

"Luke." She said his name softly, huskily, unashamed of her need.

"Lydia." He said her name, half groan, half plea. "I'm afraid I'm a little drunk. If you let me in, I can't be accountable—"

Lydia yanked him inside and slammed the door, her eyes roaming over him hungrily.

"—for my actions," Luke belatedly finished, staggering a little. He held up a bottle of champagne. "I won a little bet with the bartender.

His crooked grin melted her heart.

"I told him how I pretended to be a gigolo, and how you pretended to be a client." His grin slowly faded. He set the bottle of champagne on the floor, snagged her waist, and brought her gently against him. "Know what he said when I finished the story?"

She shook her head, stunned by how much she'd come to love him.

Luke grinned again. "He said we deserved each other because we were both nuts." He lowered his head an inch at a time, his gaze fixed on her mouth. When their lips nearly touched, he murmured, "I think he's right, don't you?"

"Yes," Lydia whispered, pulling him down so that she could deepen the kiss. Breathless minutes later, she reluctantly broke the contact.

His mouth curved into a grin just short of goofy. "Truce?"

"Truce." She couldn't help smiling. "We'll sort everything out later, okay?"

"Okay." He looked comically serious as he added, "It's really too late for talking, anyway. Don't you think so?"

"Hmm." She caught her breath as he pushed the wrap from her shoulders. "Yes, I do." Her hands went to his zipper.

She giggled when he sucked in a sharp, nervous breath and held it.

"Don't worry. I'm the *last* person who would want to do damage to that part of your anatomy." Slowly, carefully, she lowered the zipper. She could feel the heat from his erection, felt eager to circle it with her fingers.

Taste him.

Love him.

Ride him. She drew his new jeans down his hips and helped him balance as he kicked them away.

He wasn't wearing underwear.

That suited Lydia just fine because she wasn't wearing any either.

"Back up," she whispered, unbuttoning his shirt as she followed his progress to the bed. When they reached it, she pushed him backward. She jerked her nightshirt over her head and tossed it aside. Watching him watching her, she curled her fingers around him, then engulfed him slowly with her mouth.

"God, Lydia!" Luke tried to pull her up, his actions frantic and out of control.

It was the way Lydia wanted him.

"Lydia," he gasped, catching her by the shoulders and finally managing to dislodge her mouth. His eyes were blazing as she straddled him. "Lydia, if you don't slow down, I can't be accountable—"

"That word again," Lydia chided. She rose above him, moved him into position, and slowly lowered herself onto him. He felt so right. *This* felt right, she thought, biting her lip as she clasped her hands in his and began to move in a reckless rhythm.

He pulled her forward and captured her panting mouth in a rough kiss that sent her pulse pounding harder, her hips moving faster. Scant moments later, he grabbed her hips and held her still.

Startled, Lydia opened her eyes to find him watching her with an intensity that was almost painful to see.

"Do you have any idea how amazing you are?" he asked thickly.

Inside her, she felt him pulsing. He was close to climaxing, trying to prolong the moment.

Anticipating the pleasure.

Did he really think he would leave her behind? Flashing him a wicked smile, Lydia deliberately clenched her inner muscles around him.

Luke's eyes went wide with shock. Dismay quickly followed. He ground his teeth and thrust deep, his hips jerking uncontrollably.

Just the way Lydia wanted him.

And seconds later, when she felt him spurting deep inside her, she was right there with him.

Chapter Twenty-seven

"Luke! Isn't that Ivan and Jet? Oh, and there's Greg, too! What in the world are they—"

Standing behind her in line at the airport, Luke casually slipped an arm around her neck and put his hand over her mouth. He tried to ignore the enticing way her bottom wiggled against his groin as he whispered near her ear, "Shush. We don't want them to see us."

The moment he took his hand away, she whispered back, "We don't? But what are they doing here in Barbados?"

"Getting me out of jail." Luke choked back laughter at her baffled expression. "I'll explain it all on the plane."

"You'd better," Lydia muttered, moving forward to give the stewardess her ticket.

The moment they were in the air and the seatbelt sign flickered off, Lydia pounced. "Okay, tell me! I'm dying here!"

Looking into her beautiful, animated face sent a shaft of pure fear into Luke's heart. What if she didn't love him? What if all she felt for him was lust? They hadn't talked about love. Granted, between the instant combustion and the misunderstandings, they hadn't had much of an opportunity.

"Luke? Are you okay? You're not afraid to fly, are you?"

Luke swallowed hard, deciding then and there that he really should get around to telling Lydia how he felt.

But first things first.

Quickly, he explained how the guys had goaded him mercilessly before delivering the news that she'd gone to Barbados after Tony. When he told her what Jet had said to send him off on a jealous rampage, Lydia clapped a hand to her mouth to muffle her spontaneous laughter.

He tried to look fierce as he said, "I don't know how you can find it funny when it was *your* reputation he was trashing."

"He didn't really mean it. He was just goading *you*, Luke."

"Well, now he's paying for it, isn't he?" Luke's smile was supremely smug. "I heard that airline tickets to Barbados are outrageous this time of year." He loved the way her eyes widened with sudden realization.

"You called and told them you were in jail?"

"Guilty as charged."

"You're a devil!"

But Luke could tell she didn't really mean it this time. His heart expanded with cautious joy. He was on to something wonderful. He could feel it in his bones. If he was completely truthful, he'd sensed it the moment he first saw her in Danny's Bar and Grill.

Did *she* feel the same way?

Tentatively, Luke set the wheels in motion, knowing they had a lot of ground to cover before he could just blurt out that he was in love with her. "Do you think you can trust Tony to just show up?"

Lydia's expression grew instantly somber. "I think he will. If he truly loves Aunt Tempera . . ."

"You believe she'll forgive him?"

"I *know* she will. When two people truly love one another, they can't help but forgive and forget."

Luke felt a jolt in his gut. She spoke as if she knew exactly what she was talking about. He cleared his throat, suddenly nervous. "What about the video he made with Cameron?"

"What about it? He made that tape before he met Tempera. I think it's not only unrealistic, but unfair to judge people by the mistakes they've made in the past."

Her tongue swept her bottom lip, leaving a glistening sheen behind.

Betraying a nervousness that matched Luke's own.

He realized then that Lydia was just as wary and anxious of their new relationship as he was. It was a sad fact that this was their first rational conversation as Luke the man and Lydia the woman.

Not the gigolo and the client.

Not the rat and the fox.

Not dumb and dumber.

"I agree," Luke said softly. He watched the sweep of her long lashes as she blinked in surprise.

"You do?"

"I do. Is that so surprising?"

"You—you were so angry with me, Luke." Before he could respond, she rushed on. "No, wait! I have to say this. I don't blame you for thinking I'd set you up. That was what I intended to do all along, as you already know, so when it happened, I didn't blame you for not believing me."

"You don't have to explain."

"Yes, I do."

"No, you really don't. I'm just as much to blame as you are for leading you to think I was a gigolo." Luke was sitting close enough to see her pupils dilate with shock. He groaned inwardly. How long had it lasted? How long had they been having a civil conversation that was actually getting somewhere?

Ten, fifteen minutes?

"So you're saying that you *don't* believe that I had nothing to do with *our* arrest?"

"Lydia, it doesn't—"

"Yes, Luke, it *does* matter. It matters to me!" She unfastened her seatbelt and scooted farther away from him, leaving a chill in the space she'd vacated.

Luke's warm fuzzy feeling deflated like a hot air balloon. He searched for the right words to rectify yet another silly misunderstanding. "You said earlier that you believed people should forgive and forget . . . if they loved one another."

"And you agreed."

Exasperated, Luke said, "Yes, I did agree. I still agree, which is the point I'm making. Whatever you did or didn't do—it doesn't matter. I deserved to be thrown in jail for carrying the game too far." When she stared mutely at him, Luke lost his new-found patience. "Tell me, Lydia, while we're clearing the air here. When did you finally realize I wasn't a gigolo?"

As Luke watched the revealing color creep into her face, he finally realized exactly how Lydia felt.

He burst out laughing.

A split second later, a sheepish Lydia joined him.

They were both startled when the people seated around them began laughing as well.

"You two need to get your own sitcom!" someone called out to another round of laughter.

By the time the plane landed in Atlanta, Lydia knew Luke's middle name, the location of his birthmark, and his most embarrassing moment at school.

But she didn't know if Luke loved her.

"How was your flight?" Tempera asked Lydia the

second her bottom hit the leather seat inside the limo.

Lydia, not prone to cruelty, cut right to the chase. "Yes, I found him, and yes, he's agreed to come back and help us." She gave her aunt a moment to compose herself before she added softly, "He wants to see you, Aunt Tempera."

"I knew it!" Tempera's voice wobbled with emotion. "I knew that he really loved me. What happened to drive him away? Did he tell you?"

"I think he wants to explain it to you. It's rather complicated." Lydia let that information sink in before she said, "Don't you want to know about Luke?"

"Oh, him!" Tempera let out a shaky laugh. "I wasn't worried about Luke. He can take care of himself, but since we're on the subject, is he still in jail?"

"Never was." Lydia's lips twitched in remembrance. "I think it was just a . . . deliberate misunderstanding."

"Hmm. So you two made up?"

While her aunt possessed an abundance of beauty and class, she was a little lacking in the subtlety department, Lydia mused wryly. She was, however, very glad to be able to say, "Yes, we did." On the floor. On the bed.

In the shower. Twice.

"Did you tell him you loved him?"

Lacking in subtlety, but not guts. "No."

"Did he tell you that he loved you?"

Lydia swallowed an exasperated sigh. Since meeting Tony, her aunt had become the proverbial romantic. "No, he didn't. We had an audience during the entire flight." A very verbal, nosey, avid, opinionated audience. At least, that was the excuse she was clinging to.

"Take my advice," Tempera said with obvious feeling. "Don't wait a moment longer than necessary to tell him that you love him. Life is too short to waste on pigheadedness."

"I will, Aunt Tempera. I promise." And she would, as soon as she made the deal with Rhew Burgess, convinced the judge she had been used unlawfully by the police department, and reestablished Mr. Complete's reputation.

She had exactly one week before the hearing.

Luke had stated more than once, and most emphatically, that it no longer mattered. Lydia disagreed. What she'd done—however purposefully and inadvertently—to not only Luke, but to Mrs. Scuttle and the company's escorts could not be forgotten or forgiven by her.

Lydia felt very strongly on the subject, and nothing Luke or anyone could say would change her mind.

She'd done it.

She had to fix it.

Plain and simple.

"By the way," Tempera said, placing a bulky brown envelope on her lap. "I paid a little visit to Rhew Burgess while you were gone." When Lydia stared at her in open-mouthed shock, Tempera shrugged. "I had to keep myself busy, didn't I? Otherwise I would have gone insane wondering if you'd found him."

"How did you—" Lydia's mouth went dry. She

stared at the package in her lap, daring to hope. "You went to see Rhew Burgess? Alone?"

Tempera sniffed. "I'm not as helpless as some people think." A grin tugged at her lips. "Although I wished you had been there to see his face when I rattled off the names of all the influential people I know. I told that creep he'd never get another call from anyone in *this* city if he didn't hand over that tape and leave Luke and his boys alone.

As the shock wore off, horror crept in. Lydia struggled to sound casual. She traced the outline of the tape through the package with nervous fingers, remembering Tony's part in the video. "Did—did you watch it, Aunt Tempera?"

"Of course not! What's on that tape is private. It belongs to Cameron Rose, and what she wants to do with it is her business."

Another thought struck Lydia. "Aunt Tempera, why did you let me go chasing off to Barbados after Tony if you suspected you could make Rhew hand over this tape?"

Tempera blushed and looked away. "I think you know the answer to that, Lydia. You've always been a smart girl. Besides, Luke needed a little shaking up."

"Yeah, I'm really smart." Lydia's chuckle was self-deprecating. "I've been charged with soliciting a prostitute—whom I framed to begin with—and I may have cost a lot of decent people their jobs."

"Hmm. That's the other thing I wanted to talk to you about," Tempera said.

"Let me guess; the judge is a very good friend of yours."

Tempera blinked in genuine astonishment, apparently unaware that Lydia had been joking. "How did you know? His wife's a darling woman. She helped me with a fund-raiser last year. But I don't think you'll be needing my help. Brett said that once the judge finds out Detective Parker planted that nasty bug in your purse without your knowledge, he'll throw up his hands in disgust. I wouldn't be surprised if Parker didn't wind up directing traffic. According to his superior, Captain Gallant—"

"Whom you also know?"

"Well, yes. Remember that fund-raiser at the city park last fall? With pony rides and the hot air balloon and a dozen kiddy carnival rides?"

Lydia nodded, dazed by her aunt's ingenuity.

"The captain's wife, Martha, helped sell the tickets. She and I are old friends. Anyway, she told me that this wasn't the first time Detective Parker has twisted the law a bit to get what he wanted. He's been suspended before." Tempera put an arm around Lydia and squeezed. She was smiling broadly. "Now, see there? Nothing to worry about at all, and I feel so much better for helping, since I did help get you into this mess."

"I guess now Cameron doesn't have to do a charity concert at Hope House," Lydia ventured. The concert had been Lydia's backup plan if Rhew refused to trade the tape for Tony's silence on the subject of blackmail.

By showing Cameron in a favorable light, Lydia had hoped to minimize the damage if Rhew released the tape to the media.

"Nonsense! Didn't I tell you? Hmm. I knew there was something I was leaving out. She said she wanted to do the concert anyway. Hope House still needs some work, and we've got those computers to buy. . . ."

Tempera was back with a vengeance, Lydia mused, feeling a rush of love and pride. On impulse, she tapped on the dividing window. Roger pushed a button and the window silently retreated.

"Need something, Miss Lydia?" he inquired politely.

"Yes." Lydia struggled with a sudden attack of nerves. "Um, can you take me to Luke's apartment?"

"Yes, ma'am!"

Luke knew the last words Lydia remembered saying to her parents before they disappeared. He knew her favorite color, her favorite flower, and that eating strawberries caused her to break out in hives.

He knew she'd lost her virginity when she was seventeen and that she'd broken her ankle trying out for gymnastics in the sixth grade.

But he didn't know if she loved him.

Why had he let the chance slip away? Luke flung the new nylon bag he'd picked up in Barbados onto the sofa and stared around at his apartment as if the walls would give him an answer.

"Lydia, I love you." He tested the words on his tongue, then repeated them, only louder. "Lydia, I love you."

Now what was so difficult about that? Why didn't he just blurt it out to her before they landed in Atlanta? The worst that could happen was . . .

Luke didn't want to think about the worst that could happen.

"I love you, Lydia." He took out his keys and marched to the door. It would take him fifteen minutes to get to her house. Plenty of time to rehearse the words.

And he would start right now.

"I love you, Lydia!" he shouted, just as he opened the door.

Lydia stood on the threshold, looking startled and lovely and tempting. Her luscious lips broke into a wide, joyous smile. "I love you too, Luke!" she shouted back. She fell into his arms, laughing and crying and kissing him.

Her arms circled his neck. Her sweet, warm breath tickled his ear as she whispered, "You'll always be my gigolo."

He laughed and hugged her tight. "In that case," he drawled with a wicked grin, "there's this new BMW I've been coveting. . . ."

Epilogue

"Who spiked the punch?" Ms. Ruth demanded, eyeing Collin, Tyler, and Ivan with suspicion.

Collin shrugged.

Tyler shook his head.

Ivan lifted a giggling, sweaty Joey onto his shoulders as if using him for an alibi.

Lydia took a cautious sip of her punch and shrugged. "Doesn't taste spiked to me. Does it to you, Aunt Tempera? Casey? Cameron?"

All three sampled the punch.

Casey frowned. "Tastes a little like rum. . . ."

"No, it's definitely vodka," Aunt Tempera stated, draining her cup and holding it out to Ruth for more.

"Who cares?" Cameron asked, also draining her cup. "We've got numerous reasons to celebrate, don't we? I've got that awful tape, the judge cleared the charges against Lydia and Luke, and we've already got enough donations to buy a warehouse full of computers and the concert hasn't even started."

"Well, you might care," Ruth said dryly, pointing to the make-shift stage set up in the yard where Cameron was about to perform, "when you get a load—no pun intended—of those idiots up there. What *are* they doing?"

Lydia peered in the direction Ruth pointed, shading her eyes. The outdoor charity concert was turning out to be a hit. Of the three hundred chairs they'd rented, most of them were filled with Atlanta's rich and pampered. "It looks like they're fighting," Lydia ventured.

Cameron and Tempera shaded their eyes.

"Yes, I think they are," Tempera said, frowning. "Looks like they're fighting over the mike, doesn't it?"

They all jumped as a terrible, ear-splitting racket burst from the powerful speakers placed strategically around the concert area. Jet, apparently the winner of the previous struggle over the mike, tapped his finger against it.

"Testing, testing, one-two-three." His slurred voice boomed out over the crowd. Everyone fell silent. Children giggled and pointed.

"Give me that, you idiot!" Luke said, grabbing the mike from Jet. It was obvious he wasn't any steadier on his feet. "I'm not only older than you, I'm bigger than you *and* I'm your boss."

"Big deal!" Jet sneered, reaching for the mike. Luke danced clumsily out of reach. "You might be the boss, but you're not God, although I'm sure you think you're God's gift to women."

"I'll settle this," Tony said, snatching the mike from Luke. "Tempera, will you marry me?"

Tempera gasped. Her empty cup fell from her fingers to the ground.

"Not so fast, Slick," Luke snarled, recovering the mike. "I told you, I was going to ask first." His goofy grin was contagious. Everyone laughed.

Lydia held her breath.

"Lydia, will you marry me?"

He lost the mike again to Jet, who shouldered both men aside. "Just a damned minute, you worthless gigolos. Cameron Rose, will you be my wife?"

"They're crazy," Cameron whispered, but her eyes were glistening and she was smiling.

"Bonkers," Tempera muttered faintly. Her lips were trembling.

"Completely insane," Lydia agreed. With her gaze locked on Luke's grinning face, she dropped her cup on the table and headed for the stage.

Just before she reached it, a shoe flew past her head and smacked Jet in the forehead.

Laughing, Lydia stood aside to make room for Mrs. Scuttle.